His to Command

By
R.C. Wynne

His to Command
By R.C. Wynne

First Edition
Copyright © 2021 by R.C. Wynne
All rights reserved

Cover art by Beautiful Mess Graphics
Editing by CTS Editing
Formatting by CJC Formatting

www.rcwynnebooks.com

ISBN: 978-1-944984-98-4
Library of Congress Control Number: 2020919299

This book is a work of fiction. All names, characters, locations, and incidents are strictly products of the author's imagination. Any resemblance to actual persons, living or dead, is entirely coincidental.

This book is licensed for your personal enjoyment only and may not be reproduced in any form, except in assisting in a review. This book may not be resold. Thank you for respecting the hard work of this author.

For up-to-date news on R.C. Wynne's latest releases, book signing events in your area, and giveaways, follow his newsletter -
https://landing.mailerlite.com/webforms/landing/l7q0q7

You can also join R.C. Wynne's reading group one Facebook, Wynne's Romance Hideaway, for more updates, extra giveaways, and even more fan involvement - https://www.facebook.com/groups/wynnesromancehideway

To Mr. Martin, who never permitted me to skate through school.

Acknowledgments

This book has been a long time coming. The first book in the series is *Losing Faith,* and it was published in September of 2014, almost seven years ago. And there's still one more book to come, *Sharing Hearts*. Why did it take so long to make this book see the light of day, especially when I had so many people yelling at me to write, even on my own team? Partly because I wasn't ready for this series to end. It's dear to my heart for many reasons, and I wasn't ready to say goodbye. To be honest, I'm still not, but it's time. I may have to write some novellas to flesh out other side characters or give some more background on the main characters, but for the main stories, it's time to see them come to a conclusion as other stories are ready to be told.

Several people have kept me focused on this series, talking over storylines, twists and turns, even character development, and I need to take this page to thank them, and first, I need to thank the three ladies who have lived this series with me for the past six-plus years: Charleen Cox, Teri Edney, and Sarah Mick. These three ladies always seem to keep me going, as well as making me look good while keeping me organized. This is the team every author needs. I would never have published *Losing Faith* without these three ladies behind me, encouraging me, supporting me, and making sure I don't make a fool out of myself, which I would left to my own devices. I know it's hard to believe, but these ladies are why you think that. They're amazing.

I also need to thank several authors who are always uplifting me, sharing ideas with me, and helping me not go insane during this isolationist time of our careers: Linzi Baxter, Gracen Miller,

Violet Howe, and Lori Joseph. You need to look these authors up and enjoy their works. You won't be disappointed.

And I need to thank you, the reader, for keeping me in my chair, writing story after story, sharing ideas and even parts of my crazy life. You're the reason I keep doing what I do, so thank you. Your notes and messages of encouragement always brighten my day.

One

Edwin Coldwell sat in his truck, staring at the front of the Savannah office of Rutherford Construction, feeling as if he had been sent to the Russian Front of World War One. This was his punishment, he knew. His purgatory. He was sent here because he couldn't keep his pants up, and Neal Rutherford didn't need a scandal back in Brevard. Edwin blamed everyone at first—Cherish for bringing everything out into the open, exposing the fact that he had been sleeping with her and her sister, Faith for not standing by his side after everything came out, Morgan Brewer for being Neal's voice that sentenced him into this exile, and even Neal for not just firing him outright, so he could stay home where he knew everyone and everything. In the end, however, Edwin knew that the fiasco that ushered in his downfall was his fault and his alone. It had been his decision to accept the transfer, instead of just quitting, accepting the punishment he was given with aplomb. The truth was, he needed to get out of

Melbourne. He needed to run away, and Neal Rutherford provided him that opportunity.

He wanted Faith Greer to run away with him, even asked her, but she had made it abundantly clear that wasn't going to happen. Her rejection still twisted in his gut.

Faith stood in front of him, arms across her chest. The wind tugged her hair, stray strands blowing across her face. She made no attempt to move them. His gaze had returned to the river, so she allowed hers to go there, as well. He wanted to talk to her about everything, but she had called asking to meet him, so he would allow her to lead the conversation. He really didn't want her to say what he knew she would have no choice but to tell him. He wanted to live in his fantasy for just a little while longer.

"Did you ever call Morgan?"

Not the beginning he expected, but at least it showed she was concerned for him. "Yeah, I'm going to transfer to some offices in Georgia. They're going to promote Jed to my spot. I'm not sure who will take his place." Edwin shrugged. "Not really my concern, I guess." He was going to miss the crew he had surrounded himself with, dreading the idea of working with people who didn't know how he liked things, a crew he didn't hire. Savannah was a new place for Neal to open shop, but according to Barbi, Neal's personal assistant, the crew had been hired with the thought of Brian Holmstead heading up the new office. Now they were getting Edwin. Lucky them. He sighed, shaking the self-pity thoughts from his mind.

"When do you leave?"

"I start there Monday. Neal and I will be drumming up business, starting from scratch."

"Have you told Cherish?"

He gave a snort of laughter. "I doubt I'll ever talk to your sister again, not after she tried to drop kick my family jewels into a new dimension." Cherish wanted a white knight, while all Edwin wanted was a good time. The same thing he wanted when he started sleeping with Faith, but then he allowed the game to enter his heart, and he lost his focus. Losing that cost him everything.

"You deserved it, you know. Don't get me wrong. Cherish slept with you, too. It's not your fault alone. Still, you played us against each other. Dumped her so you could get into my pants and didn't even give me fair warning that you had your own game underway with someone else. Now, her marriage is over, and my nephew has a broken home. You deserved what she did and a whole lot more." Faith stopped and took a deep breath, an attempt he knew of getting her anger under control. *"You're lucky that's all she did."*

"I know." It came out as a sigh. *"I screwed up. I hurt people I never meant to hurt. To be honest, if I had ever thought I had a chance to be with you, I never would have allowed anything to happen with Cherish."* He turned and stared into her eyes. *"Faith, I have always been attracted to you. We've been great together, and you know it."* He pushed himself off the tailgate and stood in front of her, his hand raising her chin, making her look into his eyes. He had always loved her eyes. *"We still can be. Come with me to Georgia."* Not giving her time to think, he leaned down and kissed her, his lips soft and warm, yet with an urgency to them, a hunger that filled every part of him.

When he broke the kiss, he gazed into her eyes and saw her answer already there, the answer he didn't want to hear. She pushed up on her tiptoes, a sadness on her face, and kissed his cheek. "Good luck in Georgia." She patted his chest and turned back to her truck.

"Faith..."

She faced him as she opened the truck door. "Goodbye,

Edwin." She slid into the driver's seat and drove away.

He had just stood there and watched her drive away, knowing he had screwed up the one decent thing he had going in his life. Faith Greer. He hadn't reached back out to her after that, knowing she had made her decision. He couldn't blame her. She had a great relationship with her husband and a new one brewing with a fiery redhead she had yet to figure out. He hadn't reached out to Cherish, either, and he probably should have since she was the one he had hurt the most. Instead, he focused on packing and getting himself ready for the next chapter in his life, avoiding the one that had been slammed shut with Cherish's knee embedded in his groin.

Opening the door to his Ford F150, he stepped out into the cool April Savannah day, dreading the notion of starting over, but knowing he didn't have a choice. All he could do was make the best of it.

He made his way up the cobblestone walkway to the glass front door, the Rutherford Construction logo emblazoned on it. He had spent the past fifteen years of his life working for Neal, growing the Brevard office into the successful company that it had become. Neal was giving him the chance to do that here in Savannah, and while it was a great opportunity for him, it still felt like punishment, only increasing how sorry he felt for himself. He pulled the door open, stepping into the rest of his life. It still felt like a prison cell.

He wasn't the first one there. A tiny brunette sat behind a small desk, typing away at her keyboard. She glanced up as he entered the lobby, a bubbly smile decorating her lips. She wore a light blue sweater-blouse, jeans, and white sneakers. Her dark hair was pulled back into a ponytail, keeping her from having to fight with it when she answered the phones, and her green eyes sparkled with invitation as she looked up at him. "Good morning," she said, her voice perky and upbeat. She didn't have Ashlynn's store-bought tits, but she was still a delight to behold when someone first walked inside. "Welcome to Rutherford Construction. How may I help you?"

He returned her smile as he stepped up to her small desk. "Well, I suppose you could show me to my office. I'm Edwin Coldwell, the new boss."

"Oh, yes, we were told to expect you today," she said, her eyes widening a little as she pushed back in her chair, standing to her feet. She reached out to shake his hand. "I'm Samantha Herring, your receptionist. Most people just call me Sammy."

"Well, Sammy, if you'd be so kind as to show me where I need to go, I'd appreciate it." He shook her hand, keeping the smile on his face. She was a slender five-and-a-half-feet to his firm six-three, so she had to look up at him even when standing. Her grip, however, told him she wasn't someone to mess around with.

"My pleasure. Just follow me."

If he hadn't been in such a self-pity mindset, he would have appreciated the curve of her ass as she stepped in front of him and the way her sweater cupped her breasts, the V-neckline giving a small glimpse into the treasures that waited underneath. The old Edwin would have already hit on her, suggesting a different kind of tour. Today, however, it was the farthest thing from his mind.

~ ~ ~ ~ ~

Andrea Newman looked up from the contract she was looking over and saw Sammy walking him through the secretary's den, a large room in the middle of the back office area with offices along each side. It had four desks facing each other, two of which were still empty. The other two belonged to Kendra Hunsaker, in charge of human resources, and Jana Mitchell, who was in charge of inventory and equipment. Andrea's office rested on the west side of the room, the glass wall giving her a perfect view of everything that took place on the other side. She watched as Sammy escorted Mr. Edwin Coldwell to what used to be the office of Brian Holmstead, who up until last week was her new boss and the reason she transferred to Savannah in the first place when Neal Rutherford announced he intended to open an office here. Edwin smiled at Sammy, thanking her as he opened his door and stepped into his glass fishbowl. Andrea blew out a sigh. Now she was trapped in Savannah with the infamous womanizer Edwin Coldwell. *Well, have fun fucking someone in your office with those glass walls.*

Sammy left Edwin's office and weaved her way through the secretary's den, the are they referred to as the bullpen, to Andrea's office. Andrea stayed as she was, pen in hand, staring out the glass walls. Sammy just waved and then opened the door, letting herself inside. "I see you saw who has arrived." She shrugged. "He seems nice enough, though not what I really expected. He was quiet. Polite. From everything I've heard, I really expected more banter and hints of innuendo. Yet, he was the perfect gentleman."

Andrea glanced out the door to where Edwin stood in his office, taking in his new surroundings. She tapped the pen along her lips. "Well, perhaps he's moving slow until he settles in. I talked to Jed Jorrel down at the Brevard office, and it was a mess when Edwin left." She leaned back in her chair, glancing back over at Sammy. "Somehow, I suddenly feel like a babysitter and not a manager of this office. Oh, well. Neal will be here tomorrow. We'll just wait and see what the rest of the plans are for the naughty boy over there."

Sammy gave her a confused look. "What plans could there be outside of him running this office? Isn't that why he's here?"

Andrea took a deep breath. She really wasn't sure why Edwin

was there outside of ruining her perfect plans for a peaceful career. "I wish I knew."

Sammy just nodded and then left, returning to her receptionist's desk.

Andrea took a deep breath. She guessed she should go and say hello to the new boss and get it over with. However, as she stood to do just that, Edwin stepped out of his office and asked for everyone's attention. She dropped her pen on her desk as she shoved her chair back and stood. Crossing her arms over her chest, she stepped out of her office and sat on the edge of Karen's desk, waiting for whatever the man had to say, not really wanting to hear any of it. This is not what she had planned.

Edwin stood, hands on his hips as he swung his gaze around at each of them. "As you may have guessed, I'm Edwin Coldwell. I've glanced over the files of everyone in our office over the weekend, and it looks like we have a great crew. I'm looking forward to working with each of you, and I hope you'll be patient as I play catch up over the next day or two. I'd like to meet with each one of you, get to know you a little bit, and then share some thoughts for the future. For now, just keep doing what you've been doing. Thanks." He smiled at them, and then everyone turned back around to their desks and whatever they had been working on before he called their attention away.

Andrea expected him to turn back into his office and hide for the rest of the day. Instead, he weaved his way through the desks and over to where Andrea stood, a smile on his face and a quick lift in his eyebrows, stretching his hand out once he drew near. "You must be Andrea."

"Why must I be Andrea?" she asked, one brow cocked.

Edwin shrugged. "I watched you come out of that office." He pointed behind her to her office. "Just seemed to make sense, since you weren't sitting out here. Thanks for running things until

I arrived. I hope it hasn't been too much of a headache."

She shook his hand and then turned and walked back into her office, hearing him follow her. She didn't want to have any type of conversation where the others could overhear. "It was no big deal. We've only been up and running for a couple of weeks. Brian had us pretty well set up before he was transferred," she said, unable to keep the rancor from her voice. She couldn't help it. This man had just swept in and disrupted her future plans. She knew he was being punished, but it made her feel as if she was being punished, as well, and that didn't set well with her at all.

If he heard the aggravation in her voice, he chose to ignore it. "I've always heard great things about Brian. He was moved to Fort Lauderdale, right? I'm sure he's going to love the beaches there. You transferred here from Charleston, if I read the paperwork correctly?"

She nodded as she walked around her desk and stood in front of her chair. "I did," she confirmed. "I was ready for a change. When I heard Neal was opening an office here, I asked to be a part of it."

Edwin leaned back against her doorframe, his hands clasped behind his back. "And you and Brian hadn't worked together before? How did that come about that you were eager to transfer and not be in the lead position?"

"I worked for Brian a couple of times before I settled in Charleston," she said with a slight shrug. "He was down in St. Augustine, and when my office opened, he was the one who helped set it up. We stayed in touch." It was a simple answer and all she planned on giving him. He didn't need to know how much they had stayed in touch.

Edwin nodded. "Makes sense. At least you knew how the man worked, so it made it easier. How many projects do we have on the table right now?"

She shuffled through some file folders on her desk until she found the one she wanted. She lifted it to him, making him reach for it. "We only have a few so far, but I have a stack of proposals I'm working on."

He took the folder from her hands, opening it up, and glancing at the contents. His eyebrows arched, and she knew the one he had just noticed. "The Rabbit Hole?" He glanced up at her, a curious expression on his face. "We're building a sex club?"

She didn't smile, just nodded. "According to Neal, we'll build anything."

He returned his gaze back to the file, his head bobbing up and down. "True, true. I'm not sure he ever thought we'd go from building children's hospitals to BDSM clubs, however. I can't wait to see the look on his face tomorrow when he arrives."

"Do we know what time he'll be getting in?"

He closed the folder, tucking it under his arm. "Not really. Morgan will give me a call when Neal leaves just so we have a heads up."

She nodded. She knew Morgan Brewer was another one who was being punished without actually being punished. However, along with Edwin, both received new offices instead of termination. She assumed they must be really good at what they do or else they had something to hang over Neal's head. She highly doubted the latter, though. Neal was as squeaky clean as they came from everything she heard of the man.

The silence grew between them, hanging heavy in the air. She couldn't exactly ask him to leave, and she knew he wanted to say something else. He glanced up at the ceiling a moment and then turned his gaze on her, his eyes soft as he stared at her. "I know this isn't what you wanted. You expected to be working for Brian when you transferred here. I'm sorry I screwed that up for you. It wasn't my idea, trust me."

Andrea nodded. "I've heard all about it. The reason you're here and Brian isn't."

He nodded. "The gossip in this company has always been faster than any other communication."

She leaned back in her chair. "Can I be frank?"

He gestured for her to speak her mind, which surprised her.

"I respected Brian, which is why I wanted to continue to work for him. He was a good boss and knew how to keep his work separate from his...other activities. I don't want to work for someone who's going to be causing me more headaches than he is teaching me how to be the best at what I do. This is work, not high school." She leaned on her desk, her fingers intertwined in front of her. "I'm here to work, not cover for your extracurricular activities."

He nodded. "Well, no one has ever covered for me, but you're right; this is work. I'll expect you to have my back when it comes to that, and if we're going to have any problems working together just let me know, and I'll see to it that you get to work for Brian. You are not my guardian or my boss. However, I am your boss, and I hope that we'll be able to work well together. We're both here for a fresh start." He bounced himself off the wall and stood straight. "So you've heard the gossip about me. That train works both ways. Always remember that. I have just as many connections within this company as Neal, and files don't always tell a person everything, especially the parts we don't want in them." His smile was more of a smirk as he turned and left her alone.

She watched him walk away, his words ringing in her mind as she wondered what exactly he had heard about her. No one knew. There was no way they could know. They had been too careful. Hadn't they?

Two

He sat at his desk, staring out the glass door, a pile of manila folders stacked in front of him that he needed to go through but just didn't have the energy to do so. He wasn't surprised at the icy reception he was given by Andrea. It wasn't like she had asked to work for him after all. She didn't apply to be his second-in-command, and he didn't hire her. She had actually transferred here to work for Brian for some reason only she knew. No, she hadn't wanted to work for Edwin. That was quite obvious.

But she was stuck with him.

Just as he was stuck with her. She wouldn't have been his first choice to work with, but here they were together. They would have to make the best of it. He only hoped she would be willing to give it her best effort. It really didn't sound like it earlier, and he had suffered a rough enough time lately that he didn't need any more tension in his life. If she couldn't change her mindset, he would talk to Neal about replacing her.

His cell phone started ringing, jerking his attention from his self-pity party. Glancing down at his phone, he groaned as he noticed the name on his screen. Cherish Lansky. He took a deep breath. *So much for getting rid of the tension in my life.* Against his better judgment, he picked up the phone, sliding the button to answer it as he lifted it to his ear. "What now?" His voice was terse, curt, but he didn't care. Cherish was the reason he wasn't sitting in the office he had spent so much time decorating and instead was surrounded by pictures and knickknacks he didn't even comprehend. "Didn't you give me enough hell already?" Maybe he just needed to lash out at someone, and that's why he answered the phone. He was ready to explode, and Cherish was the right person to bear the brunt of his anger. If she could have just been an adult and gone her own way, none of this would be happening, his exile or her looming divorce.

"I... I'm surprised you answered." She sounded nervous, frightened almost. Good.

"So am I, to be honest." He took a deep breath, running his hand through his hair as he stared out at the bullpen of desks outside his door. He didn't need anyone coming in and catching him talking to the whole reason he was even there. He lowered his voice. They also didn't need to overhear what he actually desired to say to the woman who tumbled his world to the ground. "What do you want, Cherish? I have a new office to get accustomed to, thanks to you."

"I heard. I'm sorry Neal sent you away. Beats being fired, I guess."

It would have been better if you would have just quit and kept your mouth shut. But no, you had to stir up a hornet's nest of shit. He didn't say that, however. "That remains to be seen. Look, I highly doubt you called to wish me luck, so why *did* you call?"

She deserved his anger just as much as he had deserved her knee. He just wanted her out of his life completely so he could move on with the rest of whatever lay ahead of him.

"Why wasn't I enough? I mean, when did I push you away?" She sounded sad, almost like she was pleading to understand something he couldn't even comprehend.

Unbelievable. "Really? This is why you're calling me? Shouldn't you be worrying about Glen and your family?" She had made it fairly plain a couple of Sundays ago that she didn't want anything else from him except his suffering, so why worry about any of it now?

"I need to know."

"Why? What does it matter now?" *What does any of it matter now?*

"It just does. Please, Edwin. I need to know. I thought you were enjoying us being together. I tried to give you everything you wanted. I did everything you said. Why wasn't I enough? What did Faith have that I didn't? What did she give you that I couldn't?"

He ran his hand over his face as he took a deep breath. "You didn't do anything necessarily. Cherish, what we had wasn't supposed to be serious. We were just having fun. I was enjoying it, but you… You started needing something I wasn't ready to give. You started acting like my girlfriend at work, and it was just too much." *Way too much.* It was too late to get out of it safely when he realized she was looking for someone to save her from a boring life, and he was stuck until he figured it out. Then there was Faith… Edwin sighed. And then he didn't care how safe it was. He wanted the older of the siblings.

"And Faith? Why did you go to my sister?"

Another deep breath. "Faith *was* just wanting fun. She wasn't looking to leave her husband. They just wanted to open up their marriage to sexual adventures, and I was her adventure. But..." Silence. Faith didn't screw up what the two of them were enjoying; he did. He wanted too much from her just as Cherish wanted too much from him. After a couple of moments, he started speaking again. "But things changed on my end. I actually fell for your sister. I even asked her to come to Savannah with me, but she turned me down. I'm not sure when my heart got involved, probably just like you don't know when you started caring for me, but I crossed a line and broke one of her rules. It was just supposed to be fun, but I tried to make it more than that. It's probably good that I'm in Savannah, for both of us. I need to work on my career, and you need to work on your marriage. Trust me, this is for the best."

"I don't think Glen wants me back," she blurted out, and to his surprise, he felt sorry for her. "I've lost everything." She started crying, and even after everything, he wished he could fix things for her, knowing part of her misery was his fault.

"No, Cherish, you haven't," he assured her in a softer tone. "Not yet, anyway. You just need to work on holding onto everything. Besides, you still have that little boy to take care of. He needs you." Silence answered him. With a deep breath, he continued when it was obvious she wasn't going to say anything. "I'm sorry, Cherish. For everything. I was wrong in a lot of things I did, but I promise, I never meant to hurt you or cause problems with your family. I'm truly sorry." It was the truth. Things just got way out of hand. Way, way out of hand.

"Yeah, so am I. Goodbye, Edwin."

The phone line went dead, the sound of defeat strong in her voice. Pulling the phone away from his ear, he stared at it a moment, thinking of all the damage he had caused because he couldn't keep his pants zipped up. Still, he knew if it wasn't him, Cherish would have found someone else to screw around with.

That didn't excuse him, of course. Well, not completely.

Dropping his phone onto his desk, he stared back out at the bullpen. He had a whole new crew to get to know and learn how to work with, a group that had only been around for a short while. They were still learning to work with each other and already had another boss to deal with. He shook his head. *This is going to be so much fun.*

~ ~ ~ ~ ~

Five-thirty. Andrea was more than ready to get out of there. It wasn't that it was necessarily a bad day. It just wasn't the day she wanted. Nor was it with the person she wanted. She glanced out her glass office door across the bullpen to where Edwin Coldwell sat behind his shiny new desk thumbing through crisp new manila folders. The new office hadn't even been around long enough to put coffee stains on the work orders. *I need a drink.*

She shut down her computer and tossed everything into her purse before standing and shoving her chair under her desk. If she was lucky, she could get out of there without dear Mr. Coldwell seeing her. She was not in the mood for any after work banter. She just wanted out of there.

Before she could escape her office, however, her phone rang. Digging it out of her purse, she saw Brian's name and face come across her screen and couldn't stop the smile that spread across her face. Leaning back on her desk, she answered the phone. "Well, hello, there. How was your first day in Fort Lauderdale?"

"Funny, I was just about to ask you the same thing," he said, his voice immediately making her honey drip. "How did big bad Edwin do? You didn't kill him did you?"

She sighed as she glanced across the office to her new, unwanted boss. "Not for lack of wanting to, I assure you." She shrugged. "The day was good. He stayed in his office mostly, catching up on contracts and reading through the few employee files we have." Her smile slid into a grin. "I missed your good morning instructions," she said, lowering her voice.

He chuckled. "Sorry about that. It's a lot harder to play the dominant so far away when I'm rushing to get out the door. A whole lot easier when you're right there in the bed beside me."

"We did it for a few months before we could both find an office together," she reminded him. "I think we can make it work again until we figure things out."

"I know you do, love. And I assure you, I want to figure it out as well. However, as I told you before, you transferring here isn't the best idea right now. Not with Edwin having been moved because of his extra-curricular activities. It would make people question our motives."

She knew he was right, but she didn't want to agree. She didn't care what people thought. She had been able to have Brian in her life for two weeks rather than just through text or video calls, and that just wasn't enough. "Well, hopefully, we can figure it out quickly. I miss your imagination."

He chuckled again. "Be patient. It'll take me a little while to figure things out, but we'll get there. In the meantime, just focus on work."

"Yes, sir," she said, trying hard not to sound rejected.

They both said their goodbyes, and Andrea dumped her phone back in her purse. Now, she really needed that drink.

Kendra and Jana were already out the door by the time Andrea stepped out of her office. *Lucky them.* The office lights were just waiting for the last one out to shut them off., which would be Edwin as it appeared. Andrea was tempted to flip the switch anyway, just to be mean, but decided not to push her luck. She hoped Brian would hurry up and figure out how to transfer her down to Florida. The longer she stayed in Savannah, the worse her mood and motivation were going to get. She had invested too much into Rutherford Construction to just toss it all away, and she hated going through the interview process for a new job, but she didn't know how long she could work for the man who had cost her the future she had been waiting for. No. Moving was easier. She made a mental note to call Brian later and push him for that transfer again.

She took the outer circle of the office, avoiding going anywhere near Edwin's office, and pushed her way out into the reception area where Sammy sat, punching away at her keyboard. "Okay, Samantha, I'm out of here and heading for a beer. Have a good night."

"How did it go?" Sammy punched at her keyboard a few more times before slipping her hands into her lap and leaning back in her chair so she could focus on her boss. "First day with the new kid and all," she said as if Andrea wouldn't already know to what she was referring.

Andrea paused at the receptionist's desk, leaning on the shelf that protected Sammy from the public. "Quiet. He stayed in his office, and I stayed in mine after that initial chest thumping of his to claim ownership of our crew. He just needs to stay on his side of the office."

Sammy gave her a quizzical look. "You really don't like him that much? He just got here."

Andrea shook her head. "I don't have to know him. His reputation precedes him, and it's not a good one. From what I understand, he's here to avoid a scandal back in Brevard. Something about sleeping with one of his employees. A married one at that. Brian is being punished so Edwin gets to start over with a clean slate. Only problem is, his slate is nowhere near clean, and I don't plan on letting him get away with his shenanigans here."

"You don't think those women knew what they were doing

when they screwed around with him? I mean, they have to carry some of the blame, don't you think?"

"Only for being gullible. No. Edwin used his position to get them out of their pants. He should have shown more control."

"I don't know. He's pretty hot in my book. He could be doing anything, and I wouldn't mind letting him in my pants."

Andrea rolled her eyes. "Don't. You stay behind your desk and leave Mr. Coldwell alone. I won't have any of his chaos infecting this office."

"All right, all right. Relax." Sammy held up her hands, palms out in front of her. Whether it was an act of surrender or her way of telling Andrea to calm down, Andrea wasn't sure. Still, she took it. "I still think you're forgetting a couple of things here."

"Oh? And just what would those be?"

Sammy's grin was mischievous. "First, we're all adults, and second, Edwin is one hell of a hot looking man."

Andrea shook her head as she turned toward the double doors. "Our tastes in what constitutes a *hot man* are vastly different." She waved at the other woman from over her shoulder as she pushed the glass door open. *I really need that drink now.*

~ ~ ~ ~ ~

Edwin stretched, his muscles screaming at him for being in the same position for so long. Glancing out his office window, he noticed everyone else was gone. Curious, he glanced at his watch. Seven-ten. *Holy shit.* He stretched again, his muscles popping, and then stood and walked around the bullpen. He sneaked a peek at Andrea's office, only to notice it was dark. He walked to the front of the building, opening the door to the reception area, but it too was dark, and the front doors locked. He was alone. *No one even bothered to say goodbye. So much for a good first impression.* He knew he was going to have to do better. His reputation as the wayward child had preceded him here, whether it should have or not, and he was going to have to overcome it in order to garner control of this office. It didn't help matters that Andrea seemed to be totally against him, and the others seemed to follow her lead. Neal really should have transferred her down to Fort Lauderdale with Brian. *Maybe I'll bring it up when Neal gets here.* Edwin just knew he didn't want to face Andrea's antagonism on a daily basis. It would definitely not be a friendly work environment. For a woman who looked as hot as she did, she sure as hell had an icy exterior.

Returning to his office, he packed up for the night and shut everything off. As he reached the door between the reception area and the back offices, he paused, turning around to stare once more at his new surroundings. It was like he was starting all over again, even if it was within the same company, following the same rules, rules he had learned to work around for quite a while. He was dreading starting over, learning new people, new routines. *Boy, did I ever screw my life up.* He flicked the light switch, throwing the interior offices into darkness. There was nothing for it now but to make the best of it.

He locked the front door and headed for his truck, dreading another night of unpacking and setting up house.

The Savannah rush hour traffic was already nonexistent by the time he headed out of the office, which made it easier for him to find his way around an unknown area. Edwin had found a place only twenty minutes from the office just in case he needed to get there quick. For the time being, being in a new place, he would only have work to keep himself occupied. Another aspect of moving he was dreading—making new friends. He liked his old friends. They were comfortable. Like broken-in shoes.

Shake it off, Edwin, sheesh. He was never a gloomy person before, but since Cherish had kneed his family jewels into next week and Faith had basically kicked him to the curb, he just felt like wallowing in his misery. Granted, it was misery well-deserved, but nevertheless, he was tired of feeling sorry for himself. It was time to put some skip back in his step.

Soon, he was back at his new apartment, dropping the keys onto a stack of boxes that never made it past the front foyer, and heading for the refrigerator and a cold beer. He sat his briefcase on the kitchen counter and headed for his back balcony which overlooked a creek that ran along the west side of the property. A couple of squirrels leaped from tree to tree in a frenzied game of chase as two cardinals watched their antics from a safe distance away. Two young boys fished from the side of the creek, ignoring the rest of the world around them, lost in playing Tom and Huck for a few moments. Edwin relished the simplicity of their lives. Life should be simple. *Then stop making it so damn complicated, you idiot.* He took a long pull from his beer as he reached into his shirt pocket for his pack of Salems. He had made his life difficult, and it was time to fix that. It was time to grab hold of the pleasures this world had to offer, especially his new home. Speedbumps are not roadblocks. It was time for him to stop acting like they were.

Three

The alarm on his cell phone rang, jarring Edwin into an uncomfortable wakefulness. He rolled over on the couch, doing his best not to fall off as he reached for the phone on the cluttered coffee table to shut off the alarm. Once the place was silent once again, he collapsed back onto his pillow, his eyes closed, hoping he could recapture just a few more minutes of sleep. It was no use. He was awake and might as well get up and start his day. As he jerked the covers off his naked form, his body groaned at him, reminding him that he really needed to get his bed put together.

The chill air brought goosebumps to his flesh as he made his way into the kitchen and the first thing that he had unpacked upon his arrival—his coffeepot. While his morning pick-me-up was brewing, he decided the next thing to get out of the way was a shower. Hopefully, the hot water would jolt him awake. His mind was still a fog from sleeping in an unfamiliar place, not to mention on his couch. He desperately needed to recapture his routines to regain some semblance of normalcy.

Once out of the shower, he quickly dried off, wrapping the towel around his waist when he was finished. After a quick brushing of his hair, he made his way to the kitchen and the coffee that awaited him. Out of the cabinet to the right of the coffeepot, he pulled out a stark white cup and then filled it with half a spoonful of sugar and just a drop of two-percent milk. He then poured in his coffee, stirring slowly until the liquid was a dark cream in color. He rinsed the spoon, setting it in the drainboard when he was finished, and made his way back to his bedroom. Routines. Edwin liked his routines.

He had spent most of last night arranging his dresser drawers and unpacking his closet. He had no intention of living out of boxes any longer than necessary. He had arrived Friday with most of what he would need to set up house until the movers arrived with the rest of his belongings. He spent the weekend setting up his kitchen, bathroom, and living room. Why he waited to do his bed last, he had no idea. *Probably just thought I didn't deserve a bed.* He still hadn't gone grocery shopping really, outside of beer and the fixings for lunchmeat sandwiches, so after he was dressed—gray slacks and a baby blue button-down shirt—he decided to head to a small café he spotted while driving around this past weekend. If he was honest, he didn't feel like cooking for himself anyway. It was usually just a hassle to fix breakfast for one person.

The Tuesday morning was bright with just a light breeze. He had heard a lot about Savannah and was eager to get out and explore its history. Of course, it would have been nicer if he had someone to explore it with him. Maybe while he was discovering Savannah's secrets, someone would discover him.

As he pulled into the parking lot of Gertie's Diner, his cell phone rang. He groaned, fearing another confrontational call from Cherish. Instead, it was Morgan Brewer. Another one of Neal Rutherford's managers. Morgan's punishment had sent him to Biloxi, Mississippi to open another new office. His calling Edwin could only mean one thing. *So much for my positive mood.* He slid the button to accept the call. "Morning, Morgan."

"Edwin, my man, your world's about to get dimmer," Morgan said, just a little too chipper for Edwin's tastes.

"Neal's on his way, I take it," Edwin said with a sigh. "There goes the rest of my week."

"My gain is your loss," the other man said with a chuckle. He may have felt bad for Edwin, but Edwin doubted it. The two of them were a lot alike. Both were just looking for a good time and, most of the time, didn't care with who or even where. Usually, it didn't matter. However, Edwin had kicked the hornet's nest back in Brevard, and Neal had hauled him out of town in an attempt to quiet things down. Morgan had gotten caught up in some of it but had avoided all perceptions of wrongdoing. His transfer was more of a promotion than a punishment. "How are things in Savannah?"

"Cooler than they were back in Brevard and in more ways than one. Of course, with Neal on his way, I'm sure the heat's about to be turned up."

"You'll weather it just fine. You might face Grumpy Neal for a little bit, but he still wants you around or he would have just canned your ass. Ride it out, take your spanking, and then make sure you pick your next office fling a little better."

"I'll have to hire new people for that. The men here are prettier than the girls. It's deflating." It also wasn't true, but Edwin didn't want Morgan to think he was even tempted to go that route again. The man had Neal's ear way too much to give him any information Edwin didn't want to get out.

Morgan chuckled. "Have you heard anything from back home?"

"I've talked to Jed. They've hired someone to fill Nessa's spot and moved her to Faith's position. Then he told me he fired Grady—"

"That's not what I meant, and you know it," Morgan said, cutting Edwin off before he could continue with the meaningless chatter.

He heard Edwin take a deep breath. "No, nothing. I tried to call Faith once, but she didn't answer, nor did she call back. As for Cherish the... I don't even want to go there." He wasn't going to tell Morgan about Cherish's call. There was enough gossip going around as it was. He was ready to keep his life to himself for a while. Something he should have done since the beginning.

"I don't blame you."

The two men talked a little while longer, discussing Morgan's proposition to move to Biloxi for however long it would take to get Jacqui Karston happy and how Edwin could be successful in Savannah. After a bit, Morgan wished Edwin good luck and ended the call for which Edwin was grateful. While he was the one to screw up and get busted, he was honest with himself enough to admit that Morgan's getting away with things irritated him just a little. Okay, a lot. Just because Edwin deserved it, didn't mean it was fair. Suddenly, his appetite was gone.

~ ~ ~ ~ ~ ~

Andrea pushed her way into the building with her ass, a cup of coffee in one hand while still chewing on a bagel with blueberry cream cheese. She couldn't even say good morning to Sammy as she greeted her. Instead, she waved with two fingers from the hand holding her coffee mug. Sammy just laughed and shook her head as she waved back, the phone on her desk starting to shrill. Shoving the bagel in her mouth so she could open the door to the back offices, Andrea entered her workday, wondering what great surprises lay in store for her this Tuesday.

Kendra and Jana were already at their desks, Kendra going through files while Jana was pecking away at her keyboard. Glancing off to her left, Andrea hoped… She sighed. Edwin was in his office, already working. She was hoping he would have just decided to quit and go back home. She wasn't that lucky, obviously.

"How are we looking today?" she asked Kendra as she neared the woman's desk on the way to her own.

"We got donuts," Jana said, cutting the other woman off as she pointed to a box of donuts sitting open on a table against the wall under the giant whiteboard Andrea knew hadn't been there when she left yesterday.

"And a whiteboard, I see," Andrea said with a shake of her head.

"And soon, we'll have the owner of the company, as well," Kendra said.

"Oh, shit, that's right. That's today." Andrea closed her eyes and tilted her head back. She didn't need Neal all up in her business. It was bad enough she was going to have to babysit Edwin. Between the two men, they were going to make a mess of her office. "Okay, do we have anything to show him?" She turned her gaze back to Jana.

"The owner from that BDSM club we're negotiating a contract with is supposed to be here later," Edwin said as he came out of his office. "We also have a couple of restaurants and some houses out in Baker's Cove. That is, if I've read all those files right that Jana left on my desk this morning." He glanced at Jana as he said it, waiting for her affirmation that he was right. When she nodded at him, he just smiled. "Oh, and we have donuts." He pointed to the box on the back wall.

"And a whiteboard, I see," Andrea said, doing her best not to sound condescending. "Why do we need a whiteboard?"

He shrugged as he cast a quick glance at the whiteboard before turning back to face her. He offered her a soft smile, probably trying to be all charming and sweet and stuff. But it wasn't working. She didn't need sweet and charming. Not in her office. "I like to see all of our jobs at once, get an overview of what's happening, where it's happening, and whether it's on schedule or not. It's a big picture kind of thing."

"Ah," was all Andrea could come up with to say. She turned back to her office, rolling her eyes when no one could see her, and took another bite of her bagel. Screw the donuts.

"Hey," Edwin called out to her. "When you drop your stuff off, come to my office. I want you to look over some files with me."

She turned to face him, her brows scrunched up in confusion. "Files for..?"

"I'm hiring another assistant manager." He just smiled as he turned around and headed back to his office.

Andrea just stood there, staring after him as he walked away, her mouth slightly ajar. Kendra and Jana just stared at her, both wearing a shocked expression.

~ ~ ~ ~ ~

He waited until he was back in his office, the door shut before he allowed the chuckle he was holding in to slip past his lips. The look on her face was priceless. She probably thought he was replacing her, but he had no such thoughts. He was used to working with two assistants, and if this was going to be his office, he was going to set it up the way he wanted. He still had to hire a warehouse manager, which Brian Holmstead had never gotten around to doing the couple of weeks he was running things. Edwin also wanted to hire another girl for the bullpen. Savannah was going to be his office, ran his way. Hopefully, Andrea would get on board with that. If not, he had no problem hiring two assistant managers.

A quick glance at his watch let him know he had about two more hours before he had to get Neal from the airport. If he was lucky, he could get Andrea to stop hating him at least a little bit in that amount of time.

A knock came at his door. Glancing up, he waved Andrea inside, her expression still worried. "You said you wanted to go over some files with me?" she asked as she stepped into his office, closing the door behind her.

"Yes, please, sit." Edwin gestured to a leather chair in front of his desk. "I want to hire a few more people and thought I'd get your input on them before I do. We're both going to be working with them, so we need to both like who we bring on board."

She still looked skeptical as she sat. "Why do we need more people? We're just barely getting up and running. Shouldn't we get some jobs first?"

"Oh, we'll get jobs, and when we do, I want us to be ready. Neal will want us to be ready, too. I'm not going to disappoint him."

She nodded her head slowly, an unsure look still on her face. "How many more people were you wanting to hire?"

He listed out the main people he wanted to bring to the team as they were creating crews for the jobs. "We at least need a skeleton crew to get us in some doors. Won't do well to sign a contract and then start looking for employees. Luckily, Brian had Kendra start some of the process last week. She had a list of names for me to look at this morning when I brought it up to her." He shrugged. "We should be able to get a few good candidates."

"But…another assistant? Do you really think you and I can't handle the workload?"

Edwin sat up, resting his arms on his desk, his hands clasped together, fingers intertwined. "Can we? Of course. But do we have to? *Should* we have to?" He shook his head. "No. We'll give Neal our best, but we won't give him everything we have. We still have to have a life outside of these walls. So, we'll hire some more people. Besides, Neal believes in growth, and I want to be prepared for when it happens."

"Brian didn't think we needed anyone else. Jana handles trucks and equipment, so why do we need a warehouse manager? And I think we can handle running this office without hiring someone else." She leaned forward in her seat, her voice rising as the passion of what she believed filled her.

"Brian isn't here, and I'm running things now. I know you wanted to work for him, that you liked the way he did things, but I like to do things just a little differently. We're hiring these positions. That part isn't up for debate. Now, I'm hoping you'll help me pick who we want, but whether you do or not, I *am* filling these positions." He sat there, hands folded in front of him, just waiting for her response. He knew she would second guess him. Expected it actually. Yet, this was his office, and he would run it the way he wanted. He liked things a certain way. Routines. Structure. And his way worked damn well. Always had, which is one of the reasons Neal kept him around. She was just going to have to figure that out and go with it if she was going to continue working there.

He watched her take a deep breath, shifting slightly in her seat. He could see the argument all over her face, the way her jaw tensed, the muscles of her neck pulled taut. She wanted to debate some more with him. But she didn't. "Fine. I'll be happy to look at the candidates." She held her hand out for one of the folders.

He watched her as he handed her the one on top, the one for the warehouse manager. He heard what she said, but he didn't believe her. She was only biding her time for something. He just needed to figure out what.

~ ~ ~ ~ ~

She glanced at the information in the folder for a Ryan Slater, thirty-six years old, former warehouse manager for an auto parts store. Andrea stared at the rest of the file, but she wasn't really seeing it. Instead, she was boiling inside, her anger at what Edwin was doing to Brian's office simmering just below the surface of her nerves. They didn't need more people. They had plenty. Edwin Coldwell was just afraid of working. She couldn't wait until Neal got there and set Edwin straight. He wouldn't go for this frivolous spending.

And that smirk. Edwin was enjoying this, that was obvious. He was just trying to mark his territory. It didn't matter. This was her office until she could get Brian back up here or her down there, and she just needed Neal to tell Edwin that. These changes were not necessary and a waste of resources. Neal would see that.

She stared at the file in front of her. Two more hours. Two more hours until the owner of the company could straighten out his wayward employee. It couldn't get here fast enough.

Four

Edwin stood by the gate, waiting for Neal Rutherford to get off the plane and begin the scolding Edwin knew was coming his way. While he had already suffered a dressing down back in Brevard, he knew something would have to be said today if even just as a reminder of why Edwin was even in Savannah. Edwin didn't need any reminders. Andrea's attitude since he arrived was reminder enough. He wasn't sure what she had against him outside of the fact that he was there and Brian wasn't. He had heard of people really wanting to work with someone before, but Andrea had moved from an established office with a great reputation to help Brian start this one, bypassing becoming the boss of her own site, and Edwin had a gut feeling it wasn't just because Brian was good at his job. He was also a lot like Edwin as memory served. At a manager's gathering Neal put together last year, Edwin and Brian had started talking and the subject of the BDSM lifestyle had come up. A joke was made, but Edwin knew from the way Brian talked about it that the man had more than a passing interest in the subject. Brian, obviously, possessed a quality that intrigued Andrea enough to make her uproot her life and move to Savannah, and Edwin knew how intoxicating something like that could be, which was another reason he was confused when she balked at building The Rabbit Hole for Trent Wilson. The BDSM club should have fueled her curiosity, instead.

Edwin shook his head. Andrea's likes and dislikes were none of his business. He refused to make the same mistake in Savannah that he made in Brevard. This was his new start after all, and he was determined to make the best of it. In time, he would find that special someone to give him what he thought he had discovered in Faith Greer.

A river of people began to flow down the runway corridor as Neal's flight was finally released from their cramped seats. Edwin tucked the Salem cigarette he had been playing with behind his right ear and kept an eye out for the owner of Rutherford Construction, trying to pick Neal's salt and pepper hair out of the dozens of other businessmen on the same flight.

The fact that Neal kept Morgan and Edwin in the company didn't surprise Edwin at all. They had been with Neal since he started flipping houses fifteen years ago, helping him build his company into the giant construction company it was today. The only one closer to Neal than them was his personal secretary, Barbi. He could do without Edwin and Morgan, but he couldn't survive without Barbi, and everyone close to Neal knew it. Edwin was surprised the two of them hadn't taken their relationship out of the office. Of course, Neal traveled more than a relationship would allow for most women, so Barbi may have put a halt to anything other than what the two shared currently.

As the next stream of passengers flowed through the doorway, Edwin spotted Neal in the midst of the river of people, chatting up another older gentleman as he pulled his luggage behind him. Edwin shook his head. Neal Rutherford could make friends anywhere and in any amount of time. It was part of the reason he was so successful.

Neal waved him down, and then said goodbye to his new friend as he crossed the flow of people to reach Edwin's side. "Thanks for meeting me," he said as he stretched out an arm to shake Edwin's hand. "I hope you haven't been waiting long."

Edwin shook his head. "Just long enough to enjoy a cup of coffee and some peace and quiet. How was the flight?"

"Longer than I wanted," Neal said. "And I swear those seats get smaller and smaller."

They both turned and headed for the exit. "No baggage to claim?" Edwin asked.

Neal slipped his sunglasses over his eyes as he moved closer to the exit. "Nope. Not planning on being here long. A week tops. Everything I need is in my carry-on. I just wanted to make sure Andrea didn't murder you on your first day."

"It wasn't for lack of desire, I'll tell you that," Edwin said as he ran a hand through his dark hair. "She made sure I realized she didn't appreciate me taking over for Brian, and she thought I deserved to be fired."

"You did deserve to be fired, but luckily, we have some history and some pull within the company." Neal shot him a grin, then he shrugged. "Moving you here actually killed two birds with one stone. If I had left Brian here, I'm sure I would have had the same problem with him and Andrea as I did with you back in Brevard but keep that under your hat. Andrea's just hurt because the man she was crushing on isn't here anymore. She'll get over it. You two will actually make a good team once she gets past her disappointment."

Edwin nodded, but decided not to comment. He knew Brian Holmstead had the same proclivities as he did, which meant Andrea probably did, as well. That type of commitment wasn't an easy one to shake off, which was why Edwin was surprised Brian didn't take Andrea with him when he moved to Florida. "So, how is Morgan doing in Biloxi?"

Neal barked out a burst of laughter. "He has his hands full, that's for sure. The CEO of the Karston Foundation is an icy woman with a major chip on her shoulder with everyone she meets. If Morgan thinks he'll be able to use his typical charm to woo her his way, he's in for some major disappointment." He chuckled some more. "A perfect punishment if you ask me."

Edwin couldn't help but laugh as well as they stepped out into the Georgia sun toward his truck. "I almost feel sorry for him."

"I don't," Neal said. "It's about time someone put you both in your places. Jacqui Karston will do it for him, and I'm sure Andrea will do it for you."

"I'm sure Andrea wants me dead and buried," Edwin said with a sigh. "How long are you planning on staying again?"

"Just long enough for Andrea to know not to kill you and hide your body. I'm tired of shuffling people around." Neal walked around to the passenger side of the truck after tossing his bag in the back. "I want to look over the job proposals you guys have so far and see what we can do about making some contacts for more business. After that, I'm heading to St. Augustine."

Edwin slid behind the steering wheel. "What's in St. Augustine?" He slid the key in the ignition and started the truck, slipping it into reverse, and heading back to the office. He couldn't ignore the smile that crossed Neal's face, however, when he glanced over, shifting the truck into drive.

"Peace and quiet," Neal said. "Peace and quiet."

Edwin sighed. He wasn't sure what that felt like anymore, and he highly doubted with Andrea Newman as his manager he would ever rediscover those qualities again. She was determined to make his life miserable. He could feel it. *God, I miss Brevard.*

~ ~ ~ ~ ~

Andrea just stared at Neal as she sat across from him at his desk. While Neal Rutherford never stayed long at any one location, he made sure to have an office designated strictly for him at each one. His assistant, Barbi, called ahead and had everything ordered to decorate it according to every other office Neal had in all of his locations. Same paintings. Same desk. Same live plants. From what Andrea heard, Neal was a little obsessive that way. He liked the same things done the same way all the time, which probably explained why he insisted on keeping Edwin Coldwell. "Neal, we've got things running pretty smooth already," she said, repeating herself for the third time. "We don't need the personnel he's wanting to hire. Edwin's just afraid of doing the hard work."

Neal leaned forward in his chair, hands clasped in front of him as he stared at her. "You've only met him a day ago. How can you know what he's afraid of?" he smirked. "I know Edwin, and he's not the type to bare his soul of his deepest, darkest secrets, no matter how long you know him. So, I doubt you know the man at all. And he does work. Otherwise, I wouldn't have kept him around for fifteen years. He just does it in a way that best utilizes everyone's qualities and strengths."

"Neal, we don't have the business to take on three more people," she stressed. "I'm trying to save you money we haven't even brought in yet."

"But it's my money." He arched an eyebrow at her. "Look, Andrea, I appreciate what you're wanting, but as I said, Edwin has worked for me for over fifteen years. He knows how I like things to go, and he's doing exactly what I would want him to do.

You don't wait for the business to knock on your door before you get ready for it. If you do, then you're behind, and your client will know it. Act as if you already have all the business you can handle, and others will wonder why you're so busy and want you to work for them."

She sat back in her chair, shoulders slumped. She didn't get it. She thought for sure Neal would see things her way, want to save money, and build things slowly. The fact that he approved of Edwin's recklessness only confused her more.

And irritated her if she was honest. She wanted Neal on her side so she could get rid of Edwin. Savannah wasn't his office. It was hers. She would run it her way.

Or, at least, she would have if Neal had seen things the way she wanted him to, which he didn't, and now she was stuck working for the womanizer that had sent her domin... Sent Brian back to Florida.

She sighed. This was not how she saw this meeting going. With a deep breath, she nodded. "Can I be frank?"

Neal shrugged. "Always."

"I feel like you're wanting me to babysit, and I transferred here to help run an office." She leaned forward, her seriousness in her motions.

Neal arched an eyebrow at her, one corner of his mouth turned up in a smirk. "Andrea, I may not be in these offices, but I assure you, I know what goes on in them. You transferred here to be with Brian, and don't think I'm clueless as to why. He allowed you to run the office your way while he pretty much coasted." He shook his head. "I know you two were intimate, don't bother denying it or even asking how I know it to be true. I won't tell you either. However, I'm not putting up with that in my companies anymore. If you want to be with Brian, then by all means move to Florida, but you won't be doing it as my employee. That would be sad, though, because you're damn good at what you do, and I need you here." He settled back in his leather recliner. "Play your cards right, and the next office is yours." Then he shrugged. "Or this one when Edwin gets caught with his pants down again. However, you're not a babysitter. You're one of my managers, and I expect you to manage. Edwin has a lot to teach you if you have the guts to learn."

Andrea just stared at the man across from her, his words making her mouth fall open slightly as she absorbed them. How did he know about her and Brian? Edwin had even implied that he knew about her and her former boss. She swallowed the lump in her throat and nodded, unable to say anything else.

Neal must have taken her silence as acquiescence because he nodded once and said, "Good. Now, let's get Edwin in here and get down to work." He picked up his phone and hit a button. "Edwin, grab those files and come to my office. Let's see what we're starting with so we know where we need to go from here." He hung up the phone and turned back to Andrea. "Now, what are some of your plans for this office and generating some new business?"

~ ~ ~ ~ ~

Edwin wasn't sure what Neal and Andrea talked about, but he could tell by her expression that the conversation didn't go the way she wanted. He did his best not to let the smirk show on his face. With the cold reception she had given him since he entered the offices yesterday, he was sure she had hoped that Neal would see things her way and side with her on her grievances with the way Edwin was already doing things. Brian may have hired her, but he sure as hell didn't keep her informed on the big boss and how he worked. While Edwin hoped Neal's talk with her would calm her down some, he highly doubted it. If anything, it would probably only make her more antagonistic toward him. He knew he needed to figure out a way to bridge this gap of animosity between them, but he just didn't know how.

"Edwin, good, you're here," Neal said as he settled back in his leather desk chair. "Now, let's look at those projects and see where you're at."

Edwin passed the folders over to Neal as he sat down in the other chair beside Andrea. He chanced a glance over to her, but she refused to look at him, keeping her gaze fixed on Neal as if she was focusing on the task at hand. Edwin knew better, however. She just didn't want him to know that she was annoyed. Yet, she couldn't keep that from her expression. He gave a silent chuckle and turned his attention back to his boss, who was already glancing through the folders, nodding at what he saw.

They were tucked away in Neal's office for two hours, strategizing on how to drum up new business and make a name for themselves in the community and surrounding areas. Neal wanted them to get involved in the city, reaching out to leaders and volunteering support for different things. His goal was to make Rutherford Construction a visible force to be reckoned with in Savannah and the surrounding areas.

Once the meeting was over, Neal ordered a car and then told them he'd see them at dinner. Both of them. Edwin thought he heard Andrea groan. He definitely needed to get her to somewhat tolerate him if they were going to work together. How was the question, though.

As they left Neal's office, Edwin asked Andrea to join him in his office before returning to hers. He wasn't sure what to say to her, but he knew he needed to head off her sour mood before it affected the rest of his day. When he entered his office, he decided to take a more casual approach and perched himself on the corner of his desk, one leg draped over the side as he watched her come in and stand just inside his door. He sighed. This was not going to be easy.

"Look," he started. "I know that whatever you two discussed in Neal's office wasn't what you wanted to hear."

She crossed her arms over her chest. "Rubbing it in?"

Edwin sighed again as he shook his head. "Not at all. I'm telling you I want us to work together. I think we can make this an awesome office. Neal has a vision, but he's leaving it up to us to carry it out our way."

"You mean he's leaving it up to you to carry it out. He doesn't care what I think." She shifted, her back ramrod straight as she glared at him. "Trust me, I heard what Neal said, while you were there and before you arrived. I'm to kowtow to what you want and get in line with your agenda, whether I agree with it or not." Her lips were pressed into a thin line as she stared at him—or rather, glared at him. "He won't even permit me to transfer. I'm stuck here if I want to keep my job with this company, following you around in a subservient manner, like some obedient puppy." She narrowed her eyes at him. "I am *not* a puppy dog."

"I never even considered that you were," Edwin said. "I don't expect you to bow down to me or even placate me. I want you—no, *need* you—to speak your mind. I don't want you to always agree with me. I don't need some "Yes, sir" manager who never challenges my ideas and thoughts. That's not how we move forward. I want you to always speak your mind." He shrugged. "Of course, I have the final say, but I promise to always take your opinions and suggestions in mind before making that final decision. The only advantage I have is that I know how Neal likes his offices run for the most part. I'm the foundation upon which your new ideas can be built, but that can only happen if you get past your preconceived notion of me, and we work together to make this the best office we can make it." He cocked his head to the side. "I can do it without you, of course, but I'd rather do it with you."

She stared at him, and Edwin decided it best not to say anything else and just stare back at her. He meant what he said. He wanted her on his side, working together, but whether she decided to jump on board or not, he was determined to make Savannah a great office. This was his home now, and he wasn't going to do it half-ass.

He could see the war on her face, the battle to hate him even still. Finally, she nodded. "I'll see you at dinner." She turned and walked out of his office, leaving him staring after her.

Edwin ran a hand through his dark hair as he watched her walk away, wishing he knew how to make her change her mind. He could only do what he could do, however, and leave the rest in her hands. He could only hope she came around to his way of thinking and stop fighting against him. Yet, he knew he couldn't put too much effort into making her see that working with him was better than working against him. He needed to get to know the rest of the office and focus on the other employees. If Andrea refused to work with him, he knew she would be working against him, and he wouldn't allow her to poison the rest of his staff against him. He grinned as he said to himself, *I'm too damn good of a person for that.*

Five

Andrea sat across from Trent Wilson, a powerful looking black man with dark brown eyes and a seductive smile. If she weren't so pissed off right then, she would have enjoyed his sculpted muscles and powerful fingers, imagining his hands gripping her hips and driving into her. But she *was* pissed. She had hoped to be able to get away from Edwin for the rest of the day until she was forced to have dinner with him later that night when they joined Neal, but she had forgotten about their meeting with Trent, owner of The Rabbit Hole. She still couldn't believe Savannah was about to get their very own BDSM dungeon. She couldn't believe *she* was about to help build it.

"Have you had a chance to look over the plans?" Edwin asked Trent from behind his desk. "I know our architects have spent a long time going over your needs, making sure everything was doable." He grinned, glancing down at the files on his desk, his fingers tapping them lightly. "There are a few special, um, accommodations in the blueprints, but I think we can make it all work out."

Andrea turned and glanced at Edwin, not sure how to take his manner of speech. He seemed to be having fun with what he knew was in those plans that Trent had handed them. She wondered how much Edwin Coldwell actually knew about the lifestyle Trent seemed to be wanting to bring into his business.

Trent's smile grew as he nodded, his ankle resting on his knee, his hand cupping his shin. "I'm glad to hear that. When do you think we'll be able to get started?"

Edwin leaned forward on his desk, hands clasped together in front of him. "As soon as we get you to sign the contracts and cut that first check."

"Great," Trent said. "I'm eager to get this underway."

"Can I ask how you got this idea in the first place?" Edwin asked, his head tilted to the side.

Trent cocked an eyebrow as he stared at Edwin. "Are you sure you want to know? Some people have a limit when it comes to things of a sexual nature."

Edwin chuckled softly as he glanced over at Andrea, a smirk on his face. "My limits are pretty low," he said before he turned his attention back to Trent. "We have a few of these places back in Florida. Please. I'd love to know what gave you the idea."

Trent glanced over at Andrea. "And you?"

She stared at him for a moment, debating within herself whether now would be a good time to leave the meeting or not. Glancing at Edwin, she saw the challenge in his eyes, almost daring her to get up and leave. Straightening in her chair, she turned to Trent and said, "By all means, let's hear the story." She turned back to Edwin, smiling, letting him know he lost this round.

He just chuckled as he turned his attention back to Trent, settling back in his chair.

The other man shrugged. "It's not that big of a story really. For the past few years, I've been hosting these by-invitation-only sex parties in my house, mostly around Halloween or other holidays. Within my walls anything went as long as people consented. We've had people used like serving trays, covered in finger foods and then pleasured once the food was devoured by everyone. There was one man who enjoyed having sex with another man for the first time, and a woman who had a train ran on her."

Andrea felt her brows pinch together. "I'm sorry, a train?"

Trent nodded. "That's where she just lies there while one man after another has his way with her."

Andrea felt her eyes go wide as she made a slow nod. "Um, wow."

Trent chuckled but continued. "Everyone has to wear a mask, so no one knows who anyone else is. It helps to release people's inhibitions if they can keep their identities a secret. If they don't know who anyone else is, then they aren't afraid of what could be said once the party is over or if they run into someone at, say church or work. They feel free to truly let go and experience things they've fantasized about. I'm hoping the popularity of those parties will translate into a busy dungeon."

Andrea heard the stories Trent shared, imagining each one and how it must have felt for those people, her pussy dripping at the images he described. Were there actually people in Savannah who allowed themselves the freedom to do everything he suggested? To just enjoy sex, even if it were with strangers? How would it feel to have dozens of fingers grazing her flesh as they picked up small pieces of fruit or other finger foods from her body? If she was guaranteed total anonymity, how far would she allow herself to go to experience something? Heat pooled between her legs as she wished she had the guts to find out.

"How do people hear about your parties?" she asked before she could think better of it.

Trent turned to her, smiling. "I have a special list of names for my eyes only. People find out about the parties through word of mouth, of course, but then I screen everyone, making sure everyone is disease free, knows how to be discreet, and loves to have a hot time. The people who attend trust me to look out for their privacy as well as their safety." He turned back to Edwin. "There's always an interest, so I'm counting on that to work for me here."

"Well, we'll make sure we make it look as authentic as possible," Edwin said. "I'm sure you'll be pleased."

Trent slid out of his chair, standing as he reached out to shake Edwin's hand, the file folder with the contracts in the other. "I have no doubt. I'm looking forward to working together."

Andrea followed suit, standing, her mind full of the images Trent described. Did people really go to places like that? She had always thought sex was a private matter, kept behind closed doors. Would they really go to a public dungeon? She sighed, thinking that all this time she believed that there was no one like her in the world.

Trent reached out, shaking her hand as well, smiling at her as he gave a slight dip of his head. "Thank you for everything."

"My pleasure," Andrea said as they released their hands, arms dropping back to their sides. She glanced over at Edwin, but his focus was purely on Trent Wilson. How was he not thinking about those scenes Trent described?

"I'll get with my lawyer and get these contracts signed," Trent said, holding up a manila folder. "And when they come back, there will be a check attached."

"Sounds good," Edwin said as he moved to open his office door for the other man. "Andrea here will go ahead and get things lined up, so that as soon as we get those contracts back, we can get started right away."

"Great," Trent said. He shook Edwin's hand one more time and then Andrea offered to show him out.

As they walked, Andrea debated within herself about asking more questions about his parties but decided against it. At least, not in the workplace, not with so many eager ears close by. Although she really wanted to know more about the people who could just let themselves go.

At the door, Trent turned around once more, shaking her hand. "Thanks again," he said, his smile contagious. "I really do look forward to working with you. This dream has been a long time coming."

"I'm sure it's going to be everything you want it to be," she assured him.

He gave her a slight dip of his head before turning and walking to his sports car.

Andrea just stood there for an extra moment, watching as the man drove away, her mind still twirling over the tales he shared. So not appropriate for the workplace, but damn, they had her honey dripping.

Blowing out a sigh, she turned and made her way back inside. Edwin would want to talk over the meeting with Trent, and she'd have to sit there, enduring it when all she wanted was to get the hell out of there. She could really use some alone time with her battery-operated-boyfriend right then.

~ ~ ~ ~ ~

Edwin had a hard time containing his grin as he watched Andrea walk back into the office. He could tell by the flush to her cheeks that Trent's tales of open sexuality had stirred things inside of her, things she would never admit to Edwin. That didn't mean he didn't want to know, however. Andrea was a tough one, someone who held herself stiff most of the time, which usually meant there was some sort of pain or doubt hidden just below the surface. If he could find that out, their working relationship might loosen up a little.

"Well, what do you think?" he asked her as she entered his office, sitting back down in her chair. "You ready to build a dungeon?"

She gave him a one-shouldered shrug. "I think he's definitely eager to get people through the doors of his business and having sex. I'm just not sure there's enough people like that in Savannah to keep his idea open. If there was, wouldn't there be a dungeon already?"

Edwin nodded. "Perhaps. Or perhaps he's the first one with the ba…um, guts to build one. I'm sure there's plenty of legal hoops to leap through for permits and licensing and shit. Could be no one else wanted to take the time or be associated with something so sexual."

"And you're sure Neal's ready to be associated with something like that?" she asked, leaning back in her chair.

It took all of Edwin's power not to let his gaze drop to her ample breasts as her shirt popped open slightly because of the way she was sitting. Giving himself a mental shake, he smiled at her, nodding. "I think Neal will take just about anyone's money, including the owner of a sex dungeon. And why wouldn't he? If he doesn't do it, someone else will, and right now, we need the money to help us get a foothold here."

"I'm just not sure a sex business is the first step we should take," she pressed. "Once we get our name out there, garner a reputation in Savannah, then yeah, sure. However, one of our first gigs? It might label us as the type of business *we* are."

He shrugged. "Well, Brian must have disagreed with you, since he was the one who went after this contract before he left." The way she sat there, staring at him with her mouth ajar, told him he caught her off guard with that bit of news. Had he read the situation wrong? He would have thought with the way she railed against his taking over this office and Brian being shuffled off before he could finish unpacking, that she had been playing footsie with the man. Neal had even said as much. Yet, wouldn't Brian have told her about something like The Rabbit Hole?

"Brian started this?" she asked, her body frozen in place. "I just thought…"

"You thought I went after this? How could I? This is only my second day here. You had the contracts when I got here, remember?" He shook his head. "No, I saw the paperwork for the first time yesterday, even though Sammy forwarded me some briefs about the waiting contracts for me to look at before I arrived." He leaned forward, clasping his hands in front of him. "For the record, I did doublecheck with Neal to make sure he wanted the Rutherford name attached to a sex dungeon. He assured me that Brian told him all about it, and he was on board." He shrugged again. "So, we're building The Rabbit Hole."

She shook her head, and he could tell she wasn't nearly as upset about building Trent's dungeon as she was that Brian had kept it from her. *Someone is going to get a pretty nasty phone call.*

He tapped the top of his desk as he leaned back in his chair. "Well, that's one contract about to be signed. On to the next one."

She nodded as she rose from the chair. "I'll set up some meetings for tomorrow. See if we can get something a little less, um, carnal."

Edwin laughed. "Maybe find us a daycare or something to balance it all out."

She turned, and he thought for just a split second she was about to smile, but then she straightened her back. "I'll see you at dinner." And then she walked out of his office.

He watched her weave her way through the desks in the middle of the bullpen, not even talking to Kendra or Jana as she passed. How in the hell was he going to get her to chill out? He was surprised she even talked about things with as close to the subject of sex as they came. *That woman can suck the fun out of anything, I bet.* He stared at Andrea as she stormed into her own office and dropped down into her chair. *Oh, somewhere in this favored land the sun is shining bright; the band is playing somewhere, and somewhere hearts are light, and somewhere men are laughing, and somewhere children shout; but there is no joy in Mudville—mighty Andrea has struck out. And she's pissed off as well as a prude, it seems.* He sighed as he leaned forward, reaching for another file folder.

Staring at the papers inside, he tried to concentrate, but finally gave up, realizing it was useless. His mind kept repeating Trent's stories. God, how Edwin would have loved to have been at one of those parties. The wild abandon, the exploration, the wanton sex. And now Trent was opening a BDSM club, and Edwin would have a hand in putting it together. It would be almost like building his own sexual playground. He had never been in a dungeon before but had always wanted to visit one of the ones back in Florida. Seems he may be getting his chance in a few months right there in Savannah.

Leaning back in his chair, he stared up at the ceiling, his hands clasped behind his head as his thoughts drifted back to Faith Greer, the woman ready to do whatever he told her to do. Complete obedience. And he had pushed her at different times. In his office back in Brevard, at his house, even in his truck while driving around town. He told Faith to do something, and she did it without question. He remembered how he pressed her up against the glass window, her breasts smashed for anyone to see as he fucked her from behind. And people did see. A group of men drove by and stopped to watch, and she stood there, holding still while he took her, driving his cock into her wetness to the cheers of the other men. Then he sent her off on a week-long trip with Morgan in the hopes she would sleep with him and earn Edwin some extra points. As it turned out, she did sleep with Morgan, but it didn't have the effect Edwin had wanted. Instead, she came back and ended everything, destroying his world in the process. It was the last time he talked to her, knowing that once Faith made a decision, it was final, and he wouldn't want to do anything to ruin the life she had. He had asked her to come to Savannah with him, but she refused, choosing her new adventure with her husband and Tracey over him, not that he could blame her. That didn't take away the pain, however.

He sighed, sitting back up in his chair as he glanced back out the window to his small office. The one he had back in Brevard was bigger. Much bigger. As he stared out the window, he watched Andrea shuffling through a stack of files on her desk. Something besides Brian being transferred had her ire up, but what on earth could it be? Something had her on edge, and Edwin believed it was more than just the thought of building a dungeon. He wanted to find out what that something was. Perhaps then, he could get her to lighten up on him, and he could have some real fun. He wasn't so sure how long he could be the good boy for Neal unless he found somewhere to unwind.

He glanced toward the wall where he knew Sammy sat on the other side. She seemed like someone who might know where to go for some fun. A grin creased his face. It was time to explore Savannah's seedier side.

Six

"I really don't think Andrea is on board with this dungeon of Trent Wilson's," Edwin said as he pulled into the parking garage near Ellis Square. "She had a lot to say about it after he left."

Neal shrugged, glancing out the side window as Edwin searched out a spot. "She'll get there. Give her time. That dungeon will give us a nice cushion to get us started in this city. We only have a few other projects, and I want to make sure we can handle anything that comes our way." He glanced over at Edwin, a serious expression crossing his face. "And I expect quite a bit to come our way. I want to see this office running as smoothly as Brevard. With Morgan in Biloxi and you here, we can make a fairly decent name for Rutherford Construction. We'll be building things throughout the south."

Edwin laughed. "That's what I've always loved about you,

Neal. Ambitious as hell."

Neal nodded, chuckling softly. "And you and Morgan have helped me see those ambitions come to fruition, which is why I haven't booted your asses out of the company so far. Don't screw things up here."

A parking spot appeared up ahead, and Edwin pulled in, shaking his head. "Trust me, Andrea's not going to give me a free moment to screw up. I think she has everyone in that office watching me for any misstep. "

"Good," Neal said, bluntly. "However, that needs to work both ways. You keep your eye on her, as well." He popped the door open as Edwin turned off the car, but he didn't step out immediately. Instead, he turned and stared at Edwin. "You both should have been fired. See if you can come together and make this office a success." He stared for another moment, his face a mask of seriousness.

Edwin felt uncomfortable under the man's scrutiny, shifting slightly in his seat. "Yes, sir," he said with a curt nod, and only then did Neal slide out of the car. Edwin took a deep breath and followed suit. *So, the rumors about Andrea are true. Interesting.*

Andrea was already waiting for them outside of Hogan's, an Irish pub along River Street. Neal nodded, smiling at her as they approached, and Edwin took a moment to really look at her. Her short blond hair framed her oval face, her cheekbones a little high and leading to her soft blue eyes, eyes that seemed harder at work when she was daring him to fuck up or arguing about how he wanted to do things. She wore a tight top with a low neckline that exposed her ample breasts, her nipples soft bumps, which told Edwin she didn't go for padded bras often. Her jeans cupped her curvy ass, and when she turned to follow Neal inside, Edwin couldn't help but appreciate the sway of her hips. He wasn't sure why he had taken so long to admire her treasures. Probably because he was trying to keep her from castrating him for replacing Brian. Edwin also wondered how far she had crossed the line with her former boss. The way Neal spoke, it seemed it was as if she had almost been fired as well, which only piqued his interest even more. Trouble always loved hanging out with trouble after all.

As they slid into their seats, the hostess handed them each a menu, promising their server would be with them shortly before turning and walking back to her stand. Edwin watched her walk away before he caught himself doing it and turned back to the others at the table. Andrea stared at him, judgment clearly on her face. Neal just ignored him.

"Tonight, we're celebrating," Neal said as he reached for the drink menu. "So, I don't know about you, but I intend on having an adult beverage. Feel free to join me. This is on me."

Edwin chuckled slightly. "Now, that I like to hear." He reached for the other drink menu, and then paused, handing it over to Andrea first. "You've been here the longest. Ever eaten here?"

She stared at him and then dropped her gaze down to the menu as if it were about to bite her. "I did when I first arrived, but I don't remember what we had." She took the menu.

"So, no recommendations, huh?" Edwin nodded. "Okay, it's time to explore." He glanced over at Neal. "What are you thinking about having?" He opened the food menu as he waited for one of the others to finish with the drink menus.

Neal stared at the menu. "Probably an Old Fashioned like usual, but I always like to check out the options. What about you two?"

Edwin opened his mouth to answer, but Andrea cut him off, dropping the drink menu on the table. "I think I'll have a margarita, sugar on the rim, instead of salt."

Edwin chuckled as he reached for the drink menu, noticing she didn't bother to hand it back to him. He supposed a few moments of civility earlier was all he could expect. He dropped the menu back down, deciding not to even bother. Their server showed up at that moment, and before she could ask what they wanted, he turned to her, a frustrated grin on his face. "I'll take a Glenfiddich. Actually, make it a double."

The server took the other drink orders and Neal's appetizer order for chips and spinach dip, then turned and walked off, promising to be back as soon as she could with their drinks.

Once she was gone, Neal clasped his hands together as he leaned on the table. "So, you two ready to play nice together, or do I need to make some other arrangements for this office?" He bounced his gaze back and forth between the others, waiting for their answer.

"Not even going to wait until the drinks arrive?" Edwin asked with a slight chuckle and a shake of his head. "It's as I already said. I'm here to work, and I'll do what's necessary to make this office a success." He turned to Andrea. "I'm actually looking forward to working together. Fresh starts all the way around."

Andrea nodded, but didn't look at Edwin. "I'm here to work."

Edwin stared at her for a moment and then glanced over at Neal, giving his boss a one-shoulder shrug. He supposed that was the best he was going to get out of Andrea. He would take it, of course. He'd do what he was supposed to do to make it work. If she decided not to meet him halfway, then that was on her.

"Glad to hear it," Neal said, obviously ignoring Andrea's curt reply. "Now, what are we all having for dinner?" He pulled the menu to himself, opening it, and starting to peruse the items listed.

Andrea followed suit, her motions stiffer than her boss's.

Edwin stared at her for a moment, wondering how long she

intended to keep up the cold exterior toward him. If he had wronged her at some point, then he would understand, but this… This was carrying her grudge a little too far. Obviously, she didn't care about putting on a bad face in front of Neal. How far had she gone with Brain? It had to be pretty far, considering her behavior. This went way past Edwin being a womanizing dog. This was a pouting woman acting as if she had been ripped away from something important. What had Brian said to her when he left? He obviously didn't take her with him when he was transferred, so what actually happened between them? It had to be more than just a little fun in the sheets. Edwin wished he knew.

The server brought their drinks, and as Edwin lifted his to his lips, he determined to find out just exactly what happened between Brian Holmstead and the woman he left behind. He was sure someone somewhere knew the answer to that. In this company, someone always did.

~ ~ ~ ~ ~

Neal left them standing there, deciding to take an Uber instead of having Edwin drive him back to his hotel. She stared at the man as he walked away, wondering why on earth he would leave her alone with Edwin. What did he expect to happen? Friendship? She agreed to work with the man. Wasn't that enough?

"Well, I think he intends on us getting another round of drinks," Edwin said, turning to her and shrugging. "I say, since we have the company card, we should go ahead and do as he suggested. I'll even let you pick the bar."

Andrea shook her head. "You have fun with that. I'm heading home." She started to walk away, but Edwin grabbed her arm and brought her to a halt. She glanced down at his hand, eyebrows cocked. "Excuse me? Let go."

Edwin released his grip, hands held out at his side in a surrender gesture. "No offense. Didn't mean to ruffle the stoic

Andrea." He dropped his arms, a smirk on his face as he shrugged. "Neal is giving us a chance to get to know each other and work through whatever animosity you have toward me. Look, I get it. You don't want me here. I obviously interrupted some grand plan you had. But you're stuck with me, so let's make this work." He held up the credit card Neal told him to use, grinning. "Come on. You have time for a couple of drinks." He cocked his head as his grin grew. "I'm sure there are questions you want to ask me. Now's your chance. Join me for a couple of drinks, and I'll let you ask me anything you want."

She eyed him suspiciously. "And you'll answer any question I ask? No lying or deflecting?"

His lips twisted in a lopsided smirk. "Anything you ask, I'll answer. What do you have to lose?"

She stared at him for a moment, not sure she believed him, but knowing the offer was too good not to give it a shot. "Fine. There's a bar on the next section. We can go there." She turned, leaving it up to him to follow or not. This was his idea after all. All she wanted to do was get home and out of her bra.

A quick scurry was heard behind her, and soon, out of the corner of her eye, she saw Edwin walking beside her. She smirked but said nothing as she led him to The Exchange Tavern and straight to the wooden bar, sliding onto one of the burgundy upholstered barstools. The sound of glasses clinking and silverware rattling against ceramic plates mixed with people laughing, some a little louder than others, telling Andrea that they had been there awhile drinking and visiting with friends. Or making new ones.

Edwin wasn't so quick to sit down, though. Instead, he glanced around the place, taking in the hockey sticks pinned to the wall above the bar on two sides, the stained-glass decorations next to them, and the rest of the wooden booths and chairs along with the brick walls. A shelf loaded down with bottles of various alcohol hung from above the bar and a window on the other side gave everyone a great view of what was happening in the kitchen with the smell of hamburgers on the grill as well as chicken wings in the fryer.

Nodding, he slid onto a stool beside her, swinging around with a smile on his face. "Quaint little place," he said, turning to her as the bartender approached. "How did you find it?"

She shrugged. "Brian brought me here when I first arrived. He had already been here for a couple of weeks, getting things set up for the new office. He had time to explore before I got here."

The bartender stepped up to them, hands on the bar as she leaned on it. "What can I get the two of you?"

"Tequila," Andrea said. She wanted something stronger than what she had at dinner since she was here alone with Edwin. He was carrying this getting to know you thing just a little too far.

"I'll take a Glenfiddich, neat," Edwin said, turning sideways on his stool to face Andrea as the bartender turned around, pulling two glasses out from under the bar. "This area seems like it'd be fun on the weekends."

She nodded, keeping herself facing the bar. "River Street is a lot of fun. Shops, bars, restaurants. They have ghost tours, as well. Those wind up down the road, giving the tourists a good show for their money. I've never been to one, though. Those things give me the creeps."

He chuckled softly, nodding. "I'm sure they play it up pretty well for the best reactions. Who wants to go on a ghost tour that isn't scary, right?'

"True," she said as the bartender set their glasses in front of them. "Cheers." She picked up the thin glass of tequila, lifted it in a toast, and downed half of it, the amber liquid burning its way down her throat to set her stomach on fire. Setting the glass back on the bar, she took a deep breath and turned to see Edwin staring at her, his eyes wide. "What?"

"Do you really hate being around me that much?" he asked. "I mean, I get it. You wanted to be here with Brian, but how long are you going to hold that against me? It's not like I asked for this. You don't even know me. I deserve to at least be given the benefit of the doubt. Let me earn your scorn, at least, before you set up these barriers."

She scoffed. "I think you've already earned my scorn." She glanced over at him. "Why exactly were you transferred here again? I'm sure it wasn't because you were doing such a bang-up job back in Florida." Then she arched both brows as she nodded. "Oh wait, that's exactly why you were sent here. Banging on the job."

"And why were you sent here?" He gave her a pointed stare, one hand on his glass, a glass he had yet to lift to his lips.

She stared at those lips a moment, his silent accusation hanging on them. "I volunteered to come here," she said, still not ready to give in to his insinuations. She hadn't agreed to answer any of his questions. However, she caught herself staring at his lips still and jerked her attention back up to his eyes. "I wasn't sent here, like you were."

He cocked his head a little as he stared at her, a slight smirk twisting his lips. "And why, exactly, would you volunteer to leave where you were, your friends, your family, everything you knew, probably even a promotion eventually, to come here?"

She stared at him as he lifted his glass and took a slow sip, his gaze fixed on her over the rim of the glass. She could feel her breathing getting heavier under his gaze, feel her heart pounding. He wanted her to admit to something, to moving here because of Brian, but there was no damn way she would give Edwin the satisfaction. "Maybe I was looking for new opportunities." She gripped the thin glass to keep her nervousness from making her hand tremble.

"Maybe? You don't know?" He shrugged, leaning back in his stool. "Seems you would know why you moved your life to Savannah. Look, I don't care why you're here. All I care about is that we somehow figure out how to work together and make a go of this. Neither one of us has a choice at this point if we want to keep working for Rutherford. It's not like he's going to transfer us again. I want to see this office kick ass, and I want you to help me do it. However, I need to know if we can work together or not?" He took another sip of his drink as he watched her.

She hated that he was staring her. She finished off her tequila, rubbing her lips together as the alcohol burned its way down to her stomach. He was right, she knew, but that didn't make it any easier. Setting the glass back on the bar, she took a deep breath, nodding. "Yes. We can work together. We don't really have a choice, do we?" She turned and faced him, her lips pressed together. "We can do this."

He chuckled. "Not really ringing with confidence, but I'll take it. Besides, we have a dungeon to build."

She stared at him, realizing how forced her assurance had come across. She sighed, relaxing her shoulders a little. Edwin was right. They had to figure out how to make it work between them. She had moved there to be with Brian, but he had left her behind. She had nowhere else to go right now, so she was stuck working with Edwin. Neal made it abundantly clear that he wasn't transferring her anywhere, especially not down with Brian. She had to make this job work until she figured something else out. "I'm sorry," she said, relaxing a little where she sat. "I mean it; we'll make this work. I'll give it my all." She forced a smile on her face. "Even in building a dungeon."

Edwin nodded, setting his glass on the bar, but not letting go.

"Have you ever been to a BDSM dungeon?"

She was about to tell him how inappropriate his question was, but stopped, her mouth slightly ajar. Nothing she had done so far had been appropriate. Most other bosses would have fired her for the way she constantly attacked him, but Edwin took everything on the chin and kept smiling at her. Instead, she closed her mouth and shook her head. "No, I haven't. To be honest, I never even knew something like that existed. I thought BDSM was something people kept in their bedrooms."

He cocked an eyebrow at her, a lopsided grin creasing his face. "So, you have heard of BDSM then." He tilted his head a little, his eyes narrowing as he studied her. "Mind sharing your opinion on that topic?"

Seven

Edwin tossed his keys onto the table by th front door and headed for the kitchen counter and the bottle of whiskey he knew waited for him. He had to admit, the night went better than he expected it would, especially after Neal left. He honestly didn't expect Andrea to agree to another drink with him the way she had behaved since they met yesterday. Maybe he hadn't lost his touch after all.

After pouring himself a double, he stepped out onto the back porch, the dim lighting of the moon casting a soft glow over his backyard. Slipping his phone onto the table beside a camp chair, he sat down, propping his feet up on the railing, and settled his glass in both hands in his lap as he stared out at the quiet night, the sound of crickets off in the distance. A slight breeze whispered through the trees on the back of his property, their leaves dancing as the branches swayed. He took a slow, deep breath, the scent of magnolias filling his nose. For the first time since Cherish almost sent his family jewels into his chest, he felt relaxed and at peace. Lifting his glass, he took a slow sip, swiping his lips with his tongue when he was finished.

As he rested his head on the back of the chair, a small smile toyed at his lips. Tonight had been fun. And the look on Andrea's face when he asked her about ever venturing into a dungeon almost made him spit out his whiskey. She hadn't answered him, of course, turning back around and ordering another tequila, but the look on her face told him all he needed to know. She hadn't been in one but was definitely interested. Since then, his mind couldn't stop picturing her in several positions, serving his sexual needs. He had paid closer attention to what she had on at that point as well, and damn, the woman looked hot as hell. Her blue eyes sparkling whenever she allowed herself to laugh, her ample breasts bouncing with the motion, the creamy tops spilling over her neckline. When she leaned over the bar slightly to talk to the bartender, Edwin took the chance to stare at her heart-shaped ass in her skintight blue jeans, and he had to shift in his seat a little to keep anyone from seeing how his cock had grown. Even the way she kept her short blond hair made her look sexy, wisps curling up in front of her ears adding to her personality. Everything about Andrea Newman shouted a smoldering sexuality. That is, until she tried busting his balls in front of everyone. He shook his head, chuckling. *Fuck that, even then she looks hot as hell.*

He took another sip of his whiskey, swallowing the dirty thoughts that crept into his mind. Glancing over at his phone, he was almost tempted to text her. He would have if she hadn't seemed so hellbent on catching him at something so Neal would fire him, probably hoping Brian would be transferred back. He sighed. No. Texting Andrea was a bad idea. An extremely horrible idea.

Instead, he took another sip of his whiskey, feeling the slow burn of the liquid traveling his throat to his belly. He glanced back at his cell phone. It would be a waste of time anyway. She was clearly still hung up on Brian. Edwin wondered what the play was there. Did Brian intend to move her down to him once he was settled? Did Andrea even want to go to Florida? Would Neal permit it or would she have to leave Rutherford Construction? Edwin couldn't see Neal permitting it after what he told Edwin earlier about both of them needing a babysitter, so she would definitely have to quit. But, did she want that? Edwin hoped not. As much as he would love to work with someone who wasn't always busting his chops, he actually liked Andrea. At least from the little he knew about her, he liked her. From all reports, she was damn good at her job.

He glanced at the phone again. What possible reason would he have for texting her at this time of night? He had already told her he enjoyed himself tonight and was glad they agreed to work as a team, instead of always fighting each other. There was nothing work related that couldn't wait until morning. He sighed as he lifted his glass for another drink. There just wasn't a valid reason for him to reach out to her that wouldn't have her red flags whipping in her immediate accusations. No. Texting her was out. He would just wait and talk to her tomorrow. Besides, even if she didn't think he had some scheme up his sleeve, what would be the point? There was no way Andrea would give him the time of day. They hadn't even flirted tonight. Just sat there, sipping their drinks and sharing mundane stories. Nothing deep or personal had been shared or even offered. Why was he even thinking along these lines?

He took another drink as he shifted in his seat, reaching for the phone. Scrolling through his contacts, he found Andrea's name and opened his texting app. He stared at the blinking cursor for a moment, trying to think of what to type. *This is such a bad idea.* With a deep breath, he wrote, *Really had a good time tonight. Thanks for hanging out. Perhaps one night we should take the whole crew out. Have a good night.* He plopped the phone back down on the table and finished off his drink. *Well, let's see how much trouble that gets me in.*

~ ~ ~ ~ ~

Andrea stared at her phone, unsure what to think about Edwin's text. Was he setting her up for something? He didn't really want to keep talking to her outside of work, did he? What should she write back? Should she write back? No. Ignore it. She could pretend she didn't see it and just apologize in the morning for not answering.

But he was trying to be nice. Or so it seemed, anyway. And he was nice. She had almost died when he asked her about ever attending a BDSM dungeon, having to turn away and ask for another drink while she hoped he didn't see the blush on her cheeks. Furthermore, he looked nice. Okay, that was a lame way of putting it. Edwin Coldwell was more than nice, not that she had given him much of a chance since he arrived. That didn't mean she hadn't noticed how tight his pants fit around his ass, or the slight bulge in the front promising thicker things when not constrained. Even Sammy had noticed how powerful Edwin looked: strong arms, thick chest, broad shoulders, a jawline that begged to be caressed. And that smirk of his. Just thinking about it brought an instant heat between her legs.

She closed her eyes. *Stop this! I do not need to be fantasizing about my boss. He's the reason Brian isn't here. I can't forgive that.*

Opening her eyes once more, she glanced down at the phone again. She should answer him at least. Then she wouldn't have to worry about it in the morning. With a sigh, she plopped down on her bed. But what should she say? It was true she had a good time as well, but how would he read that? Would he think she wanted to do more with him? Was this a trap to see if she would cross the lines she had already gouged into the ground between them?

She was being silly. It was a simple thanks for a fun night. Nothing more. She needed to stop reading anything more into it. Hitting the reply button, she typed, *I had a great time, as well. Agree about taking the others out for a night on the town. Might help gel everyone together better. See you tomorrow.* She hit send and clutched onto her phone, staring at the message. She had to get Edwin Coldwell out of her mind.

Scrolling through her contacts again, she found Brian's name and hit CALL. She heard three rings and then his voice. "Well, this is a surprise," he said, and by the sound of his voice, he had almost been asleep. Or was he whispering?

She jerked her gaze to the clock on her nightstand. Eleven-Thirty. Damn. "I'm sorry," she said, weakly. "I honestly didn't realize the time. I just got in a little while ago and just assumed it was still early. You go on back to sleep. I'll call you tomorrow."

"Just got home, huh?" She could hear him shifting in his bed. "What had you out so late?"

Shit. She didn't want to tell him she was out with Edwin. Shit. Shit. Shit. "Neal took us out to dinner, and then we had some drinks at The Exchange Tavern. The one you took me to when I first got here. Remember?"

"I do," he told her. "A good place to hang out. Did they like it?"

She closed her eyes, realizing the more she spoke, the more she was digging a hole. "Well, actually, it was just Edwin and me. Neal left us to try and figure out how to work together."

"Just you and Edwin?" Brian asked, his tone holding an edge. "Wasn't that a little awkward? Did he behave himself?"

"He did," she assured him. "Actually, he seems to want this to work for both of us. Look, I'm sorry. I really didn't know how late it was. I just…" She took a deep breath, pressing the phone to the side of her face a little too hard as she dropped her chin slightly to rest on her chest. "I just missed your voice. Any chance of a visit anytime soon?"

She heard him take a deep breath. "I don't see how right now,to be honest. I'm still getting things settled here. You know how it is with a new boss in town. How are things going at your office? Edwin fitting in all right?"

"He's not you, but he's doing all right, I guess." Then she remembered the dungeon. "Hey, did you negotiate for us to build a BDSM dungeon? We're working for Trent Wilson, and Edwin says you started the ball on the project."

Brian chuckled. "Yeah, actually, I did. I was going to surprise you with it, but then I got transferred. I know how you love being my little submissive, so I thought working on a dungeon might open us both up to some steamy ideas. I was sure Trent would give me some free tickets or passes or whatever he's using to charge people for admittance, and then we could take you to your first public play scene."

She sucked in a breath as the thought sent heat straight to her sex. "You would have taken me out in public as your submissive?" Would she even be able to handle being out in public like that? What if Brian took her to The Rabbit Hole and Edwin was there? By the way he talked, Edwin seemed to know something about the BDSM lifestyle, so it stood to reason he might go just to check it out. Her pussy dripped even more at the thought of Edwin seeing her there. Giving herself a mental shake, she sat up straighter on the bed. "You'd want people to see me like that?"

"Of course," he assured her. "It would be hot as hell. Those places come with a code of discretion. If we saw someone there, they'd be there for the same thing we were and couldn't exactly go running to Neal." She heard him laugh again, his voice dropping lower. "Maybe I'll still take you. Put you in a skimpy outfit, collar and leash. Spank you in front of people right before I make you kneel and suck me off. Now that would be hot."

She bit down on a groan that threatened to slip past her lips. "Yes," she said, her voice a breathy whisper. "Yes, it would."

"Where are you?" he asked, and she could hear the devilish grin in his voice.

"I'm at home," she told him. "In my bedroom. I was just about to get ready for bed when I called you."

"So, you're still dressed?"

"Yes, sir," she said, still picturing the scene Brian described.

"Then I want you to be a good girl and strip for me," he ordered. "You may set the phone down to do so. And grab your vibrator. Since you woke me up, I think I'll have you come for me. Sweet sounds to help me go to sleep again when we hang up and I have something to dream about."

"Oh, god." She sucked in another breath, her honey dripping even more. "Yes, sir. Give me a second, please."

"I'll be waiting right here when you come back."

Andrea set the phone on the bed as she slid off and quickly stripped out of her clothes, leaving them in a rumpled pile on the floor. She then reached into her nightstand and grabbed her purple vibrator, testing it once to make sure the batteries were good. She had used it a lot since Brian left. Once she was satisfied everything would work perfectly to get herself off, she slid back onto the bed, her back on the pillows as she rested her head against the wall. Spreading her legs, she picked up the phone again. "I'm here, sir."

"That's a good girl," Brian said into her ear, his voice low, seductive. "Are you ready to play with yourself for me?"

"God, yes sir," she moaned. "Please. May I?"

"You may, love," he told her. "Turn your toy on and give that sweet pussy of yours some relief while I tell you what I would do to you at the dungeon."

"Yes, sir," she said, flipping her vibrator on and sliding it between her legs. "God, I've missed you."

"And I you, my little toy. Now, close your eyes. Picture yourself in the dungeon, a corset pushing those beautiful breasts of yours up for everyone to see, your nipples hard buds aching to be pinched and licked, your luscious ass on display for everyone's pleasure, for my pleasure."

Andrea placed her toy on her clit, feeling the vibrations pulsing against her sensitive pearl. Her body immediately tensed as a moan slipped past her lips just before her mouth popped open. God, she needed this, his voice in her ears, his wishes conveyed. She craved pleasing him.

He continued with his story, others touching her, caressing her with their hands, pinching her, her nipples hard beads, her areolas tight circles. She groaned, pushing the vibrator against her clit harder.

"Use your other hand to play with your nipple, Andrea," he ordered. "Pinch your nipple, tweak it, and stretch it a little, pulling it as your pussy drips from the attention. That's what I'm going to do to you in front of others, reach around from behind and torture your breasts with my fingers."

God! She moaned even louder, whimpering slightly as she slid her free hand to her breast, pinching her swollen nipple, twisting it between her fingers. "Yes," she begged. "Oh, god, yes. Please, Brian. I need it."

She could feel him behind her as if he were right there, feel his breath in her ear as he told her everything he would do to her in front of the others. She imagined how his rock-hard cock would feel pressed against her exposed ass, aching to be buried inside of her slick passion. Her back arched as she pushed her ass back into him, rubbing his hardness between her cheeks. God, she would love to be doing it all right then.

"And then I would make you kneel, right there in front of everyone like a little slut," he said, his voice still a husky whisper. She wondered if he was playing with himself while he tortured her with his words. "With my fist in your hair, I would make you watch as I opened my pants, pulling my hard cock out, ready for your mouth."

"God," she groaned, picturing everything he said, her mouth already slightly ajar as if he was actually about to shove his manhood between her lips. "Please."

She felt her body tighten, felt the wall of her orgasm ready to crash down upon her. "Oh, god!" she cried out. "Sir, oh god, sir. I think…oh god, may I…please? I need to…." He needed to give her permission. She needed to hear it. She *must* hear it.

But he didn't say it. At least, not right away. Instead, he continued telling her how he would make her open her mouth as he slid his cock back and forth over her lips until she begged to suck him off.

Her body shook, ready to explode, as she shoved her head back into the wall as she tried to hold off her orgasm. She knew it wouldn't be long before she failed him, but she couldn't stop. God, it felt so fucking good.

"Now, my toy," he whispered harshly, and the sound made her eyes pop open as she stared up at the ceiling. "Come." And she did, her body shuddering as she cried out, her climax ripping through her in one massive waterfall, her back arching as she clamped her legs around the hand between her legs. It felt like forever as she screamed, her body one massive electrical tremor.

When it was over, she collapsed on the bed, her breathing heavy in her own ears, her mouth still ajar, legs still clamped shut.

When she finally opened her eyes, she stared at the wall in front of her, confused. She knew it was Brian who told her to come just then, but in her mind, she heard the voice of Edwin Coldwell.

Eight

Edwin entered the offices of Rutherford Construction with a cup of coffee in one hand and a stack of files in the other. Sammy already perched behind her desk, her own cup of coffee leaving a ring on some old papers. As soon as he pulled the door open, she glanced up, a smile already decorating her lips. "Good morning, Sammy," he greeted. "How was your night?"

"Boring," she said, shaking her head as she leaned forward, hands clasped in front of him. "Nothing happens on a Tuesday night around here worth mentioning. Now, tonight, it's hump day. Ladies night everywhere. Tonight, I'll have my fun." She winked at him, giggling softly. "How about you? Didn't you have dinner with Neal and Andrea last night? How did that go?" She looked toward the doorway leading to the main offices, then glanced back at Edwin, obviously making sure she wasn't about to be overheard. "She play nice at all?" She shrugged. "I know she's been riding you fairly hard since you arrived. For the record, the rest of us are fine with your transfer here. It's not like we had a lot of time to get used to how Brian did things before he was shipped off and you arrived. He was nice. You're nice. Everyone's nice."

Edwin chuckled as he leaned on the counter, which barred visitors from getting too close to Sammy. "That's good to know. And yes, she played nice. We actually had a good time. She took me to this place called The Exchange Tavern. A neat little pub. Have you been there? I was thinking of taking everyone out on a team building night."

"Team building at a bar, huh? I love how you think." Sammy nodded, her lips pressed together. "And I have actually. It's one of the better bars on River Street. I love their French onion soup."

"I only had their whiskey," he said, smiling as he chuckled again. "But, I'll make sure to check it out next time I'm there. River Street seems like an interesting place to hang out. Ladies night, huh?" He nodded as if thinking it over. "Maybe I'll see which bars are having their own ladies night tonight."

Sammy giggled. "Can't let a good hump day go to waste now," she said, bouncing her brows as she smiled up at him.

Edwin just laughed as he stepped back away from the desk, tapping the top of the counter as he did. "And with that, I think I'll head to my office. Talk to you later." He shook his head, still laughing as he walked away. He would have loved to stand there and discover what kind of hump day fun the little brunette could get into, but with the way things went back in Brevard, it probably wasn't the brightest idea. Sammy was cute, and he was sure she was a real spitfire out on the town, but she wasn't someone he could ever see himself getting busy with, so to speak. Besides, if Andrea caught even a whiff of him flirting with the young receptionist, she'd fly to Neal crying foul faster than a Thunderbird jet during an air show. Edwin did not need to risk his job again. He was fairly sure he wouldn't survive this round, no matter how much Neal liked him.

"Edwin," Kendra called out as he entered the back den of desks and offices. "Good, you're here. I have a list of applicants for you to go over for the warehouse position."

He cast a quick glance over at Andrea's office, wondering why Kendra hadn't gone to her first. Turning back to Kendra, he nodded. "How about give me an hour, and we'll sit down with Andrea and go over them?"

"Sounds great," Kendra said. "Thanks."

He started to nod, but the dark-haired woman had already spun around toward her desk, no longer paying him any attention. Cocking an eyebrow at her abruptness, he just chuckled and continued toward his office. He couldn't expect to win them all the way over in just three days.

Setting his coffee down on his desk along with the files Kendra had just stuffed into his hands, he plopped down into his chair and cast a glance up at the white board on his wall, debating which job to dig into first. The Rabbit Hole kept coming up as the winner.

He glanced over at Andrea's office again, thinking of her reaction to building the dungeon yesterday. She acted repulsed, but Edwin somehow figured she had experience in the BDSM lifestyle. The way she dodged his question last night made him question just how repulsed she truly was. A smile toyed at the corners of his mouth as he pictured her with her hands bound over her head, breasts exposed, nipples hard buds of pleasure ready for his mouth. His smile slipped into a grin as he wondered how far into the lifestyle Andrea would go.

A hard rap on the glass to his office jerked his attention to the side. Neal stood there, glaring at him.

Oops. Edwin fell forward in his chair, wiping the grin from his face as he reached for a file on his desk, not even caring what it was about at the moment.

The owner of Edwin's future stormed into his office, his face twisted into a stern scowl. "Forget it," Neal said with a shake of his head as he entered Edwin's office. "I know damn well you weren't daydreaming about whatever is in that file you're holding. I'd bet a week's pay you couldn't even tell me what was in that folder." He pointed to Edwin's face as he took a chair in front of his desk. "That was a grin I never want to see on your face while you're inside these walls. And it better have been about something in the past and not some new conquest you're fantasizing about." He shook his head. "Forget that. It better not have even been about something in the past. It better have been something else entirely."

Edwin chuckled, dropping the file folder on his desk along with the pretense that he was working. "I get it, I get it. Promise." He shook his head. "I'm not looking for any trouble. Besides, I just got here. I know I'm a charmer, but not even I can work that fast."

"Bullshit," Neal said, sighing as he settled back in his chair. He waved off the conversation. "Forget it. You're going to do whatever the hell you want anyway. Just don't let it escalate like it did back in Brevard, all right?"

"Understood," Edwin said, leaning back in his chair.

"I highly doubt it. Now, are we ready to move on Trent Wilson's business?"

Edwin nodded. "As far as I know. If everything goes right, we should be able to break ground in two weeks. I'm heading over to Development Services to fill out the forms for the permits tomorrow. We'll get all the inspections done, and then, hopefully, we can get started. Trent's dungeon will be up and running soon. I'm sure Savannah can't wait."

"That's Savannah's problem," Neal said, crossing his legs. "Mine is to get the business, so we can get more. I have a couple of more meetings, and then I'll be leaving Friday." He gestured behind him at the office in general. "Think you can handle things from here?"

Edwin didn't hesitate. "You bet. I intend on hiring a few more office staff, and then we'll get started adding subcontractors to our list of people to work for us. Kendra's handed me some men for the warehouse manager position, so hopefully that will be taken care of by Monday. I plan on going over the list with Andrea in a few moments."

Neal nodded. "Good to see you two working together finally."

"I wouldn't go that far, but it's a start at least. She has some strong opinions of me as well as how this office should be run."

"You'll figure it out, I'm sure." Neal tapped the arms of his chair a couple of times before standing. "Now, I have to get going. I have a brunch appointment with some people from the hospital. We might get the contract for a new wing."

"Good luck," Edwin said, leaning forward and opening the file again.

As soon as Neal was gone, Edwin closed the file, still not sure what was inside of it, and leaned back in his chair, staring over at Andrea once more as Jana walked into her office. How would Andrea react to going to the dungeon when it opened? He would love to find out.

~ ~ ~ ~ ~

Andrea saw Edwin when he walked into the building but purposefully kept herself from looking up at him. She still couldn't shake the fact that it was his voice she heard when Brian had told her to come last night. How fucked up was that? Thank god she didn't call out his name. That would not have gone over too well.

She slammed the file folder she had been staring at for ten minutes closed, unable to concentrate on the contents. Leaning forward on her desk, she held her head with both hands, her fingers shoved up into her hair. What had gotten into her? She had only known the man for two days, and he had been a pain in the ass the entire time. There was no way he should have been in her head like that. She sighed, releasing her head as she plopped back in her chair. It had only been one conversation.

Right. And that conversation made me horny as hell to the point I had to call Brian up for phone sex. She shook her head, glancing up when she heard a hard knock on glass. Neal stood in front of Edwin's office for a second before marching inside, shutting the door behind him. *Already in trouble, Mr. Coldwell?* She sighed as she reached for the file again, determined to get Edwin out of her mind.

Though she would never admit it to him, the truth was, she had a good time last night. Of course, she had to skirt the subject of BDSM, but other than that, she found Edwin—oh, god, could she admit it?—charming. She wanted to hate him. Had determined to hate him actually. He was the whole reason her life had been jerked out from under her. Okay, maybe not her life, but her relationship. She had grown to count on Brian in all aspects of her life. Not that she needed him to take care of her, but rather, she had grown to desire his control, a control that bordered too close on the questions Edwin had asked last night.

A quick knock came at her door, jarring her for a moment. Looking up, she saw Jana standing there, her long, red hair pulled back in a tight ponytail. Andrea waved the woman inside.

"Hey, Kendra and I were wondering if you wanted to hit River Street tonight," Jana said. "Most of the bars have a ladies night on hump day, so we thought it might be fun to just get out and mix it up a little. We wanted to invite you to join us."

Andrea smiled, nodding. "Sounds like fun. What time and where?"

Jana shrugged. "Say eight o'clock. Meet up at the Hyatt and decide where to go from there. How does that sound?"

"Sounds good to me," she said, glancing over the woman's shoulder as Neal left the offices. *I wonder what that was all about.* She turned her attention back to Jana. "I'll meet you both there."

"Great." And then Jana simply turned and walked back to her desk.

As Andrea watched the woman walk away, she saw Edwin leaving his office, a stack of manila folders in his hand. He didn't say anything to the other two women as he passed them, making his way straight to her office. She watched as he walked, his shirt pulled taut over his powerful chest and arms, his broad shoulders, firm jaw. Her pussy throbbed as she remembered hearing his voice last night in her mind.

Sucking in a deep breath, she closed her eyes as she looked away, clamping her legs together. *I have got to get this under control.* With a slow, steadying breath, she opened her eyes once more just as Edwin knocked on her door. To her surprise, he waited for her to motion him inside before he opened the door.

"Hey," he said, lifting the handful of file folders he carried with him. "I thought we could go over some of these applications for the warehouse manager if you have a couple of minutes. Kendra is going to be reaching out to Ryan Slater about helping us out in here, so that's taken care of."

She still didn't think they needed a warehouse manager or another manager in the offices, but she was tired of protesting the matter. After all, he was the boss.

Her eyes went wide as soon as the thought entered her mind, sending heat straight to her sex. *He was the boss.* Shifting in her chair again, she nodded, forcing a smile onto her face, hoping he didn't catch her reaction. "Sure. Whatever you need." *Oh, god, stop it!* She took a deep breath in through her nose, forcing herself to focus on the first file he handed her, inwardly scolding herself for the schoolgirl thoughts she was having. Okay, not so much schoolgirl as horny college student. "See anything here you like?" She closed her eyes, biting down a groan. Thank god Edwin didn't know her inward struggles right then.

"Are you all right?" he asked, his head cocked to the side a little. "You look a little uncomfortable. We can do these later if now's not a good time."

"No, no," she said, her words coming out in more of a rush than she intended. She took another calming breath. "Now is perfect. Really."

"Good," he said as he tossed the other files on her desk. "I have a couple of thoughts, but I want to hear what you think first."

She gave him a curious look. "Why?"

He shrugged. "You're going to be working with whoever we hire as much as I am. I want you comfy with whoever that is." He cocked a brow at her. "That doesn't mean I'm going with your choice if I think it's a bad fit, mind you. But, there are some decent candidates in there, so I'm pretty sure I'll be all right with your choices."

Andrea nodded as she glanced back to the files, slowly scanning each one. Edwin had been right. There were some decent choices for her to pick from, and she did so quickly. She didn't tell Edwin that, of course. No. She continued to sit there, staring at the files while her mind wandered back to Mr. Coldwell. She hated herself for it, but she couldn't force herself to stop. He was a cocky son-of-a-bitch, smug, over-confident. And it all made him sexy as hell. She definitely needed a night out.

No, she needed Brian back in Savannah.

She stared at one word on the page, not seeing it, as she thought back to her conversation with Brian last night. They had phone sex, him saying all the perfectly naughty things in her ear she needed to hear in order to get herself off, but he balked when she asked him to come visit her. He actually seemed quite content down in Florida.

A twisting tightened her stomach, threatening to make her vomit as doubt churned inside of her, making her queasy. Had she been forgotten that fast? Then why the phone sex last night?

She couldn't think about the files anymore, but she didn't want to let Edwin know how she was struggling at the moment. Instead, she grabbed the third one down and handed it over to him. "I say go with this one." She tried to force a smile onto her face, appear normal to a degree. She wasn't sure she pulled it off, though.

Edwin kept his gaze on her as he took the folder from her hand. Nodding, he glanced down at the name. "Ethan Monroe." He glanced back up at her. "Are you sure? To be honest, I thought you'd go with one of the other guys. This one doesn't have a whole lot of warehouse experience."

Shit. That wasn't the one she meant to give him. Had she screwed up? It didn't matter. She couldn't change her mind now. If she did, he would know she hadn't really looked at the files completely. Instead, she made a weak shrug. "So, we're all about new beginnings, right? Let's give him a chance to prove himself. It's not like we're busting at the seams right now. He could work his way into things at a slower pace, learning as he goes."

Edwin stared at her for a moment, sizing her up, she knew, but then he just nodded again. "All right. I like it. New beginnings." He popped out of his chair, tossing the rest of the files back on her desk. "Look through those again and see if you think anyone would be a good fit to help us out in here in other capacities. In the meantime, I'll pass this off to Kendra, so she can get the ball rolling on bringing him in for an interview."

"Sounds good," she said as she watched him walk out of her office. Her gaze automatically went to his ass before he shut the door behind him, and she clamped down a groan as she caught herself doing it. This was not going well. She needed to get Edwin Coldwell out of her mind. *Yes, I definitely need a night out.* But first, she needed to call Brian to figure out if it was just her imagination running away with her or if she had been forgotten that fast. She silently prayed that imagination was all it was. She dreaded the thought of Brian not in control anymore.

Nine

Andrea finished brushing out her hair, almost ready for a night on the town with the girls. She had yet to call Brian, afraid to know the answer. What would he think of her going out to have drinks? Would he give her rules for the night? Set expectations? He had done it before. Taken her out and placing her at a bar, asking her to flirt with whoever approached her while he sat in a booth and watched. If the man wanted to buy her a drink, she was to let him. If he touched her thigh, she was to let him. If he leaned in to kiss her, she was to let him. The entire night had kept her panties soaked, especially when a strong-looking, dark-haired man sat down beside her, smiling at her once as he motioned for the bartender and ordered a whiskey neat. She remembered how her nerves made her hands tremble slightly but also how turned on she had been, knowing that she wasn't allowed to tell the man no to anything he wanted. She had glanced over at Brian, and he just winked at her, which sent another tremor of excitement through her.

She stared at her phone, which sat on her dresser. What would he tell her to do now? She sighed. Only one way to find out.

Dropping down on the bed, she snatched up the phone and scrolled down her contacts until she found Brian's name. She stared at his name for another moment before taking a deep breath and hitting CALL. Her nerves threatened to undo her as she lifted the phone to her ear.

Three rings, and then Brian answered, but he didn't say anything at first. Instead, she heard him shuffling as if moving around or something. When he did answer, his voice was a soft whisper. "Hey, you, sorry I needed to get somewhere so I could hear you. Kind of early for a repeat of last night. Something I should know about?" He laughed softly, and it made her feel more at ease.

"No, nothing you need to know about," she assured him. "I'm heading to River Street with Jana and Kendra for a night out."

"And no Mr. Coldwell?" Brian asked. "I thought you two had such a good time last night. You don't want to take him out again? Show him a good time?"

"No," she said, almost shouting. The truth was, she did want to show Edwin a good time, which is why she needed to avoid it at all cost. "No, I don't think he'd have a good time with us. You've seen Jana when she gets drinking. I'm not sure even he could handle that. We know we couldn't."

Brian laughed. "You're probably right." The line went silent for a moment, then he asked, "So, you doing all right? Something happen?"

She placed her free hand between her legs, pressing them together. "Nothing happened." Not yet, anyway, and she was hoping to keep anything from happening. "I was just thinking of our nights out, and how you would make me do things." She felt the smile crease her face. "I miss those nights. I miss you being here."

"I know, love," he said. "I'm sorry this happened. It wasn't my first choice, I assure you."

"And now?" The question came out before she could stop it.

"What do you mean 'and now'?"

She took a deep breath. Why the hell did she say anything? She pressed her lips into a thin line as she tried to think how she wanted to ask what she knew she needed to ask.

"Andrea? What's going on?"

She took another deep breath and just blurted it out. "I meant now that you're there and I'm here, do you feel the same way? We never discussed how this would all work with you in Florida and me still here. I know you thought it was a bad idea for me to follow you to Fort Lauderdale, but how do we keep moving forward with each of us in a different location?"

Silence answered her, which made her stomach twist into a tight knot again. She knew she should have kept her mouth shut. She was pushing him into a corner.

"You're right," he said finally. "We never did talk about how it would work. And we both knew you coming here would have stirred up all kinds of shit considering why Neal transferred Morgan and Edwin. No one knew about us, and it was the only way to make sure we didn't fall into the same stink that covered the two of them."

"I got news for you," she said. "Neal knew. He practically told me so. And I also think Edwin knows by the way he spoke to me Monday."

"What did he say?"

"Basically that he knew people didn't uproot their entire life just to follow someone they didn't even work with to a new city. A new store in the same city perhaps, but not a new city in a new state."

"Makes sense," Brian told her. "Which is why I didn't think you following me a second time would look good. They're guessing, sweetie. They don't really know anything."

"Brian, I don't care what everyone thinks or knows or believes or anything like that," she said, feeling desperation clench her heart. "I just want to be with you. I want us like we were. I submitted to you. I need you to act like my master."

"I know you do, love, but it's kind of hard to do with you up there and me down here. We just need to give it a little time."

She sighed, closing her eyes as she dropped her head. "I don't want to give it time."

"Hey, hey, it'll be all right," he assured her. "And it won't be for long. We just need to give things time to cool down around your new boss, so people won't think of us in the same light."

He was right, but that didn't mean she liked it. "Fine. But how much time?" She opened her eyes but continued to stare down at her hands. She hated that she sounded like she was whining, but she was tired of not having answers.

"As long as it takes, I'm afraid," he told her. "But, hey, we can still have some fun, right? Tonight, when you go out with your friends, see if you can have a little fun. Pick one guy to cozy up to and get to know. Make it the first guy who comes up to you and say hello if you can. Wear something on the sultry side that shows off your boobs. Something enticing. Flirt with him, and if you feel safe enough, go have some fun with him before you go home. Tomorrow night, you'll call me and give me all the dirty details. How does that sound?"

She nodded. It wasn't what she wanted exactly, but she would take what he gave her. "That sounds fine. Thank you, sir."

"Well, I'll take your words and not the sound of your tone," he said, a slight chuckle in his voice. "Go have some fun. I'll be waiting for your call tomorrow night."

"Yes, sir." She dropped the phone on the bed as she blew out a breath of frustration. She still didn't have any answers. Just a command to go out and play the flirty submissive for some stranger. She supposed it was better than nothing.

With her hands on her knees, she shoved herself into motion. *What to wear? What to wear?* She wished she knew. Something sultry. Show off the girls. She would do as he asked, but it wouldn't be as much fun without him sitting there watching her carry out his orders.

As she pulled out a slinky, burgundy dress, holding it out in front of her as she raked her gaze over it. *I can at least use his orders as a distraction. I could use a distraction.* With a shake of her head, she turned and draped the dress across her bed. It was time to get ready.

~ ~ ~ ~ ~

Edwin stared down the red brick steps at the underground entrance to The Bar Bar. *Now that's a unique name.* He chuckled, shaking his head, and then descended the steps two at a time. The sounds from the music and the patrons laughing filtered through the front doors as Edwin approached, a couple stumbling out, arms around each other's waist as they brushed past him.

The interior of the dimly lit bar was almost exactly what Edwin would have expected with wood furniture and red brick walls. The bar, a horseshoe-shaped structure toward the back, had a wall of bottles on the back end with a large wooden beam at the front. Metal barstools with red seats and backs circled the bar and off to the side was a leather couch where a couple sat facing each other, drinks in hand as they made puppy eyes at each other. Off to the other side sat a pool table and foosball, both already occupied. Lights filtered down from several spots in the ceiling casting a soft glow to the floor as music played from speakers

Edwin couldn't see and people did a little bump and grind of their own. Off the dance floor, women huddled together staring at guys while the guys stood around gawking and trying their best not to look awkward. Typical.

"Another round of shots!"

The familiar voice jerked Edwin's attention toward the far corner of the bar where he noticed Andrea pounding on the surface while Kendra and Jana laughed from each side of her. At first, Edwin was tempted to just turn and walk back out of the bar, leaving the women to enjoy their night. It was obvious they didn't want him there or they would have invited him. Then he saw Andrea's red dress, the material cupping her ass as she leaned over the bar to get the bartender's attention, her slender legs straight and alluring as she stood there. His cock stirred, making up his mind for him.

With a smirk decorating his lips, he made his way over to where the ladies enjoyed themselves.

"Mr. Coldwell," Kendra said, stiffening a little as she spotted him and pushing away from the bar. The others turned to look at him, a shocked expression on everyone's face.

He held his hand up, shaking his head. "Edwin, please." He shoved his hands into his pockets. "And it seems like everyone is having a great time. Don't let me spoil it. I was just out for a drink myself; you know, wanting to soak in some of the local scene."

Andrea cocked her head a little, her eyes narrowed, and somehow, Edwin got the feeling she was sizing something up.

Perhaps he did overstep. "Well, anyway, I just saw you ladies and thought I would say hello before moving on. I'll leave you to your night. See you tomorrow." He started to turn and walk away, but Andrea stopped him.

"You should stay and have a drink with us," she said, and he couldn't help the way her breasts spilled over the top of her little red dress.

The other two ladies turned and stared at Andrea with surprise covering their faces.

Edwin glanced at them a moment and then turned back to Andrea. "Are you sure? I mean, I don't want to intrude."

She nodded as she gestured to the bartender. "I'm sure. I'll even buy the first drink. Glenfiddich, right?" She turned back to the bartender. "And four shots of tequila."

He nodded, his lips pressed together. "Good memory."

She scoffed. "It was only last night, but thanks." She ordered the drink and then turned back around to Edwin as she leaned on the bar with one elbow. "So, what do you think of the place?"

He glanced around nodding. "Quaint. I like it. Seems to have some decent atmosphere. Looks like the locals love it."

Andrea nodded, glancing around the place as well. "They do. Monday night is usually ladies night, so you'll have to come back and see what wanders in. Right now is just happy hour."

"We'll be right back," Jana said. "We need to use the bathroom." She grabbed Kendra's arm and dragged the woman away from the bar.

"We do?" Kendra asked as Jana hauled her away.

The bartender slid the drink in front of Edwin, made sure the ladies didn't need anything else, and then moved on down to the next customer.

Edwin reached out for his glass. "Happy hour works for me," he said, lifting the glass to his lips and taking a swallow.

~ ~ ~ ~ ~

Andrea watched as Edwin drank his whiskey. his Adam's apple bobbing slightly. She couldn't believe he was actually there, his tight jeans cupping his firm legs and his... She swallowed... His cock. She jerked her gaze back up to his face just as he lowered his glass. She glanced back around at the people scattered around the bar. "See anything you like yet?" she asked, smirking a little. It was a blunt question, and one with plenty of innuendo, but she was feeling a little incorrigible after her call with Brian earlier.

He glanced down at her, a smile toying with the corners of his lips. "Well, I just got here, so I haven't really looked around yet." He dropped his gaze to the tops of her breasts, his smile growing before he glanced back up into her eyes.

Andrea didn't move, allowing him to look all he wanted. Brian's words replayed in her mind. *Tonight, when you go out with your friends, see if you can have a little fun. Pick one guy to cozy up to and get to know. Make it the first guy who comes up to you and say hello if you can. Wear something on the sultry side that shows off your boobs. Enticing. Flirt with him, and if you feel safe enough, go have some fun with him before you go home.* She was sure Brian didn't mean Edwin Coldwell, but he *was* the first man to come up to her and say hello. If she wanted to obey her master... She cocked a brow once Edwin's gaze returned to her eyes. "And now?"

He chuckled, shaking his head. "Miss Newman, you are trying to get me into trouble." He lifted his glass in a mock toast. "But, I will say, you look amazing tonight."

"Thank you," she said back, smiling. Raking him with her gaze, one eyebrow cocked, she returned the compliment. "You look pretty impressive, as well."

The bartender laid the shots down on the bar in front of them.

Andrea picked two shot glasses up and handed one to Edwin. "Shall we?"

He glanced off to where the others went. "Shouldn't we wait for Kendra and Jana?"

She shrugged. "We'll order a couple of more. This is for the two of us. Consider it a way to seal the commitment we made to each other last night."

He gave her a questioning expression but took the glass from her hand. "Just so they know it was your idea. I don't need them thinking bad of me. I'm still trying to make a good impression here."

Andrea giggled, nodding. "And I haven't exactly been helping in that area. I'm sorry."

"You're fine," he said with a slight shrug. "I wasn't who you expected to be working with. I get it. Hey, I'm just happy you're being nice to me now."

She felt the shame warm her face as she ducked her gaze. She hadn't exactly been nice to him, she knew. Neal made the decision to bring Edwin to Savannah, and Brian made the decision *not* to take her with him to Fort Lauderdale. Edwin was just trying to survive a bad situation. "I'm sorry for that. I've been pretty shitty to you since you got here. That's not how I usually work."

He smiled at her, a smile that made his eyes sparkle, which made her panties melt. "It's all right, as I said. We'll make it work." He lifted his shot glass again. "To working together."

She matched his smile and lifted her glass. "To working together." And then they tipped their glasses back and downed the tequila. Setting the empty glass back on the bar, she then turned to Edwin, steeling herself for the next question. "Care to dance?"

His brows cocked as he eyed her. "Dance? Are you sure?"

She reached out, grabbing his hand and pulling him toward the dance floor. "Why not? We're not at work. Let's have some fun." As she glanced over her shoulder, she winked at him. "Consider it a team building experience."

"All right, but no judging my sad dance skills."

As she spun on the dance floor, she grinned over at him, her ass already swaying to the music. He didn't lie about his dance moves. He stood in one place for the most part, swaying back and forth and barely moving his hands, but his eyes never left her. She expected him to scope out the other women around him, knowing Andrea was off-limits, but he didn't look away once. Oh, his eyes strayed to her bouncing breasts, and when she turned, he had showed no shame checking out her ass. She made sure to bounce her backside a little more as she glanced at him over her shoulder. She leaned back, her head on his chest as she danced, giving him a perfect view down her top. He didn't disappoint her as his gaze darted down over her cleavage, his brows popping up slightly before he forced himself to look away. Straightening up, she pushed back, grinding her ass against him, and she could feel his hard cock through his pants. She grinned back at him again, bouncing her brows a couple of times. Say what you would about Edwin Coldwell; if what she felt was just the beginning, the man had a package that would keep her sore for days.

"Hey, you're dancing without us," Jana said as the other ladies joined them out on the floor.

As soon as he heard them, Edwin took a couple of steps back, putting distance between them.

She hated to admit it, but she hated that he had to do that. She was actually enjoying feeling his body against her.

"And you did your shots without us, as well," Kendra added, shaking her head. "Now you're going to have to do another one."

Andrea stared right into Edwin's eyes. "I don't think that will be a problem." She was enjoying the way this night was going. Now to see how long Edwin Coldwell could hang out.

Ten

Edwin finished his third drink, setting the glass down on the bar. Flagging down the bartender, he pulled out his card and handed it to her. "Put all this on my tab, please," he said as she took his credit card. Turning back to the ladies, he smiled. "Thank you all for a fun night and allowing me to crash your ladies night out. I had a great time, but I need to get home. You three sure you're all right to drive home?"

"We used an Uber," Jana said. "We're good to go."

"Calling it a night so soon?" Kendra asked. "Don't tell me the boss is a lightweight?" She eyed him up and down. "You seemed to be made of stronger stuff."

Edwin laughed, shaking his head. "My first night out in a big town, I think I'll play it safe. Don't need to get lost on my way home."

The bartender stepped up to them on the other side of the bar, sliding a black card holder in front of him with his bill and credit card inside. Edwin quickly signed it and then slid his card back into his wallet. He offered the ladies one more smile. "See everyone tomorrow."

"I'll walk you out," Andrea said, moving to follow him.

He paused a second, glancing at her as he wondered once more about her sudden change in attitude. With a quick nod, he gestured for her to proceed him and then followed, his gaze dropping to her ass when no one was looking. She definitely had a way of walking that kept him focused.

"Did you have a good time?" she asked as they reached the front door and stepped outside.

"I did," he told her. "How about you? I'm sure it wasn't the night you had planned. I'm glad you talked me into hanging out though." They took the steps back up to ground level, turning toward Ellis Square. He was surprised she was still walking with him, expecting her to turn back around once they reached the front and head back to the others.

She laughed, placing her arms under her breasts, pushing them up. "It was a lot more fun than I expected, truthfully." She turned, and he could see the tops of her luscious globes in the lamplight. It was as if she wanted him to look at her breasts, and he couldn't understand why. "I had a great time. Really. And, for the record, I'm glad you stayed with us instead of running away." She bounced her eyebrows at him, giggling some more. "And," she stepped closer, gazing up into his eyes, "it was fun dancing with you."

He took a slow, steadying breath, still unsure what was happening. "It was at that." He cocked his head a little, narrowing his eyes a bit. "Are you sure everything is all right? I mean, don't get me wrong; I thoroughly enjoyed tonight and loved seeing you relax with everyone, especially me. But…how can I say this?" How *could* he say it without stepping in a massive pile of shit?

"You seemed a little more, um…"

"Flirtatious than normal?" she finished for him.

"Yeah, that would be it," he said, giving her a weak smile. "I'm just a little confused after everything you said my first two days here. You accused me of being a womanizer. Why would you flirt with me?" He held up his hand quickly, making sure she didn't think he thought she was out of line. "Not that I didn't like it, mind you." He felt his smile grow. "I did very much. Still, it seemed a little uncharacteristic."

She dipped her gaze to the ground, nodding. "To be honest, I was just having fun. I had talked to Brian earlier, and he reminded me of some of the nights we had out on the town together when…" She stopped talking, her eyes going wide as she realized she just admitted to being out alone with Brian, her former boss, something she had never come right out and told anyone.

Edwin knew it, of course, but those were just rumors and his basing an opinion on things Neal said yesterday. "Relax," he told her. "You were both consenting adults. What you did is between the two of you and no one else's business. You'll find no judgment from me."

He watched as she nodded, ducking her head down again. He knew that expression on her face. "You miss him," he said. "Why didn't you go with him?"

She shrugged. "Optics. He didn't think it would look good if I followed him one more time, especially to an office so far away, even though I didn't technically follow him. We both came from different offices in different cities. Still, he thought I should remain here."

Edwin didn't like the sound of that. Before he left Brevard, he had begged Faith to come with him. He wanted her by his side, no matter how it looked to anyone else. Why didn't Brian want the same thing with Andrea? "Hey, how about a cup of coffee? I noticed a coffeehouse around one of these corners somewhere."

She smiled, her lips pressed into a thin line. "Yeah, that sounds like fun." She laughed a little, turning toward Ellis Square again. "I'm not ready to go home anyway."

He stood there a moment, pointing back toward the bar. "Should we tell the others you're leaving?"

She waved the question off. "I told them before we left when you weren't looking. They think I'm going to see if your reputation is true or not." She glanced over her shoulder and winked. "Apparently, they both noticed your, um, package while we were dancing." She bit her lower lip as she turned back around.

Edwin stared at her for another moment before laughing and shaking his head. He started walking, jogging a couple of steps to catch up to her. "You sure you're not trying to get me fired? I don't think I need to know what my human resources person was thinking of my junk."

She looked over at him as he stepped up beside her. "Not yet." She winked. "This is turning out to be too much fun."

Edwin just laughed some more. He wasn't sure what Andrea was up to exactly, but she was right about one thing; whatever this was was turning out to be too much fun.

They stepped into House of Joe's, grabbed some coffee, and slid into a couple of chairs around an ancient-looking table. Jazz played from the overhead speakers, and the other patrons sat around pounding on the keyboards to their laptops or playing board games, some individuals sat around in plush chairs or on couches, reading or doing homework it looked like. The strong aroma of coffee brewing wafted through the air along with the sweet smells of pastries as the sound of people talking battled with the music overhead.

Edwin glanced at his clock. Ten-thirty. "How long does this

place stay open?" he asked, not realizing the time. However, no one seemed like they were about to get up and leave, so he assumed they had time.

Andrea shrugged. "Not sure. This is the first time I've been here. I guess we'll hang out until they give us the boot."

He chuckled slightly, nodding. "I guess that works." He sipped his coffee, the dark liquid still too hot to drink without scalding his lips. Setting the cup back down on the table, he glanced over at her. "So, if you don't mind me asking, how is the relationship with Brian going? I mean, I'm assuming you two are still together, right?"

He noticed the way her smile slipped into a frown, her shoulders drooping a little. "We are," she said. Then she shrugged. "At least, I suppose we are." She sighed, her shoulders drooping further. "To be honest, I don't know what we are. He's the one who suggested I dress up like this tonight and flirt with the first person who said hello to me." She gave him a weak smile. "Just so happened to be you. Sorry about that."

He chuckled. "Trust me, I'm not sorry one bit." He gave her a wink, his smile firmly in place. Cocking his head to the side a little, he asked, "Does he do that a lot? Tell you to do stuff like he did tonight?" He held up a hand, stalling any outbursts. "And if I'm getting too personal, please just tell me. I don't want to cross any lines here."

She laughed. "I'm the one who tried to cross lines, remember?" She shook her head. "And no, you're not getting personal. I brought the subject up after all." He watched her breasts rise as she took a deep breath. "Yes, he did, actually." She glanced up at him, giving him a weak smile. "Twisted, huh? He used to tell me to flirt with strangers, and I'd do it. Loved it, even."

Before he thought better of it, he asked, "And did he tell you to do other things?"

~ ~ ~ ~ ~

She couldn't believe she was sitting there baring her sexual kinks to her boss, the boss she was supposed to hate. She smiled inwardly. No, she no longer hated him. He didn't deserve that. Nodding, she replied, "He did." She glanced up at him. "I've never been in a dungeon like Mr. Wilson intends on building, but Brian introduced me to the lifestyle. I suppose that's why I took it so hard when he left and didn't take me with him. It was kind of odd how it all started, especially since we were both in different cities. It only picked up pace when we transferred here, since there wasn't any distance between us anymore." She twisted her smile into a lopsided frown. "Sorry if I misled you. A hypocrite, I know."

He waved off her apology. "Your life is yours to share or keep secret as you see fit. No apology necessary. Although, I do expect you to lighten up on me now." He chuckled when he said that last part, and the shame of how she had treated him flushed her face. "I will say, it concerns me that he had you play the same game without him here to protect you. That's a big risk he was making you take. You need to be careful about who you allow to do what to you, even under your dominant's orders."

"Yeah, I guess neither of us thought that part out all the way," she said, a little surprised that Edwin was telling her to be cautious instead of focusing on the sexier aspects of her game with Brian.

"A dominant needs to think everything through," Edwin said, still smiling at her and making a slight shrug. "Your safety needs to be his first concern, not his horniness."

"You're right," she said, sucking in a deep breath through her nose. How would Brian keep her safe if they were so far apart? "How about you? You seemed like you knew a little bit about the lifestyle all during our meeting with Trent, and now you're telling me about a dominant's priorities. Dabbled in it some yourself?"

He smiled as he leaned back in his chair, one hand still gripping his coffee cup. "I've been in it for a few years, had a couple of ladies who liked to be controlled during sex. Nothing like a dominant/submissive relationship such as you're describing with Brian. Mine was mainly in the bedroom. Or car." He shrugged, a sheepish grin on his face. "Or at the office as rumor would have it."

Andrea couldn't stop the giggle that slipped past her lips. "I guess I should have known that would play into it." She lifted her cup in a mock toast. After taking a sip, she lowered the cup and shook her head. "I can't say anything, though, as you well know." She glanced over at him, a lopsided grin on her face. "We're a couple of real fuck-ups, aren't we?"

He just laughed, nodding as he lifted his cup to his lips, the sound of his laugh making the heat pool between her legs. She had flirted, danced, showed off the girls. Brian would just have to be satisfied with that. Although, if she were honest with herself, she wouldn't have minded if Edwin had taken her up on her advances.

As he lowered his cup, he merely shrugged. "We just like to have fun," he said. "And our fun is usually had without clothes. We are who we are. Nothing wrong with that as long as we don't bring it to work again. Neal's made it pretty clear he's had it with our sexual adventures at Rutherford Construction. That's why we're both here."

She nodded, her lips pressed into a thin line as she lifted her cup into the air with both hands. He was right. Even if Brian had asked her to go with him, she highly doubted Neal would have allowed it. "Truth," she said just before taking a sip of her coffee.

They spent the next hour chitchatting about different things from where each of them were from, crazy customers they had to work with, and the fears and excitement of moving to a new town. They hadn't realized how long they had sat there talking until one of the employees came over and told them they'd be closing in ten minutes. She stared down at her empty cup, wondering how long ago she had finished her coffee.

"Now that hour went by fast," she said, glancing back up at Edwin. "Who would have thought we could have such a good conversation two nights in a row."

Edwin nodded as he slid out of his chair, his hands going to his back as he stretched a little, bending his back as he groaned. "I enjoyed it as well."

Andrea allowed her gaze to drop down to the slight bulge in his pants, wondering how it would have felt if he had allowed her to carry out Brian's orders. Closing her eyes, she gave herself a mental shake. She did not need to bring her game with Brian into the workplace.

"You all right?" Edwin asked as he glanced down at her.

She opened her eyes again as she shook her head. "I'm fine. Just random thoughts, that's all." She slid her phone out of her purse and ordered her Uber.

He laughed a little as she stood. "I can understand those," he told her. "I've been having some of those myself tonight."

She felt the heat flush her face as she smiled.

As they stepped outside, Edwin asked, "So, what exactly did Brian expect you to do tonight? If you don't mind sharing, that is."

She balked at the blunt question, even though she felt the slight humiliation of it tingle her passion. "Well, he kind of told me to flirt with the first guy that said hello to me tonight and try to have some fun with him." She shrugged, glancing up at the clear night, the quarter moon high in the sky. "I know how that sounds, but it was part of our game when he was here. He never permitted me to get too far into it before he appeared and whisked me away."

Edwin stopped just on the other side of a couple of thick magnolias and turned to face her, his hands slipped into his pockets. A smirk brightened his eyes. "And then I walked in, the first to say hello to you."

She nodded, her hands clasped in front of her. "That you did."

"Out of curiosity, you said he would only let you go so far. How far is that?"

She shrugged. "Some kissing, groping. Plenty of teasing."

"You groping or being groped?"

"Both," she simply said, watching out of the corner of her eye as her Uber car arrived.

Edwin nodded, glancing up into the sky, his lips pressed into a thin line. He kept staring up into the night as he said, "And now you have to tell him you didn't do as you were told." He dropped his gaze back down to hers.

She could feel the fluttering of her heart in her chest as she stared back at him. She rubbed her lips together before answering. "That I do."

He grinned. "We can't have that, now can we?"

She watched as he leaned down, one hand coming out of his pocket to slide around her waist. He pulled her tightly against him as he lowered his mouth to hers, his lips pressing hard against her as he slid his tongue inside to taste her. She groaned as she felt his hand slide down to cup her ass, squeezing hard, his fingers digging into her. She felt herself fall into him, her chest pressing into him as his breath whispered against her cheek.

After what seemed like forever, Edwin broke the kiss, leaning back but keeping his hand on her ass as he stared into her eyes. "Now, you can tell him you were a good girl tonight and did what he said." He winked at her. "All masters love good girls." He squeezed her ass one more time before letting go. "I'll see you tomorrow," he told her as he stepped over to her ride and opened the back door, gesturing for her to get in. Not until she reached the open car door, did he step away, moving toward the parking garage near City Market. "Be safe getting home," he said, smiling at her before he turned around again.

She stood there, watching as he walked away, his jeans cupping his firm ass. She could still feel his hand on her backside, feel his finger impressions in her flesh, the taste of him on her lips. Her chest rose and fell with her heavy breathing as she tried to recapture the breath he had stolen from her. *He kissed me. He actually kissed me.* Her eyes went wide. *How on earth am I going to tell Brian my current boss kissed me?*

Eleven

Edwin walked into House of Joe's and ordered a coffee before taking a table by the window. He had called the office and told Sammy he would be running late, blaming it on a meeting with a possible client. The truth was, however, that he just wasn't ready to go into the office and face Andrea, not after he kissed her last night, a kiss that he thought about all night long and even woke up thinking about. A kiss he enjoyed more than he thought he would.

On the drive home and until he fell asleep, he kept replaying their conversation in his head. He had been right in his assumption that she knew something about the BDSM lifestyle; he just hadn't known she was in it as much as she admitted to him last night. Her admission had kept him hard all night long, though. It had also brought to mind the last time he was with Faith Greer in the offices of Rutherford Construction before she went with Morgan to Tampa for a week to help straighten out a struggling office.

He leaned back in his seat, his hand wrapped around his cup as he watched people walking their dogs or window shopping as they walked around the edges of Jackson Square. It was a beautiful morning for it, and something he wanted to do soon. He had yet to explore the area too much, setting up his house the weekend before he started there and then getting bogged down with stirring up the new office. Outside of Neal taking Andrea and him out a couple of nights ago and then his excursion last night, he hadn't seen much of Savannah.

He felt his grin crease his face, brightening his mood, which wasn't dim to begin with. Of course, what he experienced last night was better than any historic tour. The look on Andrea's face when he pulled back after kissing her was priceless. He had completely caught her off guard, shocking her into silence, which for Andrea was a feat in and of itself. He chuckled as he shook his head.

And she likes to be controlled, he thought as he lifted his cup to his lips and took a sip. He loved to take control, to give an order, no matter what it was, and see the lady who had submitted to him obey. He had found that in Faith, and it was something that still made his cock hard thinking about it.

"I'm glad you made it," he had said as he neared where Faith stood by her truck. *"Your husband picked out a very pretty outfit."* She had worn a sexy sundress with matching bra and panties underneath, standing there in her sandals.

"Thank you," she said, and he could see the blush color her cheeks.

"Did he go all the way with the outfit?"

"Yes, sir." He loved when she called him sir.

Edwin held out his hand. "Hand me the dress and let me see."

Her eyes widened, shock covering her face "But, we're outside. Who all is here? What if someone sees us?"

He continued to hold out his hand, a smirk covering his face. "Then, they see you," he smirked. "Now, the dress." He stared at her, sure she would obey. Of course, he knew the place was deserted, had made sure of it actually. But, she didn't know that. Just that he had given her an order and expected her to obey no matter what. It was what she wanted after all, to be given orders she had to obey. It's why she had come to him in the first place.

His cock hardened as he watched her hands go to the material at her waist, and pull the dress over her head, handing it to Edwin once it was off. She stood, practically naked before him, the breeze kissing her skin. He knew she wanted to cover her body but also knew she wouldn't.

He held her dress in his hand as if it were a rag as his eyes raped her, grinning at her. He tossed the dress on the hood of her truck. "Your bra." His hand was out again.

Faith didn't question the command this time. She just reached behind her and unhooked the clasps. No sense being modest or worrying about someone's sudden appearance at this point. Sliding the straps from her shoulders, she removed the bra and handed it to him. He took it and grinned as he hung it on her truck's side mirror. He then gestured to the back door. "Now, you may go inside. Remove your sandals once inside."

She nodded, moving to obey him. He loved her obedience, and watching her walk to the building completely naked made his cock instantly hard.

Once on the beige industrial carpet, she slipped her sandals off leaving them by the door. She didn't even question him leaving her clothes outside.

She waited just inside the door, her hands hanging at her sides.

Edwin pointed her down the hall, and with a deep breath, she turned and walked. He knew his silence would drive her crazy, making her honey drip between her legs as she thought of his arousal at the sway of her naked hips.

She walked down the hall, pausing at the connecting corridor that led to the offices, but he just motioned her to go straight. She continued on, and he watched as she took the back way to the main lobby. The hall made a right turn, and way too soon, Faith walked into the front lobby of Rutherford Construction, stark naked. He had enjoyed her walking in the buff in front of him.

"Stop," he ordered.

She obeyed, but her eyes swirled in every direction making sure they were alone. Then, her eyes went to the tall window, and he knew she could see Eau Gallie Boulevard, knowing that if someone looked in, they would see her.

"Kneel facing the window."

She hesitated, her eyes wide.

"At any time you fail to do as asked, whatever I ask, the game ends."

She looked at him with nervous eyes, silently pleading.

Edwin shrugged. "This is what you asked for. It's up to you to decide when it's too much." He stood there, hands on his hips as he watched her.

She took a deep breath and then walked over to the window and knelt down facing out.

Her obedience made his cock throb. "Now turn your body to the side." She obeyed. "Good girl." Edwin walked in front of her, the bulge in his pants straining the fabric. "Do you want it?"

Faith nodded.

"No nodding. Do you want it?"

"Yes, sir. Please, may I have your cock?" She looked up into his eyes, begging for what she knew he wanted to give her, and

for what she knew she would have to earn.

"Pull it out and use that talented mouth of yours."

"Yes, sir." She practically lunged for the button of his jeans, all at once forgetting the window in her desire to have him. She slid his pants to his ankles, her lips pressing to his engorged sex even before they were completely down.

"No hands, just your mouth."

She left her hands pressing into her thighs as she buried her face in the dark curls of his balls. She breathed him in, and then she caressed him with her tongue. He placed his hand upon her head as she sucked one of his family jewels into her mouth, sliding her tongue around and over the sac. His moans filled the room as he felt her run her tongue up the underside of his thick shaft, and he felt his body tense at her talents. As she reached the tip of his hardness, she took him as far into her mouth as she could, her tongue twirling around his shaft.

"That's my girl," he growled. "Take your boss's cock all the way into that mouth. See yourself sucking me off right here in the lobby. You're naked, in front of this window, giving a blow job. You enjoy being the little slut. Too bad we don't have cameras in here."

She moaned, the sound pulsing around his cock.

"Maybe I'll make a video of you one day."

She moaned again as her head bobbed up and down on his hardness.

After a few more seconds of sucking him off, she slid her mouth off his cock and begged, her pleas making his cock ache. "Please! Please, Edwin, please fuck me! I need you to fuck me." She dropped her mouth back onto his swollen member.

He gripped her head and pulled her from him. Without a word, he pulled her up by her hair, and the pain made her scramble to her feet, the taste of him still on her swollen lips. He pushed her to the giant window facing the road. She caught herself with her hands as he gripped her hips, pulling her slightly back. As his cock teased at her sweet passage, she begged again. "Please!"

And he drove inside of her with one thrust, burying himself balls deep into her wetness. He gripped her ass with his strong fingers, digging them into her flesh, and pounded her with deep, violent thrusts. But he wanted more of her. He slid one hand off her ass, sliding it up her back and into her hair, gripping it and pulling her head back. "Open your eyes."

She obeyed, and he knew she could see the world driving by past her nude reflection, saw the panic and lust mixed in her own reflection in the glass. One group of air boaters slowed and stared, three men returning from a day on the lake. They cheered as Edwin took her right there for anyone to see.

"They enjoy seeing my slut getting fucked, it seems," Edwin smirked. "I enjoy it as well."

He felt her body tense as he spoke, her orgasm ripping through her body. She screamed, falling into the glass. He pressed her into the window, her tits going flat and giving the men more of her nipples to see. She seemed to crave it as she groaned louder.

Edwin's cock twitched inside of her, and a second later he dumped his load inside of her. His groan filled the lobby as she pushed back harder onto him, her body begging for his cum. He thrust twice more and then held her onto his cock, pinning her between him and the window.

As soon as he finished filling her, he pulled his hardness out of her and yanked her back around, pushing her to her knees. With a gentle tug, he pushed his cock back into her mouth saying only, "Clean."

She sucked with the same passion she had shown when she

first sucked him off, tasting herself on him as well as his own cum. With her tongue, she wiped their sex from his manhood as their audience watched.

When she finally pulled away and looked up, he grinned down at her. "Good girl."

"Thank you, sir." He could see the blush warm her cheeks.

"You may stand now, love." He held his hand out to help her to her feet. She took it, needing that extra leverage as her legs were weak and shaky. His smile never vanished. "Now I may survive the week."

Little did he know that would be the last time he would enjoy Faith Greer's talents. She took every demand he gave her, obeying perfectly. He sipped his coffee, wondering if Andrea Newman was just as obedient, and then wondering how he could find out.

~ ~ ~ ~ ~

Andrea jerked her attention to the door every time someone opened it from the lobby, expecting to see Edwin walking into the inner offices of Rutherford Construction. However, it was merely the others coming in for work. Jana and Kendra made a beeline straight to Andrea's office to ask what happened after she disappeared on them last night. They were highly disappointed when all she told them was that she and Edwin went for coffee and that was it. There was no way in hell she was going to tell them about the kiss. She still couldn't believe it herself. When she finally made it home, she could still feel his hand on her ass and had grabbed her battery-operated boyfriend for a quick date. Even after her release, she couldn't go to sleep right away.

Now, she worried how Edwin would act around her when he finally did make it to work. Would he regret kissing her? Would he be smug toward her now? And how would she act around him? Her pussy dripped just thinking about that kiss. For a man she started out desperately wanting to hate, she couldn't get him out of her mind.

Her phone rang, making her jump. Glancing down, she noticed Brian's name across her screen. "Great." What the hell would she tell him about last night? With a sigh, she answered the phone, placing it against her ear. "Hey, there. I thought I wasn't going to hear from you until tonight."

"What can I say? I'm impatient. So, how did it go? Get lucky for me?"

"Um, aren't you at work? Where is everybody?"

She could hear the squeak of his desk chair. "They're busy doing their jobs, and my door is closed anyway. No one can hear me. Now, tell me all the naughty parts. What did you wear?"

She leaned back in her chair, spinning so she could keep an eye on her glass door so that no one sneaked up on her. "I wore that burgundy dress you liked, the one that hugs my ass and pushes the girls up into clear view."

"Nice! I should have made you take a picture for me."

She giggled, feeling the blush warm her face. "I'll have to remember that for next time."

"So, who was the lucky man to say hello to you first? And how far did you go?"

Out of the corner of her eye, she saw Edwin walk into the cluster of offices, her pussy instantly growing wet and her breathing heavier. "You won't believe me." She took a deep breath as she watched Edwin walk around the desks in the center of the room toward his office. "Edwin actually popped in. We didn't know he would be there, and of course, he didn't know we were going out. Naturally, he came over to say hello."

"Your boss, the one who took my place, was the first man who said hello to you?" Brian chuckled. "That is just too wild. So, I guess the rest of the night was a complete bust, huh?"

When Edwin reached his door, he turned and stared across the office at her, a soft smile playing at the corners of his mouth. He dipped his head once and then turned to enter his office, closing his door behind him.

"Yeah," Andrea said. "A complete bust. You know there's no way anything would happen with him. Besides, he didn't stay long, and the girls wanted to dance, so we kind of went our different ways. Sorry, I failed you."

"Oh, sweetie, you didn't fail me," Brian assured her, and guilt filled her at having lied to him. She wasn't sure why she did it. He probably would have loved the irony of it all, but she just wanted to keep last night to herself for now. "I just wanted you to have some fun, that's all. When you called me last night, you seemed so bummed. I was hoping if I got you to do something risky, it would get you to lighten up a little, have some fun."

She nodded, her gaze still fixed on Edwin as he sat down behind his desk. "Well, I did have fun, just not the kind you wanted me to have."

"Well, it must have worked, because you sound better."

"Thanks. It did. I'm feeling much better about things now." Much better than she should if she were honest. There was no way anything could go further with Edwin. They were both there because of already crossing a line they never should have crossed. If they were caught, Neal would can both their asses.

"Just out of curiosity, what would you have done if Edwin did go for it?" Brian asked.

Edwin glanced up, noticing her looking at him. He cocked his head, his face pinched in question, as if asking if she was all right.

She nodded, hopefully assuring him she was fine. She just enjoyed looking at him, weird as that was to admit. Biting her lower lip, she remembered the way it felt when he pressed her against him, his mouth devouring hers. She could feel the heat pooling between her legs once more.

"Andrea? You still there?"

"What?" She sat up in her seat, realizing she never answered his question. "Sorry, sorry. Jana was trying to get my attention. What was the question?"

"Just how far would you have gone with Edwin last night?"

She glanced over at Edwin again, but he had turned his attention back to whatever was on his desk. Smiling, she said, "I wouldn't have done anything with Edwin. I don't play around with the boss."

Yet, she so desperately wanted to play around with the boss.

Twelve

Edwin yawned, placing his hand over his mouth as he cocked his head to the side. He glanced at his watch, shocked that it wasn't even near quitting time yet. Looking up, he noticed the others gathered around Kendra's desk, laughing, the sight making him smile. A team that laughed together, had fun together, worked better. Tossing his pen down onto his desk, he slid out of his chair and moved to see what the laughter was all about. He had been locked in his office way too long as it was.

As he stepped out of his office, the others jerked their attention toward him, and Jana leaped to her feet as if busted doing something wrong. "Please, stay as you are," he said, waving her back to her seat. "Don't let me interrupt a good time."

Kendra smirked, and he noticed Andrea blushing as she looked away. Sammy just sat on the corner of Kendra's desk, her legs swinging back and forth. Jana eased back down into her seat, a smile decorating her lips.

He stared at them all a moment, wondering if perhaps they had been laughing about him. He highly doubted Andrea would have told them about him kissing her, unless she had done it to make him look bad, and somehow, he highly doubted she would do that. Maybe on Monday, she would have, but something he read in her last night told him her opinion of him had changed, at least a little.

He sat on the edge of one of the empty desks, his hands clasped together and in his lap. "You know, I've been here almost a week, and I don't know much about anyone yet, other than Jana likes to dance and is damn good at it, and Kendra prefers rum over tequila."

The others laughed, Kendra shrugging at the statement. "I like what I like," she said.

"So, let's spend a few minutes getting to know each other," Edwin said. "I'll even start. What would you like to know?"

Andrea's eyebrow arched. "Are you sure you want to leave it open like that? We can be a dangerous group with open questions."

He chuckled, nodding. "I'm sure."

"Like living on the edge, huh?" Andrea teased, crossing her arms over her chest.

Edwin couldn't help but allow his gaze to drift over her cleavage, remembering how hot she looked last night in her burgundy dress. He hadn't had a chance to talk to her yet, but knew he needed to soon. Things left hanging like that had a way of stirring up more trouble than anyone intended. "What can I say? I'm a glutton for punishment. Besides, the edge has such a rush, right?" He winked at her, and to his surprise, she blushed, a soft smile decorating her lips. He turned his gaze to the others, slapping his thighs. "So, who's first?"

"You don't like to dance, do you?" Jana asked, a smirk on her face.

Edwin laughed, as did the others, and shook his head. "No. No, I don't like to dance. Mainly because I suck at it. I'd much rather sit on the sidelines and drink while watching others dance."

Again, everyone laughed.

"How are you enjoying Savannah so far?" Sammy asked. "Meet any wild women yet?"

Edwin glanced over at Andrea catching her staring at him with one brow cocked. "No wild women," he said, smiling. "Just pleasant ladies who enjoy themselves." He turned back to Sammy. "Tell me Savannah isn't always this boring."

Sammy giggled, shaking her head. "You just need to know where to go, that's all. I'd be more than happy to show you some hot spots if you like."

"Thanks," he said, noticing Andrea's look. He knew she was waiting to see if he would take Sammy up on her offer. "But maybe just write a few down for me. I don't need Kendra coming after me with a harassment warning."

"With the way I saw you dance, you should be written up already," Kendra said, chuckling.

"I never said I could dance," Edwin told them. "Someone should have warned you before dragging me out onto the floor. I could have saved us all the embarrassment."

"But it was so much fun watching you fake it," Andrea said, a mischievous grin on her face.

"I bet it was." Edwin turned to Kendra. "How about you? Tell us about yourself."

They continued like that for about an hour, each one sharing bits and pieces of themselves, nothing too personal or embarrassing. Well, not unless they were asking Edwin questions.

Then, they all seemed eager to see how much they could pry out of him.

He noticed Andrea sitting there watching him the entire time, a smile on her face as she seemed to study him. He wished he knew what was going through her head, how she felt about last night. He also wondered if she told Brian about it, and what the other man's reaction was. Trying not to focus on Andrea too much, he still managed to sneak a peek at her while the others were talking, and each time, she was staring at him. The last time he looked her way, he smiled back, locking gazes with her and holding them for a moment. He had sworn to himself that he wouldn't cross the sexual line at work when he was forced out of Brevard, but there was just something about Andrea that made him question his vow. By the way she stared at him, he wondered if she questioned it, as well.

~ ~ ~ ~ ~

As everyone got back to work, Andrea followed Edwin into his office. She was impressed with his little get-to-know-you chat with everyone, taking each question fairly well and even laughing at most. Of course, he gave as well as he got, still maintaining a safe workplace environment while having fun. Just the fact that he wanted to take the time to get to know his employees surprised her. It was just one of several things about Edwin Coldwell that was surprising her lately.

"I think that was a good idea," she said as she sat down in one of the chairs in front of his desk. "It'll make them see you as more of a person and not just their boss." She stared at his ass as he circled his desk, only pulling her eyes away as he turned to sit down.

Leaning back in his chair, he crossed his legs as he looked across his desk at her. "I've found that an office that gets along well, works well. Happy people are productive people."

Andrea laughed, unable to help herself. "You've been reading motivational posters, haven't you?"

He smiled over at her, which brought a sparkle to his eyes as well as a tingle to her passion. "I was at Barnes & Noble a few days back. Browsed through some wall calendars."

She laughed, nodding. "Nice." She glanced over her shoulder at the others through the windows, each one back at their desk, Sammy already back out front in the lobby. As she turned back around to face Edwin, she decided to broach the subject neither one of them had brought up yet. "Edwin, about last night—"

"I know, I know," he said, his lips downturned into a frown. "I overstepped. I'm just thankful you haven't turned me in yet. I'm sorry for my brazenness." He smiled, giving her a sheepish shrug. "You mentioned your, um, game with Brian, and I guess I allowed myself to get swept up in it. I should have been in better control."

She stared at him for a moment, not sure if she believed him or not. Was he really sitting there telling her he regretted kissing her? Shifting in her seat, she took a moment to collect her thoughts, now suddenly feeling embarrassed for all the thoughts she had been having. And slightly annoyed. "Are you saying, you wish you hadn't kissed me? Are you saying I'm a bad kisser?" Now she was really getting pissed off the more she thought about it and struggled to keep her voice down.

His eyes went wide with panic as he sat up in his chair, clasping his hands together. "What? No. No, I don't regret anything. How could you think that?"

She slid forward in her seat, ready to spring to her feet. "Because you're sitting there making apologies for what happened." She clutched the arms of the chair, trying to rein in her temper, but it was almost impossible. Here she was about to tell him that she actually enjoyed the fact that he kissed her, that he had the balls to risk her anger by crossing that line, when he spews his asinine apology. Of all the dick moves! "What's wrong with the way I kiss?"

He held his hands up in a placating manner. "Nothing. I swear." He smiled at her as he lowered his hands to the top of his desk. He chanced a glance over her shoulder to make sure no one else had heard her, she was sure, before focusing on her once more. "Look, my bad," he said. "Truly. The truth is, I did enjoy kissing you last night, as well as," he made a weak shrug, "well, allowing my hands to roam so to speak. But, you're the one who's been lecturing me about workplace romances and how I fucked up back in Brevard. I was just trying to put us back on the right ground, that's all. What you have with Brian, if I were honest, makes me jealous. I thought I had that with Faith in Brevard, but I was the one being played." She watched as he settled back in his chair, his shoulders slumped a little. "That's not fair. I'm pretty sure she cared for me as much as I cared for her. She just loved her husband more. Still, I guess I just wanted to experience a part of that once more, even if I wasn't the one who gave the order. I intruded on something between you and Brian. For that, I'm sorry."

She stared at him, annoyance still making her muscles shake as she stared at him. "You were jealous?"

He nodded. "I was, and I shouldn't have been. You're lucky to have what you have, and I'm sure I'll find my own submissive here in Savannah at some point. For now, I just need to get this office busy."

She stared at him for a moment and then slid out of the chair, slower than she intended to a moment ago. "We'll just forget it happened then if that's what you want." She turned and walked to his door. Before she opened it, however, she paused and took a deep breath, her insides twisting in a knot she didn't understand.

Turning, she smiled over at him. "For the record, I enjoyed the kiss, too." She gave him a curt nod and opened the door before he could say anything else.

She smiled at the girls, Jana giving her a questioning smirk. Andrea just rolled her eyes as she weaved her way through to her own office. She still wasn't sure what all was just said. Edwin was a strange man to figure out. Did he want her or not?

Shoving her way into her office, she closed the door and plopped down in her chair. Why did she even care whether he did or not? She glanced over at Edwin's office, his head bent as he studied something on his desk. She had Brian, so why was she suddenly feeling so obsessed with Mr. Coldwell?

Snatching her phone off her desk, she opened her text messages and found Brian's name. *I really miss you being here,* she typed out. She stared at the message for a moment, debating on even sending the text. With a deep breath, she hit SEND, needing to get Edwin out of her mind.

Again.

~ ~ ~ ~ ~

Edwin watched as Andrea walked across the main office to her smaller one on the other side. By the look on Jana's face when Andrea passed her, it was obvious the other woman thought Edwin and Andrea were having some sexy talk behind closed doors. He should have asked what the others knew about their night after they left them at The Bar Bar, just so he would at least have a heads up about any scuttlebutt around the office. He knew he upset Andrea when he backtracked on the kiss, but what choice did he truly have? He didn't need her to have a change of heart and use it against him. He took a deep breath, realizing he still didn't have the full measure of the woman, and until he did, he wasn't going to risk losing everything for the second time in just a few weeks.

With a sigh, he shook his head and reached for one of the contracts put on the corner of his desk by he had no idea who. *Maybe I need to hire someone who can handle this part of the job.* He browsed down the facts of the contract, not really seeing them. What he told Andrea was the truth, or so he hoped. He would find his own submissive again one day, but for now, he truly needed to make this office a success. He didn't have time for anything else.

He glanced up again, staring across at Andrea. *Of course, I would love to make the time.* Cocking his head to the side, he wondered, how Brian and Andrea would make their relationship work over such a distance. Was she the type to wait? Was Brian? Leaning back in his chair, that last question kept replaying over and over in his mind. What was Brian Holmstead like? Perhaps it was time for him to find out. *Now, who do I know in that office?*

Reaching for his phone, he scrolled his contacts, searching for someone who could answer his curiosity. A smile pushed up his cheeks as he came across an old friend. If anyone would know the dirt on Brian Holmstead, it would be her. He hit the CALL button and leaned back in his chair, his phone to his ear.

"This can't be Edwin Coldwell," the female voice said on the other end, a flirtatious lilt in her voice. "I thought you had been sent to Alaska or the Russian Front or something. Do they even still have a Russian Front?"

"Such a history buff," he said back into the phone, chuckling softly. "What's up, Katrina? How are you doing?"

"I'm doing well," she said. "Could definitely use another visit from you, but other than that, everything is going well. How about yourself?"

Edwin found himself smiling as he recalled the last time he and Katrina Maxwell had enjoyed their dalliance. He had to admit, he was the dog everyone else thought he was. Of course, he was all right with that, as well. "I'm starting to get settled in. I'm actually in charge of building a dungeon."

She laughed loudly, which came out in a burst that caused him to pull the phone away from his ear a little. Chuckling, he returned the phone to the side of his head. "Oh, my god, that is so you," Katrina said, still laughing. "I hope you take me when it opens. I still remember that night when you tied me up out on our hotel balcony and—"

He listened to her share her story, laughing at the memory. It had been such a risky move, but damn, it was worth it. He could still see the moonlight shimmering against her olive skin as her breasts ached for his touch.

Once she finished her nostalgic trip, he asked, "How are you getting along with your new boss?"

"Pah. Like he's a new boss," she scoffed. "But, don't worry. I'll get him trained eventually. He seemed eager to get out of Savannah, though."

"Oh?" He felt his brow arch as he leaned forward in his chair, staring over at Andrea. "Why is that?"

"His wife was bitching all the time that she didn't want to move to Savannah," Katrina said. "From what I heard, she hadn't even left Charleston when Brian was transferred."

"I'm sorry, did you say Brian's wife?"

Thirteen

Edwin slid into the air-conditioning of Rutherford Construction feeling a little easier now that Neal was on a plane and heading out of there. With the big boss away, Edwin felt like he could move around without worrying about making a wrong move. Now there was only one person scrutinizing him.

"Welcome back," Sammy said, glancing up at him. "Everything go all right?"

He nodded as he leaned on the high counter to her desk, his arms stacked on top of each other. "The package has safely been delivered," he said with a chuckle. "Now that the big boss is gone, we can all walk a little easier. No more eggshells."

She giggled, nodding. "It's always a little tense when the owner of a company comes around and you're not sure how to act. I much prefer just being me."

"Same here. And, with that in mind, what's the night life like on the weekends here? It's time to explore a little."

"Well, it just so happens some friends of mine and me are heading to the Pipes & Drum tonight," Sammy said as she leaned back in her chair, a mischievous grin over her face. "You'll like it. The girls wear short, short kilts with long white stockings that hit mid-thigh. Extremely nice on the eyes. You should come join us."

He nodded. "Sounds like a good time. When?"

"Nine o'clock? Nothing really happens until later in the evening, so no use wasting time," she said. "You in?"

He thought about it for a moment, and was about to turn her down, thinking it was skirting too close to crossing work boundaries. Then he decided it would be no different than the other night with Andrea and the others at The Bar Bar. "Definitely," he said, tapping the counter. "I'll see you then." He gave her a short nod and then turned to the main office area with something to look forward to later that night.

Stepping into the bullpen, he saw Kendra and Jana busy at their desks and Andrea tucked into her small office, talking on the phone. He paused for a moment and stared at her. He was still not sure what to do with what Katrina told him yesterday. He had avoided Andrea all morning, not wanting to believe that after all the bullshit she gave him that she would have the audacity to sleep with a married man. At first, he wondered if she even knew the man was married, but then, how could she not know? Surely, Brian's wife would have called to check in with him while he was here, even if she didn't want to live in Savannah. Of course, Edwin was just assuming that was the case. Perhaps Brian and his wife were on the outs and a divorce was looming over them. If he was honest with himself, Edwin would admit he knew nothing of their relationship and probably never should have called Katrina and stuck his nose into it. He was better off just forgetting everything and focusing on the work relationship between Andrea and himself. He didn't need the headache of anything else.

With a deep breath, he continued to his office, saying hello to the others on his way. Once he settled into his chair, dropping his cell phone on his desk, he took a moment, closing his eyes and blowing out a slow breath as if he were blowing out the stress of the past week. He felt his shoulders loosen up, his heart slow its hectic drumming, and the tightness in his chest loosen its grip. When he opened his eyes again, he just stared over at a lighthouse painting, a soft smile curling up the corners of his mouth as he leaned back in his chair. However, though the tension may have left his body, the questions remained.

Pushing his doubts about Andrea's situation out of his mind, he allowed his thoughts to drift back to Faith Greer. She had been the closest he had come to actually dominating someone in a way more than just in the bedroom. She trusted him with everything, never doubting or second guessing his orders. At least, not once they got started. He felt the smile creep across his face as he thought back to a time they were alone in the office back in Brevard.

"Have you ever done this before? Controlled someone like this?" Faith asked, following him as he entered his office.

He sat on the edge of his desk, leaving her standing nude in front of him. He loved her nude, her body an intoxication to which he would always be addicted. That and her obedience. "Not to this degree," he admitted. "I've had dalliances before, even affairs, but none like you or what you are wanting." The truth was, Faith had allowed him to explore a deeper level of the master/submissive relationship, one that he had always dreamed about.

"What happened to those?" She no longer tried to cover up

her body, proud, it seemed, to be standing there before him like she was.

He shrugged. "Most just ended. We either grew apart, found something else that interested us more, or just became bored with what was going on. I am a lot like you. I want the adventure, the excitement of new things and new experiences. You offered me that whereas my last encounter didn't."

His last encounter had been Faith's sister, Cherish, and well, that didn't end so much as explode. He had made mistakes in the past, mistakes Andrea seemed to be making right now. A master/submissive relationship had to be built on mutual trust, and if Brian was lying to his wife or to Andrea, then how could there be trust? Yet, was it Edwin's place to mention it to her? Wasn't that crossing a line he had been told to stay the hell away from?

He sighed as he leaned forward in his chair and reached for some unfinished paperwork on his desk, unable to shake the feeling that he needed to do something, just unsure of what that something was. He glanced up, looking across the way at Andrea behind her desk. She, at least, had the relationship she wanted, even with its flaws. He couldn't take that from her. It was her choice. Not his.

He reached for his phone, opening the photo gallery. Faith had sent him a picture of herself naked on her back deck a few weeks ago. She had even made her husband take it for her to send, which had cracked Edwin up at the time, but also filled him with a power rush. That she would make her husband do that for him made Edwin realize how far she would go in their relationship.

He opened the photo, but instead of staring at her nude body, he zoomed in to her face, staring into her sparkling, green eyes. He touched the edge of the photo, then ran his finger down across her nose and chin. His heart still ached when he thought of her.

She made the right decision for herself, he knew, but for him... For him, it left him wanting what had been just within reach. What had started out as a game of sex turned into something much, much more. He knew she felt it as well. He could see it in her eyes the day she said goodbye to him by the river. Her life lay with Selby, her husband, and the woman they had brought into their home. It didn't belong with him.

He caressed Faith's photo one more time and then closed his photo gallery, dropping his phone back onto the desk. He glanced back across to Andrea. There was no way he could interfere in something that seemed to fulfill her, not after what he lost.

A knock came at his door, jerking his attention off Andrea. Kendra stood there, and he waved her inside.

"I just wanted you to know Ryan Slater and Ethan Monroe are both set to come in Monday morning for an interview," Kendra said. "Once you make a decision, I'll get started on the background checks and send them for drug tests."

Edwin nodded. "Thanks. That'll be perfect. I also want us on the lookout for another person to fill those desks in the bullpen. I don't want you or Jana overloaded when we get busy. We'll keep the person part time for now."

Kendra smiled. "I'll get started on putting the word out." She nodded, still smiling as she closed the office door.

He watched as she walked over to her desk. Sitting down, she glanced over at Andrea and then back at Edwin, her smile growing. He shook his head, sure she had noticed him staring at Andrea. He just shook his head again, chuckling as he reached for the paperwork again. Ah well, he had at least gone a week without anyone thinking something bad about him.

~ ~ ~ ~ ~

"Any weekend plans?" Brian asked her. "Not going out with your boss again, are you?"

"The only boss I want to go out with is in Florida," Andrea said, making sure she kept her voice low so the ladies in the bullpen wouldn't hear her. "And no, I have no weekend plans. I think I'm going to work around the house some. How about you?"

"Nothing fun, I assure you," he said. "I might catch up on some reading, maybe check out the beaches." She heard him shift a little in his seat. "He hasn't come onto you, has he? Edwin, that is. I mean, he was sent there for screwing with his employees. He hasn't slipped back into old habits, has he?"

She pressed her lips into a thin line, shaking her head. Why, she had no idea. It wasn't like he could see her. "No, he hasn't been doing anything like that. What makes you ask that?"

"No reason," Brian said. "Sometimes, people have a hard time breaking old patterns."

"Ah," was all she said. She had no idea why he would even worry about Edwin. Brian had to know she only wanted him. "Are you sure you can't make a weekend trip up here? We could hide out in my townhome all weekend."

"Sweetie, that's more than a seven-hour drive," he told her. "By the time I got there, I'd have to turn around and come back. Besides, I'm still getting things settled in here. I wish I could, but there's no way I can see it happening right now. I'm sorry."

"What about a flight?" she persisted. "I'm sure that would only take a couple of hours, three at the most. I really need to see you, Brian."

"I know, Andrea, and I wish I could make it happen. But I can't. I'm sorry. There's just no time right now. Maybe when I get settled in more."

She sighed. "I understand." She didn't, of course. She wanted more, and she was impatient about getting it.

Glancing up, she watched as Sammy entered the bullpen and

headed toward Edwin's office. *What's that about?*

"Look, I need to go," Brian said. "One of our clients is here. I'll check in on you later. Send me a text."

"Yes, sir," she said, but he had already hung up before she said the second word.

She dropped her phone to the table as she glanced across the bullpen as Sammy handed Edwin a piece of paper. Andrea felt her brows furrow as she watched him smile at the younger woman, nodding. Sammy laughed and then left, not saying anything to anyone else as she returned to her desk. *Curiouser and curiouser.*

Andrea sat there for a few more moments and then, when she felt the cat was about to die, she slid out of her seat to try and sate her curiosity. She opened the door to her office, making sure she was smiling as she passed Jana and Kendra. "What are you working on?" she asked Kendra while still staring at Edwin's office. He was already looking down at something on his desk.

"Edwin wanted me to find someone to fill one of the other desks," she said as she stopped what she was working on. "I'm to put some applications together for him."

Andrea turned, glancing down at the other woman. "Another woman?"

Kendra shrugged. "He didn't say that. He just said he wanted someone in here to answer phones, so Jana and I can work on what we need to work on without too much interruption. He doesn't want us distracted."

Andrea glanced back at Edwin. "That's nice of him." She continued on to his office, knocking before letting herself in. "We're hiring more people for the bullpen?"

He glanced up from the file he was looking at, his eyes widening as he tried to focus on her after staring at the paper for so long. "I'm sorry. What?" His brows furrowed over his head in confusion as he looked over at her.

"Kendra says we're hiring more people for the bullpen," Andrea repeated. "Is that true?"

Edwin nodded, settling back in his chair. "It is. She's putting a list of possible candidates together for us to go over. I don't want to be caught with our pants down when we get busy and one of them needs a day off or are too busy to answer phones. I'm thinking of hiring someone to keep the contracts organized and to run permits, answer phones. That sort of thing. I'd rather have too many people than not enough." He cocked his head at her. "Is that all right? Do you see a problem with it?"

She nodded. They had already been down this road when he wanted to hire another assistant manager and someone to run the warehouse. She saw no sense in wasting her breath now arguing against what he wanted to do. "Is everything all right with Sammy? I saw her pop in here a little bit ago."

He shrugged. "She's fine. I had asked about the Friday night offerings around town, and she invited me to join her and some friends at some Irish pub." He picked up the piece of paper from the desk, staring at the words with squinting eyes. "A place called the Pipes & Drum." He dropped the paper on the desk again as he looked back up at her. "Ever heard of it?"

She shook her head as she thought of how Sammy had practically drooled over Edwin on his first day there. "No, I haven't, but then again, Sammy's lived here her entire life. All twenty-five years of it." She hoped that by mentioning the other woman's age, he might reconsider his plans.

"That's why I figured she'd know all the hot spots," he told her. "I've busted my ass getting my place in order. There's only a little more to do before it's finished, so I thought I would take the weekend and explore some of the fun spots in Savannah. Treat myself a little, so to speak."

"With Sammy?"

He cocked his head a little as he studied her with narrowed eyes. "I'm not going there *with* Sammy. I'm meeting her friends and checking out a new bar. Nothing untoward, I promise."

She bristled as she realized how her questions must have come across. "I wasn't implying there was." She straightened as she stepped back to the door. "I look forward to seeing who Kendra brings us." With a knot in her stomach she couldn't explain, Andrea turned and walked out of his office. She debated for a moment about confronting Sammy about their night out but decided against it as she weaved her way through the bullpen to her office. She didn't need Sammy thinking she was some jealous woman or still out for Edwin's blood. It wasn't her job to keep an eye on everyone.

She slid into her desk chair, leaning back as she glanced over at Edwin again, who was already studying more paperwork. As she watched him, her mind drifted back to his kiss Wednesday night, his hands gripping her ass. She had fun dancing with him and hanging out at the bar. She was jealous that Sammy was going to have that same experience, and that admission made her pussy drip. She didn't need to be jealous of Edwin Coldwell. She had Brian, after all.

Still, Edwin was the one who filled her thoughts.

Fourteen

Edwin stepped into the Pipes & Drum, impressed with the location. While it was on the outskirts of the historic section of Savannah, it was close enough to catch some of the overflow of partiers. Off to the right set a massive wooden bar that appeared to have seen better days with wooden barstools possessing low backs lining the front of it. Toward the back was a small dance floor with a stage adjacent to that now filled with a live band playing some eighties tunes while people danced the night away. The rest of the area was filled with wooden tables and chairs, most already filled with patrons enjoying the company of their friends.

"Edwin!" a familiar voice called out, jerking his attention to the left where he saw Sammy standing and waving him over.

Edwin nodded that he had seen her and weaved his way through the crowd to join her and her friends.

"Glad you made it," she said. "Any problem finding the

place?"

Edwin slid into one of the empty chairs as he shook his head. "Nope. Google Maps is great if I turn up the volume. It's been my lifesaver so far since I arrived in town."

"Welcome to Pipes & Drum," a small blonde said as she sidled up to him. "What can I start you with tonight?"

Turning, Edwin raked the server with his gaze, his brows arched. Sammy was not joking when she said they wore skimpy kilts. He bet if the girl bent over he'd see all her secrets. He wondered if, like the men, women went commando under their kilts. If Sammy wasn't sitting there, he would have asked to find out. Glancing back up into the server's eyes, he ordered a Manhattan.

When he turned back to Sammy, she took the time to introduce the others around the table. "This is Brandy Wallace," she began, pointing to an ash-blonde with her arms wrapped tightly around a tall, stocky man with curly red hair and bright green eyes. He had a beard and mustache to match, trimmed close to his jawline. "And the refrigerator she's magnetized herself to is Kirk Russel. Next to them is Jodi Taylor, Jake Meyers, and, um, Ryan Slater."

Edwin greeted each one as Sammy introduced them, but balked when she mentioned Ryan, one brow arched. "Ryan Slater?" he questioned, turning to Sammy. "Is this..?"

She nodded, a sheepish smile toying at the corners of her mouth. "You're interviewing him Monday. Sorry I didn't give you a heads up. I had asked Kendra to take his application."

Edwin just nodded. "Friends or..?" He left the question hanging in the air, waiting to see if he needed to search out a new applicant for an assistant manager.

"Just friends," Ryan was quick to say, and Edwin noticed the downturn of Sammy's lips when he said it. *So, friends, but she obviously wants something more.*

"Well, Ryan, I'm out for a night of fun," Edwin told the younger man. "So, there will be no talk of work, and nothing that happens tonight gets brought to the office on Monday. Deal?" He glanced at Sammy, offering her a reassuring smile.

"Deal," Ryan agreed, looking a little more relaxed.

"So, what's everyone drinking?" Edwin asked, glancing around the table.

When the server came back with his drink, he ordered another round for the table, and then settled back with his drink to watch the crowd gyrating out on the dance floor. As the server left to fill the latest drink order, the song changed, and Brandy and Jodi pulled the men up to hit the dance floor. Edwin declined to join them, stressing he was more a voyeur than a dancer. Sammy chose to remain behind as well, and he had the feeling work was about to be brought up even after his declaration about not having it as a topic of conversation.

As he watched the others making their place out on the dance floor, he noticed the one Sammy introduced as Brandy grinding against her boyfriend before they had even finished moving. "She's an interesting one," he said with slight chuckle, putting off the conversation he felt looming. He had to remind himself how young these men and women were compared to him, as well. Most of the inside of Pipes & Drum was filled with twenty-somethings ready for the night's hook-up,

Sammy giggled, nodding as she leaned forward on the table, her hands clasped together. "She's definitely a wild one. She actually dated his brother, John, before Kirk, and by date, I mean she got freaky as often as possible. Then she got bored and moved on to his brother." She laughed again. "Brandy has always wanted sex more than your average person. The stories I've heard her and her best friend, Emma, share make me feel like a prude."

Edwin nodded, his eyes wide a little. "Fun while it lasts, but not a basis for a relationship," he said, lifting his glass to his lips. Once he took a small swallow, with his gaze still on the others out on the dance floor, he asked, "Tell me about Ryan. Was he telling the truth when he said you two were just friends?" Now he glanced over at her as her expression fell.

"He was," she admitted. "We've been friends for a while, although I wish it were more." She shrugged. "I don't think it'll ever happen, though."

Edwin shifted in his seat, so he faced her more, one hand around his glass, the other in his lap. "Never say never," he told her. "Some men are just too stupid to see what's right in front of their face. However, that being said, if we do wind up hiring Ryan, is it going to be a problem with the two of you working together and him being your boss? I don't want any drama at the office." He had definitely had enough of that at work to last him the rest of his life. His family jewels still ached whenever he thought about it.

Sammy shook her head, smiling. "There won't be any drama, and yes, I can work for Ryan, no problem. He's a good guy. If he wasn't, I wouldn't have recommended him. He's a hard worker. You'll be lucky to have him."

Edwin nodded. "All right. We'll see how he does in the interview process Monday and what Andrea thinks about him, since she'll be working with him the most more than likely." Then he held up a finger, pointing it at her as he narrowed his gaze. "But, the first sign of drama you're both gone. Understood? So make sure this is really someone you want to risk your job over."

She laughed softly, nodding again. "He is, sir. And thank you. I appreciate it."

The server arrived then with the second round of drinks,

setting them about the table.

"Okay then. Now, drink up," he said as soon as the server left. "You need to show me those dance moves of yours."

She laughed harder, dipping her head in mock obedience. "Yes, sir," she said as she reached for her glass. "Your wish is my command."

~ ~ ~ ~ ~

Andrea weaved her way through the Friday night traffic, still arguing with herself about what she was doing. *You're just being a nosy, sneaky busybody. It's none of your business. He's a grown man for crying out loud.* And then the argument would sway in the opposite direction. *Yes, but a grown man who was told to keep his pants zipped up. And who the hell is he to hit on little Sammy? There has to be more than a decade between them. And what happened to no screwing around at work? That sure as hell went out the window, didn't it?*

And over and over the argument went until she had herself worked up into a tight tizzy of conflicting emotions.

Finally, she pulled into the parking lot of the Pipes & Drum, her hands twisting around the steering wheel as she stared at the neon open sign. Did she really want to do this? To go in there and bust her boss doing exactly what he swore he wouldn't do. She had warned Sammy to stay away from Edwin, that he was a player, someone who would merely use her. Obviously, Sammy didn't care. Or perhaps that was what enticed her to the man.

Andrea had thought Edwin had changed. Each conversation the two of them shared made her feel as if he were someone she could respect and admire, even someone she could care about.

And that was the rub, she realized. Edwin Coldwell *was* someone she could come to care about. He had looked out for her when they were out Wednesday night, making sure she wasn't left alone waiting for a ride and not going home with some strange man because Brian wanted it, had taken her words seriously when she shared her struggles, and seemed to be treating her as an equal. Had she read everything wrong?

She stared at the front door again, her lips pressed firmly together as she worried about whether or not she should get out of her car. No. She was fine. Edwin wouldn't have told her about it if he meant to keep his intentions with Sammy a secret, so odds were, it was all on the up and up. She made a curt nod, lips pressed into a thin line as determination filled her. With her mind made up, she opened the car door. Everything was going to be fine.

As she entered the pub, she stood in the entrance for a moment, allowing her eyes to adjust to the dim lighting. People crowded the bar, some sitting and talking while others waited for drinks. The dance floor was rocking with people bumping and grinding, the band on stage making them feel the beat their bodies were imitating. Glasses clinked as servers cleaned tables, stacking as many glasses and bottles as they could on trays before walking off so another round of patrons could swarm down on the empty table. She could smell the sweat and beer in the air and noticed the servers in the skimpy outfits. What she didn't notice was…

Then she saw them. Sammy sat next to Edwin, leaning forward, a smile on her face that appeared more than platonic. Edwin leaned toward her, one hand on his drink and the other resting in his lap. Wasn't there supposed to be friends with them? She stared for another moment, straining to hear what they were talking about. It was difficult to do with the band playing and everyone shouting to be heard.

Feeling silly, she started to move toward them to say hello when she heard Sammy say, "He is, sir. And thank you. I appreciate it."

Sir? Andrea stared at the younger woman as the server then walked up with several drinks, setting them on the table.

"Okay then. Now, drink up," Edwin said as soon as the server left. "You need to show me those dance moves of yours."

Sammy laughed harder, dipping her head as if in obedience. "Yes, sir," Andrea heard Sammy say as she reached for her glass. "Your wish is my command."

Andrea spun around and shoved herself out of the pub, her throat filling with bile as she stormed her way to her car. How could he? He had only been here a week and already he had found someone for his twisted games. And Sammy? How could she go after the boss like that?

Andrea snatched her keys out of her purse and unlocked her door. Yanking it open, it bounced back at her with the force she used, hitting her in the side because she attempted to slide in before the door was all the way open. "Fuck!" she yelped as she gripped her side, her face scrunched up in pain. Blowing out an agonizing breath through clenched teeth, she dropped down into her seat, fighting the tears that threatened to fall. How could she have been so stupid?

She slipped her keys into the ignition, starting her car as she closed her door. She should have listened to her gut before she even walked into that bar. Pulling out of the parking lot, she swore to keep her nose out of everyone's business from now on. There was just no telling who was the scoundrel and who wasn't. She had given Edwin the benefit of the doubt, and he had shoved it in her face. What would he have done if she had shown up? Would he have kept his orders to Sammy a secret or flaunted them in front of everyone? *Your wish is my command. Pah! That girl doesn't know what she's setting herself up for, that's for sure.*

Andrea seethed all the way home, wanting desperately to call and talk to Brian, to tell him that she had caught Edwin with his hand in the proverbial cookie jar. She should. She should call

Neal as well. Then maybe Brian could get his position in Savannah back and her life would be back on track. Yes, she should do it.

She swiped at a tear that trickled down her face, rubbing her eyes with the back of her palm. *I'm such a fucking idiot.*

~ ~ ~ ~ ~

Edwin watched as Sammy pulled her glass toward her, and then she tilted her head to the side as she stared at something behind him. He turned, trying to find out what she was looking at. "What's up?" he asked as he searched the area, seeing nothing. Finally, he turned back around. "See someone you know?"

She shrugged before taking a drink. Licking her lips as she lowered her glass, she said, "I could have sworn I saw Andrea leave." She leaned back in her chair, shaking her head. "Couldn't have been her, though, right? I mean, if she was here, she would have come over and said hello."

Edwin glanced back over his shoulder at the front door. Had Andrea been there? He had told her about hitting the bar tonight, so it wouldn't have surprised him really if she did show up. Now that he thought about it, he should have asked her to join them tonight when she asked about it earlier. He wasn't sure why he didn't, except he was still torn over what Katrina had told him last night. Still, he wished she would have hung out. He enjoyed the two nights they had been out together, especially when she wore that tight-ass burgundy dress.

Spinning back around, he took another sip of his drink. "Maybe she didn't see us sitting here if it was her," he said as he lowered his glass. "Should we text her? Invite her back?"

Sammy shook her head. "Nah, she's a big girl. If she didn't see us and left, then maybe she had somewhere else to go."

He nodded. "Perhaps."

"Now, I think you said something about dance moves." She

grinned at him, waggling her brows.

"I, uh, don't dance. You heard the others. It's not pretty, I assure you."

"That makes it all the better," Sammy said, setting her glass down and reaching for his arm. "I promise I won't take any pictures. Videos on the other hand…" She grinned as she dragged him toward the dance floor.

Edwin allowed himself to be hauled to his humiliation, but his thoughts were on Andrea. Had it been her Sammy had seen? And why didn't she stay? He sighed as he stared at the young kids crowding the dance floor. He really wished she would have stayed.

Fifteen

Edwin entered the offices of Rutherford Construction, coffee cup in hand and feeling as if things were finally on the right track. He had a great time with Sammy and her friends Friday night, even though they were more than a decade younger than him, and Saturday he had managed to get more of his possessions out of boxes and where they belonged. He had even set up his bed and had a couple of amazing night's sleeps. Just what the doctor ordered. Sunday, he lounged around one of the squares listening to a busker play who had brought in a massive xylophone. How the man had even managed to haul it there was beyond Edwin's imagination. He felt rested as well as rejuvenated, something he hadn't felt in a couple of weeks.

He smiled at Sammy as he passed her desk, wishing her a good morning as he entered the bullpen of Rutherford Construction. Kendra was already standing, waiting for him, file folders in hand.

"You're way too eager so early in the morning," he teased as he took the folders she handed him.

Kendra turned and followed him toward his office. "Ryan Slater will be here at ten, and Ethan Monroe at eleven for their interviews," Kendra said, her tone all business. "Those are their files in case you wanted to go over them one more time before they arrive. I've set up the extra office next to Andrea for the interviews. Is there anything else you would like?"

Edwin entered his office, thinking he should have promoted Kendra to the other assistant manager position. Or maybe as a personal assistant to him. He had never had one before, and the way she carried herself, she would be perfect at it. Of course, her disposition while at work left a little chill in the air. He much preferred nightclub Kendra in tone. "No, I think that'll be great. Just tell Sammy to take them there when they arrive." He circled his desk, dropping the folders on top as he lifted his coffee mug to his lips and took a sip. Lowering it, he asked, "Did you give Andrea those candidates for the bullpen. Has she made her choices about who else we want in there?" He had told Kendra to give the applications to Andrea for her to decide, hoping it would show Andrea he had confidence in her choices.

Kendra stood in front of his desk, shaking her head. "Not that she's told me. Do you want me to ask her about it?"

He shook his head, glancing across the way at Andrea, her head bowed over whatever she was looking at on her desk. "No, I can do it. I was just wondering how far along we were, that's all. Thanks."

"Anytime," she said with a slight dip of her head as she turned to leave.

He glanced back at the files on his desk, opening Ryan's and glancing over the information one more time. He had decided Friday night to give Sammy some leeway on the matter of Ryan working there, trusting her to be able to handle things whichever direction they went between the two of them. Looking up, he glanced over at Andrea, a smile toying at the corners of his mouth as he wondered if the two of them would be able to handle it if anything ever stirred between them. Not that he expected it to ever happen, of course. No, she seemed too caught up in Brian Holmstead. However, it was fun to fantasize about, her taking orders from him, down on her knees right there at the corner of his desk. His cock started to harden as he allowed the images to play out in his mind. Last Wednesday when he kissed her, he had thought of her lips for the next couple of days, the way her ass felt in his hand. He could see her flesh wiggling as he spanked her, imagined her bent over his desk, begging for it, as well.

Sucking in a breath, he shifted in his seat, reaching down and repositioning his hardening shaft in his pants. If things were different, he could imagine having those fun games she had with Brian and so much more. So much more. It had been careless of Brian to send her out to find someone that night to play with without his protection. But, then again, Brian had a wife, so he probably only saw Andrea as a plaything for his twisted imagination. Edwin sighed, shaking his head. He shouldn't assume such things, he knew. Brian could very well care for Andrea deeply and just didn't understand the consequences he was risking by sending Andrea into the arms of a stranger without him there to keep an eye on her. And Andrea knew what she was getting into when she decided to hook up with a married man. If she knew he was married, that is. Edwin still hadn't discovered whether that was the case or not. Nor would he. It wasn't his business or concern.

He leaned back in his chair. He wanted to make it his concern, however, which was driving him crazy. He didn't need this distraction at work. Not now. Not when things were going so well.

Out of the corner of his eye, he saw Sammy lead Ryan into the bullpen and over to the office across from him and beside Andrea. He leaned forward, watching the two of them as they crossed the office area, paying attention to how they interacted. Sammy merely walked, not really paying Ryan any attention. He, on the other hand, kept ducking his gaze to check out Sammy's ass in her tight jeans.

Edwin shook his head. *I hope I won't regret this.*

With an exasperated sigh, he pushed himself out of his chair, snatched up Ryan's application, and headed for the other office. As he stepped into the bullpen, he saw Sammy usher Ryan inside the empty office and then turn and knock on Andrea's door. The small brunette informed Andrea of Ryan's arrival, but Andrea never even glanced up. She merely held her hand up, indicating that she heard the other woman, and then continued doing whatever she was doing.

Edwin stared at Andrea as he crossed the room, thinking the scene odd for her. *Someone must have had a rough weekend.* With a shake of his head, he rounded Jana's desk and entered the office where Ryan waited, making a mental note to ask Andrea if everything was all right later.

"Hello, Ryan," Edwin said as he stepped into the glass office to move behind the desk.

Ryan sat in one of the two chairs in front of the desk, back straight, knees together. He had his hands clasped and resting on top of his knees, his face a slight pale as he sat there. Not the bubbling man Edwin had met Friday night, but then, interviews had a way of screwing with people's confidence. "Good morning," Ryan said, nodding once. "Hope your weekend went well."

Edwin opened the file as he sat down, nodding. "It did. A

rather lazy one overall, but I did manage to get some things done from my recent move. How about you? Any weekend excitement?"

Ryan shook his head, glancing up as the door opened and Andrea stepped inside. "No, no. Just hung out at home mostly."

"Sometimes, that's needed more than venturing out," Edwin said as he watched Andrea move over to the empty chair and plop down, her back almost as rigid as Ryan's. Edwin felt his brows pinch together as he watched her, his lips pressed together. Something had definitely happened to annoy her. "Ryan, this is Andrea. She'll be your partner-in-crime for the most part. If hired, it would be your job to help her out, keep the crews on target, make sure people had what they needed, that sort of thing." He took Ryan's file, lifting it and handing it to Andrea so she could see all the pertinent facts.

She took it, but left it lying closed on her lap, not even bothering to look at Edwin.

He stared at her for a moment, confusion pinching his face. *This feels just like last Monday. Something has definitely crawled up her ass.* Shaking his head, he turned back to Ryan. "Our staff is small for now, but we're in the process of hiring more people. Any problem managing large groups?"

The interview continued for another thirty minutes with Edwin being the only one to ask any questions. Andrea just sat there, staring at the kid as he answered everything, which didn't make Ryan relax any. How could he with the scowl on Andrea's face?

"One last question," Edwin said as he leaned back in his chair. "You and Sammy are friends. Is that going to be any problem? You'll be in charge of her in some areas. I don't want to see any, um, friendship drama brought into the office."

For the first time, Andrea glanced over at Edwin, her eyes narrowed slits. He could see the question on her lips. Yet, she still remained silent.

"No, sir," Ryan assured him. "We can keep our friendship from interfering with work. Promise."

Edwin nodded as he tapped the top of the desk. "All right then. Everything looks good to me." He turned to Andrea. "Do you have any other questions for him?"

She just shook her head.

Edwin fought the urge to roll his eyes. Instead, he stood, reaching out his arm to shake Ryan's hand. "Fine. I'll have Kendra reach out when everything else is complete and if everything checks out, we'll give you a call Friday and see about getting you started. Probably next week sometime, I would think."

Andrea and Ryan both stood, Ryan shaking first Edwin's hand and then Andrea's. "Thanks," Ryan said. "I appreciate the opportunity."

"My pleasure," Edwin said. "Here, I'll show you out."

He indicated for Ryan to leave the office first, and Edwin stood for a moment, looking at Andrea, his brows pinched in question.

She just stared back a second before moving past him to return to her own office.

Edwin just watched her disappear before he followed Ryan, leading the other man to the front lobby. Shaking his head, Edwin wondered if he should ask Andrea what was wrong, or just assume she was still upset about him hiring another manager for the company. Then he decided, he simply did not want to get into another argument with her. She would figure things out on her own and move past whatever had her annoyed.

As they entered the office, Ryan smiled over at Sammy. "Looks like I got the job," he said, his excitement clear in his voice. "Now, I get to boss you around some." He winked at that last part, but Edwin could see the blush color Sammy's cheeks. He would definitely need to keep an eye on both of them.

~ ~ ~ ~ ~

Andrea dropped down into her chair, wondering how the hell Edwin knew Ryan and Sammy were friends. *How far up that girl's ass is he? They probably spent the entire weekend together, and now the little girl thinks she's going to get her way in things. I won't have it. Not in my office.*

Blowing out a breath of frustration, she leaned back in her chair and closed her eyes. How could she have been so wrong about Edwin? She thought for sure that there had been something there between them, that he had stopped being the womanizer she had heard he was back in Florida. Had he been playing her the entire time? Then why kiss her last week? Was that just part of his plan to weaken her anger toward him? He had hoped that by being all sweet and caring, she would ignore his dalliances around the office? If that was it, he was sadly mistaken.

She heard the door between the bullpen and the lobby open and glanced that way, her brows pinched. Edwin didn't even chance a look in her direction, instead making a beeline to his own office, closing the door behind him. Why did he have to be so damn…hot?

She blew out a breath, running her hand through her hair as she leaned back in her chair. Glancing down at the stack of applications Kendra had given her for the new woman in the bullpen, Andrea wondered if she should even hire someone else. Another skirt would only give Edwin another target for his wily ways. Suddenly, she felt as if he was asking her to pick out his next conquest. She wouldn't do it.

Reaching out, she yanked the files off her desk and thumbed through them. If there was even one male in the bunch, that is who she would have Kendra pursue. Andrea didn't even care what kind of qualifications he possessed. He was a man, and that's all that mattered. She would not bring another female into this office.

A knock came at her door, jarring her out of her thoughts. Glancing up, she watched as Sammy opened her door, poking her head inside.

"Your next interview is here," the brunette said, all bubbly and smiles. "Ethan Monroe."

"I know his name," Andrea snapped. "Thanks." She handed Sammy a file. It turned out there was a man in the stack after all. "Give this to Kendra and tell her to set up an interview."

Sammy took the file, giving Andrea a curious look. "Yes, ma'am." She cocked her head to the side. "Are you all right? You seem a little put out with something."

"Never mind how I am. Get this done and get back to your desk. We don't need you away from it in case someone comes in looking for a contractor."

Sammy nodded. "It has gotten busier, for sure, but I think anyone who came in would wait a minute or two."

"It's not up to you to think," Andrea said as she stood. "It's up to you to be at your desk during work hours. Just because we hired your friend, doesn't mean you get to skip out on your duties."

Sammy's eyes went wide. "I would never do that. Have I done something to make you think I'm not doing my job?"

Andrea stared at her, wanting to stay pissed but knowing it would only cause bigger issues. "No, you're fine," she said. "Just get back to your desk after you hand those to Kendra." Then she pushed past Sammy, heading to the office next to hers.

Edwin was on his way, but she saw him stop and ask Jana to join them.

As Jana slid past her, Andrea gave Edwin a quizzical look.

"What? You don't think I can handle an interview?"

"Sure you can," he said, nonplussed. "But, she'll be working with him the most, since she's in charge of equipment paperwork and stuff, so I thought she might like to sit in on the interview and give her opinion." He stared at her for a moment, obviously studying her for something. "Are you all right? You seem extremely on edge today." He then leaned in and lowered his voice. "Did something happen between you and Brian?"

She felt her eyes widen at the question, leaning back as she stared at Edwin. "That subject is none of your business. I never should have told you what I did. Forget I said anything." She turned and entered the office, taking the chair behind the desk. If Edwin wanted Jana in the interview, he could damn well be the one standing.

She glanced at the doorway, waiting for him to enter, but he just stood there, staring at her. After a moment, he shook his head and stepped inside the small office, stretching out his arm as he approached Ethan to shake the man's hand.

"Ethan, thanks for joining us," Edwin said. "This won't take long. I appreciate you coming in to talk to us." He eased back on the edge of the desk, clutching it with his hands.

Andrea caught herself staring at his ass and jerked her gaze toward Ethan, clasping her hands together as she leaned on the desk. She was close enough to Edwin to smell his cologne, and out of the corner of her eye, she noticed how tight the muscles in his arms were as he held onto the desk, his back appearing powerful through his shirt that stretched over his flesh. Her breathing grew heavier as she tried to not focus on his body, which was just inches away from her, but she couldn't stop the heat that pooled between her legs. It was easy to see how Sammy could be swept up in his charisma. The man had both a gorgeous body and the charm to go with it. What he didn't have, apparently, were boundaries. Well, that was fine. She would give him plenty of boundaries when it came to herself. She was done being played by Mr. Edwin Coldwell.

Sixteen

Edwin had heard Savannah could get cold, but damn he didn't expect it to be freezing inside the building of Rutherford Construction. For the past several days, Andrea had been the ice queen in the office, and not just toward him. She seemed to be casting her frosty disposition on everyone, and no one knew why. He had even asked the other ladies in the bullpen, but no one seemed to know what had caused Andrea's icy shift in temperament. The only thing he could assume was that Brian had somehow pissed her off, and she was taking it out on everyone around her. At least, he hoped that's what it was. He couldn't think of anything he had done wrong lately, anyway.

"Edwin," Kendra called out as he walked through the bullpen. "Ryan and Ethan's drug tests cleared, and the background checks should be here a week from today. Did you want to make a contingent offer based on what comes back or wait until we have everything?"

"Go ahead and make the offers," he told her as he slid onto the corner of her desk, his hands folded in his lap. "They interviewed well Monday, so I see nothing to hold us up as long as they were honest about anything in their past that could trigger a bad report."

"Will do," she said as she reached for a stack of files. "Also, the man Andrea picked to help us out in here is scheduled for an interview tomorrow at ten in the morning."

He shook his head, lips pressed together. The fact that Andrea had chosen a male to work in the bullpen didn't bother him as much as the quality of her choice. There were at least half a dozen better candidates in that stack for her to pick, so why did she pick this guy? "Sounds good," he said, choosing to keep his thoughts to himself. He didn't need it getting back to Andrea that he was second guessing a decision he said he would allow her to make. "Keep me posted."

Kendra shook her head, one brow cocked. "Are you sure you don't want me to schedule a couple of the others, as well?" she asked. "I read his application, and he really doesn't appear to have much experience in offices of this nature."

He glanced over at Andrea who had locked herself in her office whenever she wasn't needed anywhere else since Monday. For three days, she avoided even those people Edwin thought she liked, which was everyone in the office but him. "No. No, this is fine." He turned back to Kendra, smiling. "I'm sure Andrea saw something in him we missed. She did say she wanted to offer some new beginnings to people."

"Easy enough to do when you're not the one working with them day in and day out," Kendra said, sighing. She then held up a hand. "I know. I shouldn't have complained. Sorry. He'll be here tomorrow."

"I'm sure it'll be fine," he said, rapping the top of her desk with his knuckles as he stood. He paused before turning to his office. "However, keep those other applications handy just in case."

"Yes, sir," Kendra said, smiling.

As he slid back into his seat, Edwin glanced across the way at Andrea again. Something had her acting the way she was, so what was it? He wished he knew, wished he could make it right for her, whatever it was. He hated to see her like this. They had just started to make some headway in their friendship and now this. He shook his head, leaning forward, and reaching for a contract he had been studying earlier. She would come out of it soon enough.

Or so he hoped.

He spent the next hour looking over proposals and contracts for upcoming job prospects. He had been right in how busy Rutherford Construction would be soon. Trent Wilson had even recommended them to some others he knew who were building various things, and the hospital had sent the specs on their new wing for an estimate. Soon, Rutherford would have more employees and plenty of subcontractors to help them carry out the business that would be knocking on their door. Everything was starting to kick into place.

He leaned back in his chair, glancing across the bullpen to Andrea's office. Almost everything, that is. Running his hand through his hair, he wondered once again what had gotten under her skin.

He watched as Sammy walked into Andrea's office, handing her some note or something, only to be chewed out. Sammy held her hands up in surrender as she turned and walked back out of the office, glancing at the others, and shaking her head as she made her way back to the lobby. He followed the young brunette out with his gaze, wondering what the hell that was all about.

Glancing over at the others, he wasn't surprised that they were both already looking at him for answers. He only wished he had some.

He gave a weak shrug and then turned his attention back to Andrea. For three days she had been a grouchy bear to people who had come to count on her. If this wasn't about Brian, then something at work was pissing her off, and he needed to know what that was before morale hit the shitter.

Snatching up the phone on his desk, he called the main number for the office, knowing Sammy would pick up.

"Rutherford Construction," the young woman said, and Edwin could hear the smile in her voice. "How can I help you?"

"Are you alone up there?" he asked.

"Edwin?" Confusion tinged her tone. "Yes, I'm alone. What's up? Need me to come back there?"

"No, no," he told her, keeping his eyes on Andrea in case she decided to go to the front. "And this is between us, so if anyone comes in up there, don't let them know you're talking to me. What happened in Andrea's office just now?"

Sammy blew out a frustrated breath. "I wish I knew. One of the contractors called to leave her a message, and I was just passing it on. She almost bit my head off when I did, telling me I should have just patched him through, but the man didn't want to be patched through. I had offered, but he said he didn't have time for a conversation and to just give her the message. She didn't seem to care. She said if these people wanted to talk to her, they could wait five minutes. She wasn't—and these are her words, sir—their bitch to be calling them back."

"Wow, that's, uh, pretty abrasive." Edwin felt his brows furrow in confusion. "And doesn't really sound like her at all. Do you know of anything that could be causing her moods lately? You three have known her longer than me."

"Trust me, I wish I did," Sammy replied. "She's been this way since Monday."

He sighed, feeling Sammy's frustration as well. "All right. Thanks. I'll see what I can dig out of her."

Sammy scoffed. "I'd wear a shield and a cup before I walk into her office if I were you."

He chuckled. "I'll be all right. Just listen out for a high-pitched wail and then come rescue me."

"You got it, sir. Good luck."

Edwin hung up, still focused on Andrea. Blowing out a breath, he pushed himself out of his chair, ready to face the grizzly in her den.

As he stepped out of his office, the others gave him warning looks, and Jana offered him a white doily off her desk to use as a flag of surrender. He just chuckled, shaking his head as he walked on by. He had worked hard on building his relationship with Andrea; he wasn't going to do anything to set that bridge on fire now. She probably just needed someone to yell at for a while. He could give her that.

He knocked on her door, opening it before she had a chance to tell him to go away. "Hey, got a minute?"

She leaned back in her chair, throwing her pen on the desk. "You're the boss."

Closing the door behind him, he went to the wall opposite her desk, leaning back with his hands clasped behind him. "I just wanted to ask if everything was all right. Since Monday, you've seemed a little on edge. Something happen I should know about?"

"Nope," she said, intertwining her fingers as she laid her hands on her stomach, leaning back in her chair. "Everything's just fine. Working away here."

He nodded, dropping his gaze to the floor as he thought about his next question. Looking back up at Andrea, he asked, "And shouting at Sammy just now? Was that your idea of fine, or did she do something to piss you off?"

Andrea's eyes went wide as she leaned back in her chair. "What? Poor Sammy go running to you saying I was being mean to your girl?"

"My girl?" Edwin stared at her, his brows pinched. "Wow. What the hell does that mean?"

"Nothing," she said, dropping forward in her chair and turning her attention to some paperwork on her desk Edwin was sure she wasn't even seeing. "I'm fine, as I said. Now, can I get back to work?"

"No," he said, still staring at her. *What the hell is wrong with her?* "Something is bothering you, and I want to know what it is. Obviously, you can't hide what it's doing to you. You've been snapping at everyone since the beginning of the week, not even participating in the interviews, and you picked the worst possible applicant for the bullpen. Something has you off your game, and I want to know what it is."

"Oh?" She jerked her head up, glaring at him. "The wrong applicant? Why? Because he's a guy? I didn't pick some skirt for you to chase around the desks, so you think I made a bad choice?"

"What the hell are you talking about? I thought we managed to get through all of this last week? What's bringing this on suddenly? I haven't chased—" He stopped talking, suddenly realizing that Sammy had been right Friday night. Andrea was at the Pipes & Drum. Apparently, she saw him with Sammy and misinterpreted what she saw. Sighing, he shook his head. "You know, if you had just come over to the table, you would have saved yourself a grumpy mood and everyone else a lot of headache and tiptoeing."

"Are you saying I didn't hear Sammy call you 'sir' and tell

you that your 'wish was her command'? I just imagined all of that?"

He shrugged. "To be honest, I don't know what you heard, nor do I remember what all was said. But I know whatever you overheard, you took the wrong way. I am not chasing after Sammy, and she is not 'obeying' me in the way you think."

"Right," Andrea scoffed. "Whatever you say, boss."

"Oh, for crying out loud, Andrea," he said in a huff. "Do you remember the guy we—or rather, I—interviewed Monday? Ryan Slater?"

She looked up again, nodding. "Yup. Nice of you to hire one of your new girlfriend's friends. Will any more of her friends be joining our team?" She clasped her hands together, sitting there and glaring at him. "Maybe I should have had her pick the new person for the bullpen."

Edwin ignored her jabs, knowing she was going to feel like an ass once she realized how wrong she was and how she treated everyone because of it. "Sammy is hoping he becomes more than a friend," he said. "She invited me out Friday night, I'm sure, so I could see him as a person before I interviewed him as an employee." He cocked his head to the side, studying her through narrowed eyes. "Are you really this upset because you thought I was sleeping with Sammy? Do you really think I would screw around with someone more than a decade younger than me?" He shook his head as he bumped his ass against the wall, forcing himself into motion. "And here I thought you had started to see me in a better light." At the door, he stopped and turned back toward her, her expression unreadable as she stared back at him. "I'm not sleeping with Sammy or anyone else for that matter. And even if I were, that's none of your business. You don't get to judge my life. Not with how you're living yours. Now, get your attitude under control or go home until you do. I won't have you stinking up this office with your sour mood."

He watched as she visibly bristled. "How I live my life? What the hell is that supposed to mean?"

His hand on the doorknob, he stared at her. "I mean, a woman who's sleeping with a married man shouldn't be judging anyone else."

Her eyes narrowed, brows pinched as her mouth fell open. "Married man? What the hell are you talking about? I'm not sleeping with a married man."

Taking his hand off the doorknob, he stood straighter, studying her for any sign of duplicity, but he found none. "You really don't know, do you?"

He could see her hands start to tremble as she just sat there, a dumbfounded look on her face. Closing his eyes, he sucked in a deep breath. *Okay, I royally fucked that up.* Opening his eyes again, he moved over to the desk, taking one of the chairs in front. Scooting the chair closer to the desk, he leaned forward, arms across each other as he stared across at her. Andrea still stared at the door as if he hadn't moved. "Thursday, I was concerned about you after finding out Brian would have sent you out to fool around with some stranger when he wasn't close by to protect you, so I called a friend down in his office. She told me that his wife had just arrived the same night you and I were at The Bar Bar. It turns out she didn't want to live in Savannah, so he actually volunteered for the transfer to Fort Lauderdale. I'm sorry. I thought you knew."

She kept her gaze fixed on the door. "He's married?" She took a deep breath, running her hand through her hair. "I, uh, didn't know. We didn't work in the same city, so I only knew what he told me. We started talking when he came to my office in Charleston to help out and continued texting after that. I should have known when he had strict rules about when to call, but I just assumed it was part of his guidelines as my dominant." She glanced over at him, a weak grimace on her lips. "This was my first foray into this lifestyle. Pretty dumb, huh?"

He shook his head. "Not at all. You trusted him, and he broke that trust. This isn't on you."

She scoffed. "Yes, it is. I'm a grown fucking woman for crying out loud. I should have known when I was being played. I should have dug into his background a little more. I allowed the excitement of what he opened up to me to overshadow my caution." Her eyes went wide as she shook her head. "Oh, he's an asshole for what he did to me, don't get me wrong. But, I was a fool for not questioning the red flags that kept popping up. I only have myself to blame for being played." She leaned back in her chair, blowing out another breath. "What an idiot I was."

"You weren't an idiot," he told her. "You just fell in love with the wrong guy, that's all. It happens. The question now is what are you going to do about it?"

"What can I do?" she asked, shrugging. "If I go kick his ass, which is truly what I want to do, then all hell will break loose, and Neal will have my ass in a sling. This is exactly what he warned us about." She shook her head, a tear snaking its way down her cheek that she refused to wipe away. "I can't even warn his wife without it causing problems."

"A man like Brian will do this again," he said. "He'll get his sooner or later. Trust me."

She sighed, dropping her gaze to her desk. "I'm sorry for how I treated everyone. I was wrong, it seems."

He nodded. "You were," he said, grinning. "But, I'll make you a deal. If you ever need to ask me a tough question, I promise to answer it, especially if you think it's me crossing into dangerous territory. No matter what."

She smiled, and it stirred his heart. "Deal."

He hit her desk once with a flat hand and heaved himself out of his seat. "You know what? Let's close up shop early and take the crew out for a drink. I think we all deserve it."

"Edwin, we really shouldn't—"

"Hey," he said, spinning and cutting her off. "The boss wants a drink, so we're going out for a drink. Close it down. We're heading to The Bar Bar, mainly because I don't know of too many other bars." He winked at her before moving over to her office door and opening it. As he stood in the doorway, he called out, "Shut her down, folks. We're heading out for drinks." He turned back to Andrea, a grin spreading across his face. "First round's on Andrea."

Cheers filled the bullpen.

Seventeen

Edwin sat on his back porch, a glass of whiskey in one hand and a cigar in the other, staring out at the creek that drifted by his apartment. The team had all met at The Bar Bar shortly after he made the announcement earlier, and true to his word, Andrea bought the first round of drinks as way of an apology for how she had behaved toward everyone over the past three days. Edwin had even told Sammy to call Ryan and have him meet them there. After all, Andrea had been rude to him as well. He also thought it would do her good if she saw how Sammy acted around the other man, making Andrea realize just how wrong she was about the two of them.

The crew drank, laughed, and danced—well, he didn't dance, and they were all glad for it—sharing stories and just having a great time all the way around. He sat back and smiled at it all but made sure he kept an eye on Andrea. Even behind her laughter, he could see the anguish in her eyes, and it tore at his heart. He wanted so badly to thrash Brian for what he did to her. While Edwin didn't enjoy the way he told her the truth about the man, he was glad he followed his gut and checked Brian out. Andrea deserved better. She deserved someone who would give her his all. She was a strong woman, and he was sure she would make an amazing submissive.

Taking a sip of his whiskey, he worried about her being alone tonight with everything that happened today. He was sure grief at the loss of her relationship would be eating her up, worrying over every decision she ever made, every conversation they had. He knew that was how she would spend her night, because that's how he had spent that Monday night when Faith said goodbye to him. Lowering his glass, he leaned his head back against the wall, closing his eyes and feeling the familiar pain wrap around his heart. Would he ever not feel that agony?

Lowering his head, he reached out for his phone and scrolled through the contacts until Andrea's name came up. She would be feeling the same agony, he knew. He just wished there was a way to ease that pain for her, but he knew from experience nothing could.

Setting his glass on the table beside him, he decided to check in with a text. *I just wanted to see how you were doing.* He hit send before he could think better of it, picking his glass back up after dropping his phone in his lap and taking a pull from his cigar. He wondered if she had reached out to Brian and confronted him. Probably not as satisfying as if she had been able to do it face-to-face, but still, she couldn't allow it to just sit there. He wouldn't mind having a go at the man himself for that matter.

His phone dinged, and he picked it up, glancing at Andrea's name across the top. *About as well as a foolish woman could, I suppose. I called him.*

And what did he say? Edwin's first fear was that Brian had wormed his way out of what he had coming, denying that he was married, and convincing Andrea to remain with him. Edwin hated to admit it, but he had seen it happen before. It would all depend on how much Andrea would allow herself to be duped.

His phone dinged again, drawing his attention back to his lap. *I'd love to tell you about it if you'd open your door.*

He stared at the words, brows pinched. *Open my door?* He glanced over his shoulder. *Surely, she's not...*

Setting his cigar in the ashtray, he stood and made his way to the front door, wondering how Andrea would have even known where he lived. Sure enough, however, when he opened his front door, there stood Andrea, a dejected expression on her face and a bottle of Glenfiddich in her hand.

Holding the bottle out to him, her purse resting over her shoulder, she asked, "This is your drink of choice, right? Feel like having a drink with me?"

Smiling, he took the bottle from her hand, motioning for her to enter. "I'm always up for a drink." He didn't ask why she was there; he knew the answer to that. Instead, he kept smiling and offered her what she was silently asking for—not to be alone. "I'll get you a glass. You drink it neat or on the rocks?"

"However you're drinking it is fine," she said as she stepped inside, glancing around his small apartment. "I see you're almost all put together. Looks good."

He motioned with a tilt of his head for her to follow him and then led the way to the kitchen. "I have more stuff coming, but for now this is where I'm at. It's smaller than my home back in Brevard, but it'll do for now. I have a creek out back, which makes sitting out there relaxing. Later, I might upgrade to something bigger, but for what I need right now, this is perfect."

She nodded, lips pressed into a thin line as she plopped her purse down on the counter. "It's home," she said. "And that's all that really matters."

He turned, staring at her for a moment before nodding and reaching for a highball glass. "It's starting to feel that way." He poured her a double, knowing she could probably use it since she was there at his house, and handed her the glass. "I already have a drink on the porch, but we'll take the bottle with us." He shrugged. "Saves time getting refills."

She gave a soft laugh, and the sound warmed his heart.

He motioned to his back patio, grabbing the bottle and leading the way. "So, how do you think today went?"

"You mean closing the office and taking your crew out for alcoholic drinks?" she asked with a chuckle. "I think you boosted their morale, but not sure Neal would approve."

Edwin nodded, sliding the glass door open, and gesturing for her to lead the way. "I already called Neal and told him it was a necessary team building moment."

"Always thinking ahead, aren't you?"

He watched as she slid into a chair, her shoulders slumped a little from the weight of her emotions. "You just have to learn to get what you want while giving them what they want. It's all about perspective and a little semantics." He sat down, setting the bottle on the floor beside him and then reaching for his glass and cigar. "Everyone wins in the end. Besides, I think it was much needed, and Neal would have agreed, I'm sure." He held the cigar up, his brows pinched in question. "This doesn't bother you, does it?

"No, I'm fine. I actually enjoy the smell of a cigar. And I did apologize to everyone, especially Sammy and Ryan. Told him I was looking forward to working with him." She lifted her glass, taking a long swallow. She pinched her face as the whiskey burned its way down her throat, shivering a little with that first taste. "Wow. And you drink this stuff regularly."

He laughed, watching her take a deep breath. "Not as regularly as you make it sound, but yes, I do enjoy it."

"I would hate to see the lining of your stomach." She lifted the glass in a toast, and Edwin matched her. "To new beginnings."

He smiled, nodding. "To new beginnings."

After he finished swallowing, he leaned back, glancing out at the creek again. He didn't say anything; instead, he gave her the space she required to say what she needed to say when she was ready. He had questions, but those could wait. Right now, it was about meeting Andrea's needs, and he knew that what she needed was his patience and presence.

~ ~ ~ ~ ~

It didn't take long for her to open up, however. By the time she poured herself another drink, she was ready to bare all to Edwin so to speak. If anyone could understand her heartache, it would be the man who had just gone through an emotional upheaval himself.

She took another swallow, licking her lips when she was done and taking a deep breath in through her nose. "I called Brian," she said, staring out at the creek as a couple of mallards floated by. "This time I paid attention when he answered the phone. He shuffled around, covering up the mic until he finally said hello, and even then, his voice was low, almost like a whisper." She shook her head, dropping her gaze to her glass, which she held in her lap with both hands. "How had I been so stupid not to notice something like that before? He obviously had to get somewhere safe where he could talk. Stupid."

"What did he say?" She could feel Edwin's gaze as he studied her, his expression soft, concerned.

"I asked how his wife was doing with the new move, and it took him a full minute to answer me." Her breathing grew heavier as she replayed the entire conversation in her head, a fist clenching around her heart. "Then he asked how I found out, and if I had told anyone about the two of us." A small burst of laughter escaped her lips as disgust filled her. "Not an 'I'm sorry' or 'Look, it's not what you think'. No, that would have showed at least a little remorse or even a slight concern for me. Instead, he went into immediate cover his ass mode." She glanced over at him, a sad grimace twisting her lips. "I told him you filled me in about his wife. I'm sorry. I shouldn't have done that."

Edwin shrugged. "Doesn't matter to me, and besides, it's the truth."

"But he might make trouble for you," she said, truly concerned that she had made her drama his. "I don't want to drag you into this after what you just went through."

He had been taking a long drag from his cigar as she spoke, his lips wrapped around the stick as smoke filled his mouth. He blew it out, his lips in a slight pucker as he glanced back out at the lake, and all she could think about was how his lips had felt last week when he kissed her. Edwin had showed more concern for her safety in a few days than Brian ever had. "I dragged myself into it," he said, "when I called my friend." He gave her a slight shrug. "Besides, what's he going to do? Run to Neal?" he scoffed. "He's the one who was cheating on his wife. He'll keep quiet and pray you don't make a scene and cost him his marriage. Oh, he may bluster a lot, but I promise you, you can ignore it all. You're the one with all the cards."

She downed the rest of her whiskey and poured herself another glass, ignoring Edwin's cocked brow. She didn't need to be lectured on how much she was drinking. She just needed to numb the pain. "I'm not even sure what game we're playing now. Hell, I didn't even know the rules of the game *he* was playing." She sighed as she drank half of the whiskey in her glass, settling back in her chair. "I actually loved him. I would have done anything he wanted. Hell, I *did* everything he wanted. I was his to command, and he betrayed me." She swallowed the rest of her glass, and then held it in her lap.

"It sucks, I know," Edwin said, his glass resting on his knee. She had noticed he had barely touched it since they sat down. A soft smile decorated her lips, knowing he was being the protective one at the moment, giving her space to cope in any way she needed. "And it hurts like hell, but if I were you, I'd focus on the good things you shared and then just forget the rest. It's over." He turned to her, one brow cocked as he stared at her. "It is over, right? You didn't permit him to worm his way into remaining in your life, did you?"

She shook her head. "I didn't. It's over." She reached for the bottle, filling her glass almost to the rim. "I told him that as long as he left me alone, his wife would never hear about it from me." She took a large swallow, the whiskey no longer burning her throat. "Hopefully, that's the end of it. He'll have pictures and memories, but that's it. I deleted everything off my phone and tossed whatever he gave me. I don't need those reminders."

Edwin grinned, winking at her. "You could have kept the pictures."

She laughed. She couldn't help it. His statement was completely over the line as far as a work relationship went, but she laughed anyway. And the laughter felt good, even though tears flowed from her eyes again.

With the back of her hand, she swiped them away, but more just took their place. "I don't know why I'm still crying," she said. "I thought I had this out of my system before I even came over here."

"Oh, sweetie, I doubt it will be out of your system for a while. I don't know how long the two of you were together, but a BDSM relationship is intense. It goes deep inside of you and not just your heart. It penetrates every crevice of your mind, emotions, even your soul. If you surrendered to him the way you said, to the point that you would have gone home with a stranger just so Brian had a dirty story to listen to, then you went pretty deep. He's an ass for abusing that trust. You gave him something extremely special and of which he wasn't worthy."

She turned, staring at Edwin, a soft smile decorating her lips. He always seemed to know the perfect thing to say. "Thanks," she said. "And thanks for allowing me to barge in on your solitude." She went to take another drink and then realized her glass was empty. With a slight inebriated shrug, she reached for the bottle and filled her glass again.

"Speaking of which," Edwin started, his gaze fixed on how much she poured into her glass, "how did you even know where I lived?"

She giggled, scrunching her shoulders up, her nose bunching up to match. "I have connections," she told him. "I happen to know the person who has control of your personnel file."

He chortled, shaking his head. "Kendra. I should have known. Well, you're welcome here anytime." He reached for the bottle, made a point of noticing how much had already been drank, and then filled his glass. "I think you owe me a bottle of Glenfiddich. Unless, of course, this wasn't meant as a housewarming gift."

She laughed again, hating that she did because she had just giggled a moment ago. Nothing was that funny. "I, uh, meant it as a, uh, hmmmmm." Her brows pinched together as she studied the bottle. Then she shrugged, giving up on even figuring it out. "I meant it as a thank you. That's it. A thank you for opening my eyes to that dipshit Brian Humsteader."

He laughed. "You mean Holmstead?"

"Of course I do. That's what I said, isn't it?"

"Yeah, that's what you said. I just heard it wrong. My bad."

"You know, Edwin, I tried my damnedest to hate you when you first got here," she said, noticing how thick her tongue suddenly felt. She shook her head, waving the hand holding her glass, whiskey sloshing over the rim and splashing onto her hand. "Oops. Alcohol abuse." She licked the liquid from her thumb, and then turned back to Edwin. "Now, about hating you."

"Yes, about hating me," Edwin said, chuckling. His shoulders bounced as he laughed, and she couldn't take her eyes off how strong they were under his shirt.

"You got nice shoulders," she said, rubbing her lips against each other as she allowed her gaze to rake over the rest of him. "Your arms aren't bad, either."

"Thanks. I appreciate that."

"Dun mentun it," she said, or she thought she said it. Now, she wasn't so sure. *Oh, well, it doesn't matter. He gets it.* She lifted her glass and took another swig, barely even tasting the whiskey now. When she finished swallowing, she blew out a dramatic breath. She turned toward him, and her head felt like one of those Pop Vinyls the kids collected these days, bouncing in all directions. A grin slowly spread across her face. "You know, I actually enjoyed that kiss last week." She pointed at him with her index finger, narrowing her eyes at him. "You're a really good kisser."

"I'm glad you think so," he said as he stood, setting his glass on the table. "I enjoyed it, too."

She felt his hand on her arm, lifting her from her seat as he took her glass from her hand. Was he going to kiss her again? Oh, god, she hoped so. She could really use one of his kisses right now.

Instead, however, he set her glass on the table and helped her stumble her way inside the apartment. Her eyes went wide as he escorted her through the place and down the hall. Where was he— *Shit! He's taking me to his bedroom!*

When they entered, she spun, throwing her arms around his shoulders. "Now, Edwin, I know you like to screw around with coworkers, but I already told you, I'm not that type of gal." She straightened, stiffening a little. "Well, all right, I was with Brian, but I learned my lesson there, I'll tell you." She slid an arm off his shoulder and waggled a finger at him. "Just because you think I had too much to drink, doesn't mean you can take advantage of me. No, sir." She grinned, giggling. "I called you sir. Ha!" Taking a deep breath, she gazed into his eyes. "Do you want to kiss me again?"

Edwin leaned in, kissing her forehead. "There, I kissed you again," he said as he led her to the bed. "Now, you take my bed, and I'll sleep on the couch. I'm not sending you home like this, not even in an Uber."

"But, what will people say?" She felt her eyes go wide as he eased her into the bed, slipping her shoes off before pulling the covers over her. "I won't have no buttscuttle spreading that we did the funky funk."

"Buttscuttle?" Edwin repeated, chuckling. "Now that one I have to remember." As he pulled the covers up to her shoulders, he leaned down and kissed her forehead again, his lips warm against her flesh. "Get some sleep, and I'll see you in the morning with some strong coffee."

She nodded as he turned and walked back to the doorway. "Hey, Edwin," she called out, just as he reached the doorway. When he turned, his brows raised in question, she grinned and said, "You have a nice ass."

And then sleep claimed her.

Eighteen

Andrea groaned as she rolled over, her head feeling as if the high school drumline were rehearsing inside. She reached for her head, hoping to keep it from exploding, as she forced her eyes open. She blinked a few times, hoping to focus, but nothing seemed right. *That's not my ceiling fan.* She lifted her head slightly, regretting it the moment she did, and realized it wasn't her room, either. *Where the hell am I?* And then everything flooded back in, and she wished she was truly drowning. "Oh, my god. What did I do?"

Picking up the covers, she glanced at her body, expecting to see flesh, but was shocked when she noticed she was still fully clothed. Not even her socks had been removed. "All right, so maybe I didn't screw up that badly."

Kicking the covers off, she groaned, her entire body protesting against the movement. She glanced around the bedroom, her brows pinched. If she slept in Edwin's bed, where did he sleep?

How much did I actually drink last night?

She eased herself off the bed, hoping to keep her head from spinning and causing her to throw up. She probably looked bad enough in Edwin's eyes as it was; she didn't need to add to it. Making use of the master bathroom, she used the toilet and then took the time to wash her face. Borrowing his toothpaste, she brushed her teeth with her finger. Her hair was a mess, but there wasn't much she could do about that now other than comb her fingers through it, praying for some semblance of order.

Once she had procrastinated all she could in her attempt to avoid dealing with Edwin and her shame, she left the bedroom to face the music. Folk music played throughout the rest of the house. Not loud, but high enough that it offered a soothing white noise to the morning. *He likes banjo music?* She made her way down the hall, following the stomach-growling aroma of food.

Crossing through the living room, she finally found Edwin in the kitchen, stirring scrambled eggs. He stood there in a pair of pajama pants that cupped his firm ass and a tight T-shirt, his arms thick even when relaxed. His hair was perfectly combed, of course, but his feet were bare as he stood there preparing breakfast. He looked adorable, and Andrea had to fight the urge not to go over there and slide her hands up his chest as she pressed against his back. She had often wanted mornings just like this with Brian, but now she knew why she was never allowed them.

On the counter set a plate stacked with more bacon than she thought either of them could eat and a tray of biscuits with steam still rising from the browned tops. *And he cooks. Of course, he cooks.* She was about to say hello when a loud ping sounded from the counter as two pieces of toast popped up. She sighed, shaking her head. "Good morning," she finally offered.

Edwin turned, smiling as he stirred the eggs, raking her with his gaze. "Good morning." He pointed to the coffeepot. "Freshly brewed. Help yourself. Cups are in the second cabinet on the right. I didn't know if you preferred biscuits or toast, so I made both." He turned back to his eggs. "How do you feel?"

"My head is pounding," she admitted. "And my mouth feels as dry as sand. Look, I'm sorry about last night."

"No biggie," he assured her. He stepped to the side and opened one of the small drawers. Reaching inside, he pulled out a bottle and tossed it to her with a grin. "For your head." He turned back around taking the eggs off the stove and dumped them in a ceramic bowl. "And I meant it about last night. You needed a safe place to let it all go." He turned to her, a tender smile turning up his lips. "I'm glad I was able to give you that." He moved over to the table, motioning for her to get some coffee and then join him. "And don't worry about the office. I called Sammy and told her we had a meeting downtown. She'll cover for us. We still have that interview at ten, though, so we can't be too late."

"Thanks," she said as she opened the cabinet and pulled out a coffee mug with a picture of Grumpy on it. Somehow, the fact that Edwin Coldwell had a Disney mug in his cabinet warmed her heart. Shaking her head, she moved over to the coffeepot and poured a cup before joining him at the table. "I'm sorry you slept on the couch. You should have just dumped me on it. I doubt I would have noticed in my condition."

He chuckled as he scooped out some of the eggs, dumping them first on her plate and then his. "Easier to clean the sheets than the couch in case you got sick," he said, grinning. He gestured for her to take some bacon while he turned to fetch the toast. "Besides, I didn't want you waking up, thinking you could drive, and then disappearing on me." He made a sheepish shrug as he slid into his seat. "I needed to make sure you were safe in your condition."

She felt the blush warm her cheeks. "I appreciate it. Really." She finished fixing her plate, warring within herself whether to reveal just how much of last night she didn't remember. Finally, the need to know outweighed her embarrassment. "I hate to ask this, but did we, I mean, last night, while I was blitzed, did I make, did we…?"

He smirked at her. "Did we do the funky funk, as I think you called it?" He grinned as her eyes went wide. Shaking his head, he said, "No, we didn't do anything like that. Although, you did want me to kiss you again, and you did say I possessed a nice ass. Other than that, you were just your typical heartbroken drunk." He winked at her as he took a bite of bacon. "All perfectly harmless." Then his eyes went wide as his face lit up. "Oh, but you did create a new word. Buttscuttle."

She felt her brows furrow. "Buttscuttle?"

He laughed, nodding. "Yeah. I'm pretty sure in context you meant scuttlebutt, but you kind of flipped the words around." His smile softened as he reached for his coffee. "I kind of like it myself."

Andrea covered her face, her embarrassment burning up her cheeks. "Oh, god, how humiliating."

Edwin laughed harder, but it wasn't in a mocking way. More like he thought she was being cute. "It's all good, I promise. You needed to get a lot out. I'm glad you came to me. Truly."

She smiled over at him, dipping her head slightly as she shoved some scrambled eggs into her mouth. How could she have allowed herself to get so out of control in front of Edwin? She never wanted him to see her in this kind of light. A warmth filled her, her smile growing, as she realized just how perfectly safe she was with him last night. He could have taken advantage, but he didn't. He could have called a cab and sent her home, but he didn't. He could have simply slammed the door in her face as awfully as she had treated him since he arrived, but he didn't. Instead, he took care of her, giving up his bed and fixing her breakfast. He was everything she wanted in Brian, the other side of a sexual relationship, the tender, caring part.

A vibration sounded from her purse, which was setting on the counter still from where she put it last night. She turned staring at it, feeling a panic grip her.

"It's been going off most of the morning," Edwin said, watching her. "You don't need to answer him, you know? You can even block his number."

She nodded, still staring at her purse. "I know. I didn't even think about that last night." She turned back toward Edwin, concern about dragging him into everything filling her. "He hasn't reached out to you, has he? I'm sorry about mentioning your name. I should have never told him where I heard it from."

"Like I told you last night, it's no big deal. And no, he hasn't reached out to me. He won't because he's still hoping I won't keep talking to you about it. Talking to me makes it all real, and he'll have to do something at that point about what he's done. Right now, he's in the avoidance stage."

"So why is he calling me?"

Edwin shrugged, picking up a stick of bacon. "Either he needs to make sure you're not going to stir up shit for him, or he thinks he can convince you I was lying. He might come back with some sad story about his marriage, an attempt to make you feel sorry for him and return to his side." He stared at her for a moment, and she felt herself squirming under his scrutiny. "Look, what you do is up to you. It's your life after all. But, if you want my opinion, you deserve someone so much better, someone who won't keep you as a dirty little secret. You deserve to be escorted out in the daylight as someone's treasure, not their naughty little toy, at least not in a whispered sort of way. Be the naughty little toy when you both can be completely open and honest about it."

She smiled at what he said, nodding. She agreed, but sometimes, it was just so damn hard.

"Now, eat more bacon," he said, his tone stern as he glanced at her. "The grease is good for a hangover."

"Yes, sir," she said with a soft laugh as she reached for the bacon, and then she thought of what Sammy told him the other night. "Your wish is my command." She winked at him as she bit down on the piece of bacon.

~ ~ ~ ~ ~

The words kept repeating in his mind. *Your wish is my command.* And from Andrea's lips they meant so much more than when Sammy said them. He knew Andrea was making fun of the situation, but he would have loved to have given her a few commands right then while it was just the two of them. He wanted to take care of her, protect her, but he didn't want to be some rebound she used to get over Brian. He wanted to take her as his submissive, own her as his treasure, but it was simply too soon for either of them.

At least, that's what he kept telling himself as he drove to work. The truth was, however, that he knew there would never be anything with Faith. She had made her decision, but that didn't mean he hadn't held out hope. It was easy to ignore the pain with her out of sight and safely in Brevard. It would be the same with Andrea and Brian. But, every once in a while, a song would come on or a breeze would carry a certain aroma to him, and suddenly he had to fight to keep his chest from caving in with the heartache as tears threatened to blind him. Brian had opened a door for Andrea, and Faith had done the same for him, allowing him to experience that type of control over someone. He missed her, and he knew there would always be a spot reserved in his heart for her. But there would never be a place in her life for him, not the way he wanted, the way he needed.

He pulled into his parking spot and shut off the engine. With a deep breath, he reached for his phone, scrolling his contacts until he found Faith's number, and hit call. He knew she would be at work but hoped she would answer anyway.

He almost gave up and ended the call when her voice filled his ear.

"Hello, Edwin," she said, her voice soft. He could hear her smile. "How are you doing? How are things in Savannah?"

He felt the constriction in his chest as he sat there, forcing himself to breathe and not lose control. "Savannah's great, actually. Lots of history. I've even found a couple of bars I like. How about things back home? You doing all right? How's the office?"

"A few changes but not many," Faith said. "Grady's gone, thank god. Cherish, of course. Other than that, everything's pretty much the same. Morgan asked me to fly out to Biloxi and help him with his new crew. I'll be going out Tuesday night and coming back Friday, and before you ask, no, there will be no extra fun."

He chuckled softly. "Still focused on your new adventure at home?" He swiped at the tear that pooled at the corner of his eye, forcing his voice to remain steady.

"I am. Tracey is part of our family now, and we're trying hard to figure out what that exactly means for all of us. Luckily, there's a big learning curve."

He nodded, rubbing a palm up and down his thigh as he sat in his truck. "Look, I won't keep you. I know you're busy. I just..." He took a deep breath. "I just wanted to call and say I was sorry. I never should have asked you to leave your husband. I guess... I guess I just got in too deep, you know?"

Silence. He pulled the phone away to make sure he hadn't lost connection. "Faith, are you still there?"

After a moment, he heard her take a deep breath. "Yeah, I'm still here," she assured him. "Truth is, Edwin, I was getting in too deep myself. I allowed myself to get caught up in the emotions of everything going on, and the way things were with my family, and then what you offered..." she made a soft laugh. "It was easy to get lost. I did fall in love with you, Edwin, but I love Selby more. He's my life. I don't know what the future holds with Tracey, but I do know Selby will always be the center of my world. I'm sorry for hurting you. If I had been able to keep my walls up, keep that distance between us while we were exploring, things may have gone quite differently."

He pressed his lips together, nodding. "I fell in love with you, too. And I get it. Really, I do. I pushed. I shouldn't have. I'm sorry. I hope you know I'll always be here if you ever need anything no matter what it is. I'm always here for you. I truly hope the best for you and Selby."

"Thanks. That means a lot. And the same goes for me. I'm always here for you. Always. I want to see you get everything you desire, Edwin. I honestly hope you find that special person."

"So do I," he said. "Take care of yourself, Faith Greer."

"You, too, Edwin."

He hung up, knowing he would probably never talk to Faith again, but at least he was happy with the way things had ended.

As he slid his phone into his pocket, he heard a car pull up beside him. Glancing over, he saw Andrea as she parked and looked over at him, a soft smile creasing her face. Perhaps that special someone was closer than he thought.

Nineteen

The weekend was finally here, and Andrea couldn't wait to close the books on this week after everything she had been through. It had been a rollercoaster of emotions, most of which she hoped to never feel again. At least Edwin didn't make a big deal about what happened a couple of nights ago. He hadn't even brought it up since fixing her breakfast yesterday morning. He treated her as if nothing happened and she hadn't been fucking a married man. He did, however, keep glancing over at her when he didn't think she was watching, and every time she caught him, it brought a smile to her face.

"We're out of here," Kendra said after knocking on Andrea's open door, Jana right behind her. "See you Monday."

Andrea waved at them. "Have a great weekend."

As they walked away, she glanced across the bullpen. Edwin was still in his chair, leaning back and reading over more contracts. She smiled as she stared at him, biting her lower lip.

Even reading boring paperwork, he looked sexy as hell. She giggled softly, shaking her head at her thoughts. *Nothing good can come from this line of thinking, Andrea.* She blew out an exasperated breath as she scolded herself.

Her desk phone rang, indicating Sammy was calling. "What's up?"

"Just letting you know I'm leaving. I locked the front. If you or Edwin would turn out the lights when you leave, please."

"Will do," Andrea said, glancing across the way at Edwin again. "I think I'm going to be close behind you. I hear a glass of wine calling my name."

"I hear the dance floor calling mine," Sammy said, laughing. "It's Friday night. Why are you staying home? You know you're more than welcome to come hang out with me. I can text you where I wind up if you want."

"Sounds good, but no promises," Andrea replied. "I'm feeling kind of worn down. I may need a night of me time if you know what I mean."

"Please. Me time is for when you're old and can't shake your ass anymore."

"I am old," Andrea said, leaning back in her chair. "I'll leave the ass shaking to you. See you Monday."

"Have a great weekend," Sammy said, and then she hung up.

Replacing the phone in its cradle, a slight tingle went through Andrea as she realized she was in the office alone with Edwin. Is this how he had sex with Faith Greer? Or her sister? Brian had never risked them getting caught at work, and of course, she knew why now. Edwin, however, seemed to have enjoyed the thrill of that particular risk. What would it be like to fuck Edwin in this very office? Heat pooled between her thighs as she imagined it, down on her knees at his desk, obeying him.

She shot out of her chair, more to end that particular line of thought than anything else. Closing down her computer, she decided that was enough work for one day. It was time for a little fun.

After locking her office, she made her way across the bullpen to Edwin. Knocking on his door, she leaned on the doorframe, arms over her chest as she watched him look up. "Plan on working late?" she asked.

He started to say something, but it turned into a yawn as he covered his mouth and stretched. When he was done, he gave his head a slight shake, chuckling. "I guess I was in that position longer than I thought. What time is it?"

"Almost six," she answered. "Everyone else has left. It's just the two of us." She waggled her brows at him, smiling.

He chuckled as he leaned back in his chair. "Just the two of us. That sounds ominous."

"And here I thought you'd say something more like, um, enticing."

He laughed even harder, shaking his head. "Andrea Newman, you're becoming incorrigible. Do you know that?"

She gave him a one-shoulder shrug. "Would you prefer grouchy? Cause I can turn back to grouchy in a second. It's like a switch these days."

He held up his hands. "No, no, no. I'll stick with incorrigible." He blew out a breath. "We need to enjoy having weekends off while we can. As soon as things really take off, some of us will be working Saturdays and Sundays."

"Then we definitely need to make the most of the weekends while we can. Do you have any plans for the night?"

Edwin shook his head. "Nope. Just more work around the apartment. You?"

"Nothing." She took a deep breath, screwing up her courage. "You should let me cook you dinner tonight. You know, for allowing me to get drunk on you Wednesday night. It won't be anything fancy, but it beats eating alone. Since you have no plans, that is."

He smiled at her, which brought a twinkle to his eyes that melted her panties. "All right. Sounds good. Anything I can bring? Some more whiskey?" He winked at her, grinning. "What time should I come by?"

"Seven sound good?"

"Works for me. Now for the big question. Where do you live?"

She grinned. "I guess that would be important to know, huh? I'll text you my address." She shoved herself off the doorframe, ready to head to the store because she knew she had nothing at home to cook. "You're not allergic to anything, are you? I would hate to kill the boss with my cooking. Wouldn't look good on my resume."

He stood, chuckling. "Anything you cook will be fine." He powered down his computer as he flipped the file folder he had been studying closed. Then joined her at the door, standing close enough that she could feel his breath on her face as he glanced down at her. "I'm looking forward to it. See you at seven." He gestured for her to lead the way out of the office.

Andrea nodded once and then turned and walked toward the front lobby, making sure she shook her ass as she walked just for Edwin's pleasure. All right, it pleased her to do it as well.

~ ~ ~ ~ ~

Edwin walked up to Andrea's door, nerves rattling his insides. He had no idea why he was so nervous. It wasn't like he had never been invited to a woman's house before, and this wasn't like any of those times. This was Andrea, his second-in-command. She was going through a hard time and just needed some company right now. That's all it was.

But damn, her ass looked so fucking good when she walked out of the office earlier.

A quick knock on her door, and a few seconds later she answered it, wearing a short sundress, her breasts pushing over the neckline, her feet bare. Edwin swallowed the lust that filled his throat as he stared at her. He looked down at his jeans and T-shirt. "I, uh, feel like I'm a little under dressed."

She waved off his comment. "Not at all. Trust me. This is just comfortable. I wear jeans at work all day and much prefer the looser feel of sundresses." Then her expression twisted in a panic as she glanced down at herself. "Do I look bad?"

"No," he told her. "Actually, you look amazing." Her face colored at his compliment. He handed her the bottle of Glenfiddich he had brought with him. "Since you might not remember enjoying it the other night, I thought I'd bring you another bottle."

"Can't we just let that fade into the background of our minds," she said, her face pinched in a wince as she took the bottle. "I mean, I can't even remember most of it anyway."

He laughed as he followed her into the apartment, his gaze dropping to her ass again. It looked just as awesome in her sundress as it had in her jeans earlier. He took a deep breath as he felt his cock growing. Tonight would be a difficult struggle to keep himself in check. God, why was he supposed to behave?

"I hope you like lasagna," she said once they entered the kitchen.

"I should have brought wine," he said, setting the bottle of whiskey on the table.

She turned, grinning at him. "Luckily, I keep a few bottles on hand at all times."

"Smart woman." He glanced around the kitchen, her decor simple but colorful. A small table sat in the middle with wooden chairs, each with a burgundy cushion to sit on. The color made him think of the dress she wore while out the other night, the way it hugged her hips, pushing up her breasts. A lot like the dress she wore now was doing.

He watched as she reached for a highball glass out of her cabinet, stretching up on her tiptoes slightly to reach it, her dress sliding up her backside and almost revealing her ass. It still slid high enough, though, that Edwin doubted she was wearing panties. His brow cocked at that, wondering what exactly Andrea had in mind when she invited him over for dinner.

"Anything I can do to help?" he asked, slipping his hands into his pockets.

"Nope, I got it," she said, turning back to the counter and pouring him some whiskey. "Just sit down and relax. Dinner is almost ready." After pouring his drink, she sashayed over to him and handed him the glass. He took it, but she didn't release the drink right off, their fingers lingering on each other for a moment. She smiled as she allowed her hand to slide from the glass, gliding across his fingers as she let go.

He took a deep breath in through his nose, feeling his eyes widen slightly as he watched her, his cock twitching in his pants. "If you're sure," he said, his voice low, husky.

"I'm sure," she told him. "It's my turn to take care of you for the night." She winked at him as she turned back to the stove.

He stared at her for a moment and not just at her ass. Her entire body expressed sexuality, her back, shoulders, the way she moved, how she carried herself. Hell, even her bare feet. Andrea Newman was seduction in a sundress.

Taking a sip of his drink, he moved over to one of the chairs around the kitchen table and sat down. "Any backlash from Brian? I remember yesterday morning how your phone was blowing up. Did you ever answer him?"

"Nope. I already said what I needed to say when I confronted him. As far as I'm concerned it's done. He texted a couple of times today, begging me to talk to him, promising it wasn't what I thought." She shrugged as she pulled the lasagna from the oven, and slid the garlic bread inside. "I don't know what he thinks I think it is, but it can only be one thing. I was his playmate behind his wife's back. It's as simple as that. He lied to both of us."

Edwin watched as she placed the lasagna on the stove and closed the oven, loving the way she bent over and pushed her ass up in the air. For all he knew, she was probably doing it on purpose for his benefit. He appreciated the effort.

She turned back around, leaning back on the counter, her arms crossed over her stomach, pushing her breasts up slightly. "He didn't even give me the benefit of telling me I was the mistress in his life." She shook her head. "I loved what we did, but not how he went about it."

Edwin cocked his head to the side, studying her. "And if he had told you he was married, would you have still submitted to him?"

She shrugged, shaking her head again. "I honestly don't know," she admitted. "I really did care for him. Hell, part of me still does, but he lied to me and deceived me. I hate being lied to. Just tell me the truth, no matter what it is, or how hard you think it'll hurt me."

He gave her a soft nod. "I'll remember that."

She smiled over at him, and he noticed the blush color her cheeks. "I can handle a lot. I just won't be lied to."

~ ~ ~ ~ ~

After fixing their plates and pouring them both a glass of wine, Andrea slid into her seat, taking a deep breath. Her entire intention tonight was to serve Edwin, to give him what she had wanted to give Brian, but for which Brian didn't deserve. Edwin deserved it. He took care of her, even before her night of drunkenness. He protected her while they were out, he dug into Brian when she should have done it, and he made sure she was safe when her world came crashing down upon her. He was the man Brian was supposed to be for her, and she was just beginning to see that.

"Any plans for the weekend?" she asked as she picked up her glass.

"I have some movers arriving tomorrow with the rest of my possessions." He lifted his glass, taking another small sip. She had noticed he still drank cautiously, probably still wanting to protect her in case she went off the deep end again. "I'll start emptying the rest of the boxes once they arrive, deciding what to keep in the apartment and what to put into storage."

"Would you like some help? I have no plans as of yet."

He glanced over at her, one brow cocked. "Are you sure? It'll be fairly boring and tedious. I'm sure you could find better things to do with your Saturday than watch me sort through kitchen utensils and old books."

"Old books, huh? So, Edwin Coldwell reads? Now you have to let me help if for no other reason than to see the evidence of that for myself. I mean, I'm just dying to know what types of books the boss reads." She bounced her brows at him, a playful grin stretched across her face.

He made a slight shrug. "All right, but don't say I didn't warn you."

"Great. What time are they arriving?" She couldn't think of anything she wanted to do more right then than help him put his apartment together.

He gave her the time as they finished their meal, Andrea downing the rest of her wine before standing and collecting the plates. As he reached to help her, she told him she had it. "After all, you're the guest. Finish your drink. I'm just going to put these in the dishwasher, and then we can move to the living room where it's more comfortable." She made a point of looking down at his glass. "And please, don't avoid drinking because of me. I promise, I'm in control of my emotions tonight and my drinking."

"Well, I did drive here," he told her. "I need to be able to drive home, too."

She giggled. "Well, if you drink too much, it'll be my turn to sleep on the couch. After all, it's only fair."

He laughed, shaking his head as he lifted his glass to his lips. She stared at them for a moment as he took a drink, remembering how they felt meshed against hers, his tongue tasting her. Her chest tightened with passion as she forced herself to look away and finish her task. She wanted him. If she were honest with herself, she had to admit she had wanted him since last Wednesday, when he was both gentleman and scoundrel at the same time. He was the perfect mix, she was discovering, and it soaked her panties. Or, rather, it would have if she was wearing any. Her goal for tonight was not only to serve him but to leave the door open in case he made a move, a move she hungrily wanted him to make, but which she feared he wouldn't because of both their pasts. How would she get him to see past that, past her relationship with Brian that technically just ended?

Once she was finished with loading the dishwasher, she refilled her wineglass and then motioned toward the living room. "Shall we?"

He gave a quick nod as he stood, one hand wrapped around his glass. "After you."

She smiled over at him as she led the way into the living room, setting the wineglass on the end table. As she turned, she watched him place his glass on a coaster, and somehow that simple act of protecting her furniture touched her heart in the same way it did when he protected her last week.

Before he could sit down, she eased over to him, one hand on his chest. He glanced at her, his expression soft, his breathing heavy. "If I promise not to drink too much, will you kiss me again?" she asked, staring up into his eyes.

He smiled at her as he slid one hand around her waist, pulling her tightly against him. She could feel his hardness against her abdomen, and the feel of it made her suck in a breath. "Are you sure it won't be something you'll regret in the morning?"

She shook her head, her hair swishing across her shoulders. "No. I'll only regret it if you say no."

His smile grew. "Then I guess I better not say no, huh?"

She bounced her gaze between his eyes and his lips, hoping he would kiss her right then. Her honey dripped as she leaned closer, noticing him leaning into her, his mouth coming to claim her.

And then her doorbell rang.

Edwin bounced his brows at her, a mischievous grin toying at his lips. "Seems the universe wants us to wait a little bit longer."

She groaned. "I am so not a fan of the universe right now."

He held her tighter. "You'll get your kiss. I want it just as badly, I assure you."

She nodded as he released her, the doorbell ringing again. Moving over to answer it, she couldn't imagine who the hell would be visiting her at eight on a Friday night, unless it was Sammy come to drag her out to a bar. As she reached for the doorknob, she worried that if it was Sammy and the younger woman saw Edwin there what the girl would think. They didn't need a scandal after everything that happened already. Taking a deep breath, she decided she was simply not letting Sammy into her apartment and would give her the brush-off at the door.

But then, it wasn't Sammy she needed to worry about. As she

opened the door, Brian stood there, bouncing from foot to foot in his impatience.

Twenty

Panic mixed with confusion clutched at Andrea's heart. "What the hell are you doing here?" she asked, still not sure she was actually staring at Brian on her doorstep. Anger raged throughout her body, and she could feel her hands shaking. "I thought the drive between Fort Lauderdale and Savannah was just too long of a drive. You couldn't spare the time, remember? Couldn't get away. What changed? Oh, yeah, that's right. I found out you were fucking married. Now you suddenly have the time? Amazing how that works. What did you even tell your wife that she permitted you to come and try to save your nuts?"

He sighed, hands on his hips as he stared at her. "I told her I had to come up here to close out some business. Andrea, I needed to talk to you. To explain. Look, can I come in? Talk. Just to talk. After everything we shared, can't you at least give me a few more minutes to explain?"

She stared at him, her heart pounding in her chest but not for the reasons it had the last time she saw Brian. This was the man who lied to her, used her for his own games without even giving her the chance to play along fully in the know. She heard shuffling behind her, and then by the look on Brian's face, she knew Edwin had stepped up behind her. She couldn't stop the grin that spread across her face.

"What the fuck is he doing here?" Brian shouted, pointing at Edwin and glaring. He turned back to Andrea, his head tilted to the side. "You're sleeping with him now?"

"I'd be careful with your accusations," Edwin said as he placed his hand on Andrea's back, stepping up beside her. Turning to face her, a soft smile on his lips, he said, "I think I should leave you two to figure this out. Thanks for dinner. I loved it." He glanced back at Brian, one brow cocked before looking back to Andrea, the concern quite apparent on his face. "I'll check on you later."

She nodded, her arms over her chest. This was *so* not the way she wanted this evening to go. She had been so damn close to getting another kiss! "I'll be there tomorrow." She took a deep breath as she said it, expecting Brian to question where 'there' was, but the man just stood there, glaring at Edwin as if willing him to hurry up and leave.

Edwin gave her a curt nod before turning and walking past Brian, not even bothering to say excuse me.

Andrea smiled at his retreating back, wishing she could just call him back and slam the door on Brian's face.

"You two seem to have gotten pretty chummy since he arrived," Brian sneered. "Now I see why he told you about my wife. He was eager to worm his way into your bed."

Andrea let her head tilt to the side as she glared at Brian. "We're not sleeping together, thank you very much. And he shouldn't have *had* to tell me about your wife. You should have done that on your own. Instead, you lied to me, just like you lied to her."

He glanced around at the other apartments. "Can I at least come in so your neighbors don't hear something they shouldn't? You don't want them all up in your private business, do you?"

She scoffed at him. "I'm not the one with anything to hide. That would be you. I don't care what they hear."

He took a slow breath before asking again. "Please? Can we do this inside?"

She pursed her lips together, almost deciding to leave the man standing there on her doorstep. The humiliation of it would do him some good. In the end, however, she stepped to the side and gestured for him to enter.

He nodded once as he stepped past her and into her apartment. It was the first time, actually, that he had ever been there. She had gone to his a few times whenever he wanted sex, but never to her place. This would also be his last time to be there, as well.

"If you're not sleeping together, why did he feel the need to tell you about my wife if it wasn't to get into your pants?" Brian asked as soon as she closed the door. "What was the purpose if not to split us up so he could have you for himself?"

Andrea ducked her gaze to her feet, her lips pressed together. "Because I was being a judgmental bitch." She doubted Edwin would have told her the way he did if she had not been riding his case about Sammy, accusing him of already fucking the young receptionist. She glanced back up at Brian, smiling as she thought of how Edwin's demeanor changed when he realized she didn't know about Brian's wife. He had gone from angry bear to caring puppy in a split second, worried about her being hurt and feeling as if he had even caused it. He hadn't, of course. No, that blame fell solely on Brian's shoulders. "Edwin has actually been nothing but the gentleman, protecting me where you didn't." She sighed, shaking her head. "Brian, look, I'm sorry you made the trip, but it was a wasted drive. We're through. There were a lot of red flags I ignored, but I just can't anymore. You're married and will never be able to give me what I need in the end, a man who can commit to me in all areas. Go back to your wife. I wish you both the best."

"But you don't understand how it is," he said, falling back and sitting on the arm of her sofa, his hands on his thighs. "She doesn't want what we have. This is a part of me I'm not willing to give up."

"Then divorce her, but don't cheat on her. Or, somehow, convince her to explore it with you. It doesn't matter to me anymore. There can't be an us as long as there is a two of you. A dominant/submissive relationship is based on trust, and you broke mine. It's over. I'm sorry."

She could see his shoulders rising and falling with his heavy breathing as he just sat there and stared at her. More than likely, he was struggling to come up with another reason for his infidelity and deceit, but it didn't matter. Whatever he said would never be anything she could trust to be true. Once doubt enters a person's mind, it's hard to shake it out, and she had major doubts about Brian Holmstead.

She took a step toward the door, turning her back to Brian. "I think you should go." Once she reached the front door, she opened it, standing there waiting for him to leave. "Go call your wife. Do right by her for a change."

He stared at her for another moment, and for a second, she didn't think he would get up and leave. However, he finally nodded, pushing himself off the arm of her sofa, and walked over to where she stood. When he reached her, he paused, his hands in his front pockets. "Are you sure there isn't anything I can say to make you stay with me? I'll make trips. I'll give you whatever you need to make this work. Just name it."

"You can't give me my trust back," she said, shrugging slightly. "And you can't be single when you're already married. I'd be helping you cheat on your wife, and I've already done that enough unknowingly. There's nothing here for you anymore. I'm sorry."

He nodded, breathing heavily. "I'm sorry, too," he said, his voice almost a whisper. "I'm going to miss you." He reached out, placing his hand softly on her arm as he leaned in and kissed her cheek.

Andrea closed her eyes, a fist squeezing her heart as she fought the tears that threatened to fall. "I'll miss you, too, Brian," she whispered.

He pulled away, his lips a straight line as he looked at her. "Take care of yourself. Reach out if you need anything."

She gave him a soft smile. "I won't need anything, but thanks. Goodbye, Brian."

He nodded once. "Goodbye, Andrea."

She watched as he turned and walked away, his hands in his front pockets again, his shoulders slumped, head drooping forward. She took a deep breath in through her nose before closing her door on that chapter of her life. It wasn't until the door was shut and locked that she allowed herself to slump to the floor, arms over her chest, and cry her pain away.

~ ~ ~ ~ ~

Edwin tossed his keys on the table by his front door as he entered his house. He was still worried about Andrea, but she was a grown woman and needed to handle Brian without him hovering there on the edge of their conversation. As much as he wanted to protect her, and he very much wanted to protect her, she still had to deal with this on her own.

He sighed as he reached for a highball glass and filled it with the little Glenfiddich Andrea had left him the other night. He smiled as he recalled how drunk she was as well as how silly. The fact that she trusted him enough to let herself go and feel her pain made him swell with pride. He liked being her safe place and hoped she would always see him that way.

Grabbing a cigar from his humidor, he made his way to the back porch and sat down in his chair, feet up on the rail as he stared out at the creek. He also had to admit to being a little jealous right then, which surprised him. He was worried that Brian would be able to justify everything out to her, and she would forgive him and take him back. Edwin didn't want her to take Brian back. He wanted her to... He took a deep breath. He wanted her to explore the lifestyle with him. Neither one of them had the people in their lives they had set their sights on, but in losing them, they had found each other. He didn't want to lose that before they even had a chance to see where it would lead. It was a journey he wanted to take with Andrea, no matter how many rules it broke.

He used his punch to cut a hole in the end of his cigar and then lit it. Taking a long pull, he tasted the smoke and then blew it out as if blowing out his anxiety. He then took a slow sip of his whiskey as he pulled his phone from his back pocket and set it on the table beside him, wondering if he would hear from Andrea tonight. He hated leaving her side just when things were beginning to heat up between them. He would have loved to have seen how far they would have gone tonight, how far he would have attempted to take things. She seemed to have wanted it as much as he did, which was a great sign of course. It meant it wasn't all in his head. Or in his pants, so to speak.

As he lifted his glass to take another swig, his phone rang. Andrea's name came across the top, making his brows arch. *Now, that was quick.* He wasn't sure what he expected, but for her to have dealt with Brian one way or another this fast was not it, not with their history.

Reaching out, he picked up his phone and answered it. "Hey, there," he said. "You doing all right?"

"Yeah, I'm fine," she said, and he could hear the tears in her voice. "I was shocked that he actually drove up here to be honest. I had been asking him for a visit since he left, and he always swore there just wasn't time."

"Well, I'm sure he thought if he could see you face-to-face, it would go a long way into changing your mind. I'm taking it he's gone?" He took another pull from his cigar, mainly to have something to do with his hands.

"He is," she assured him. "For good. I told him to go back and work on his marriage. I also blocked his number, like you suggested."

"Smart move. Less temptation to get into it again with him if you can't see what he's saying." He felt the smile spread across his face that she had listened to him. "You might want to hide him for now from your social media accounts, as well. Less of you seeing him in your newsfeeds. It can be like a slap in the face for a while when you do."

"I'll work on that next," she assured him. "I'm sorry about tonight. I really was looking forward to that kiss."

He sighed. "I was, as well, but that's something we should probably talk about, too. I don't want you regretting later something you do now, especially if you're not thinking clearly. Plus, there's the punishment that may come if Neal ever catches wind of it in a negative light. We need to do this right if we do it. As much as I would love to feel your lips on me again, are you sure this is something you want?"

Silence answered him, and he was actually glad she took the

time to think about her reply. She was just coming off an emotional relationship. He didn't want her to just toss herself at him to feel something besides the pain of that heartache.

When she did answer him finally, her voice was soft, almost a whisper. "We can take it day-by-day if you want, see if the opportunity ever presents itself again. I get it, though. You're worried about me getting pissed off and using it against you like that one woman did. I wouldn't do that, just so you know. You're not the one tricking me. I can be tricky, too, you know?" She giggled softly.

"Actually, I *don't* think you would do that," he assured her. "If so, you would have done it to Brian already, especially when he showed up on your doorstep unannounced tonight." He felt the grin crease his face. "You didn't drop kick his nuts into next week, did you? I would have rather stuck around and seen that if you did."

She giggled, her voice sounding lighter, less full of tears. "No, there was no ball racking. Weird that I didn't even think about it, huh? Basically, I just told him he could never give me what I needed. I would always be a part time thing for him, someone he could toy with when he was horny and his wife was busy somewhere else, but never fully committed to me. I'm greedy in that I want it all, not just a tiny sliver."

"You deserve it all," he told her. "No one deserves to be someone's side dish. You're the main course, sweetheart. Never forget that."

"Thank you," she said, and he could hear the smile in her tone. "I won't. I'd still like to come over and help you tomorrow if you'll let me. I might need the distraction."

"You're welcome here anytime." He stared out at the creek, the moon shimmering over the surface. "Come over whenever you're ready. I'd love the help as well as the company. Now, not to sound too bossy here, but you should pour yourself a glass of wine, fill the tub with hot water and bubble bath if you have it, and just soak there with your eyes closed, allowing the hot water to soothe your body and soul. It'll do you good. Promise."

"Sounds like an amazing idea," she said. "I think I'll do that. Thank you. I'll see you tomorrow morning. Need me to bring anything?"

"Just yourself," he told her. "Hey, call me if you need anything tonight. I mean it."

"Yes, sir," she said, her smile even stronger in her voice. "Goodnight."

He said goodnight, as well, and then hung up the phone. He hoped she listened to him and allowed herself the luxury of soaking in the tub. It's the closest he could come to taking care of her right then. Hopefully, Brain Holmstead had taken the hint and was gone for good. She didn't need him on her doorstep again first thing in the morning. Sometimes, though, bad pennies had a way of always turning up.

Taking another sip of his whiskey, he realized just how much he was looking forward to tomorrow morning and seeing Andrea again. *Maybe she'll wear that sundress for me.* He grinned as he took a long pull from his cigar, picturing her up on her tiptoes once more as the hem of her dress just barely covered the bottom of her ass cheeks. *I'll have to get her to bend over a lot.*

Twenty-One

The movers arrived an hour early, waking Edwin out of a sound sleep. Dressed in his pajama pants, he made a pot of coffee while they stacked everything in his living room. As he leaned back on the counter, arms over his chest, waiting on the coffee to brew so he could truly wake up, he wondered how Andrea was feeling that morning and if Brian had actually left Savannah. She didn't need him hovering around the edges of her emotions, trying to coax her back into his arms. If he was smart, he would leave her alone while everything was still quiet and under Neal's radar.

The coffeepot dinged, and Edwin immediately filled his Grumpy mug. Standing there in his bare feet, he turned and headed into the living room to check on the movers' progress. Most of his furniture was already there, Edwin having brought it with him in a small trailer when he moved to Savannah. He refused to sit on the floor until the rest arrived. Still there was plenty left in storage back in Brevard he needed to go through and make decisions on.

"We're all done," a thick-bodied man said as he handed Edwin a clipboard with paperwork to sign.

"Thanks. I appreciate it." Edwin scribbled his name on the paper and handed the man back his pen. He offered him a couple of twenties for his time as well as that of his crew. "Have a safe trip back."

As he was about to close his door, Andrea stepped up wearing a tight pair of jean shorts and a T-shirt that cupped her breasts perfectly. "Well, hello," he said. "I honestly didn't think I'd see you until later after the night you had." He stepped to the side, allowing her to enter his apartment.

"I slept hard, but once I woke up, there was no chance of going back to sleep again," she said as she walked past him. "I see I missed all the strong, muscular men moving about your apartment."

He chuckled as he led her back to the kitchen and a cup of coffee. "There was only one muscular man. The other one was kind of on the scrawny side. I was actually surprised he could lift half of what he did. Still, they managed to get it all inside fairly quick." He reached into the cabinet, pulled out a cup, and filled it with coffee. He turned to her, handing her the cup, steam slithering out the top. "Any more from Brian?"

She took the cup, shaking her head. "Nope. All quiet. Amazing how blocking his number will do that."

"That he didn't figure out another way to reach you actually surprises me," Edwin told her as they walked back out to the living room. "I'm glad for it, don't get me wrong. But after making that drive for a dramatic confrontation, I honestly expected more out of him."

"Same here," she said as she sat down on the arm of his sofa, holding her coffee cup with both hands. "Who knows? He may just wait a while and try again. It won't work, though. Besides, what would be the point? It's not like he can make a relationship work. I want the best for him, just not with me."

"I hear ya," he said, lifting his cup to his lips and taking a sip.

She glanced around the place at all the boxes. "So, what can I do to help?"

He blew out a breath as he glanced around at the many stacks of his stored possessions. His life pretty much in a box. "Well, I guess we start with one box and see what's inside. I'll either know where to put it, stick it to the side until I do, or shove it back into the box for later."

Andrea laughed. "Sounds like a plan."

He noticed she didn't try to kiss him again after arriving and wondered if it was just timing or if she had changed her mind after what all he said last night. Only time would tell, he supposed.

Setting their coffee on the table, they picked a box and started unpacking.

Most everything he remembered shoving into the boxes as he prepared to leave his home in Florida. Others had been in boxes for longer than he could remember, shuffled from one place to another, only to be shoved into a corner of the garage or crammed into a storage unit. He laughed at old pictures, books he didn't remember if he ever read or not, and old Avon cologne bottles his father gave him years ago. His life had been an eclectic journey to be sure.

"What's this?" Andrea asked, her lips twisted in a smirk as she pulled a purple flogger out of a box.

Edwin felt his eyes go wide as he stared at it. *Damn. I forgot about that box.*

Andrea reached in, pulling out a riding crop as well as some leather restraints. "This box just keeps getting better and better," she said with a giggle. "I didn't know you had a goodie box." She grinned over at him as she reached inside the box to see what else she could find.

"Um, maybe we should leave that box until later," he said, taking the flogger from her hand. "I can sort through this one on my own."

"Are you kidding?" she scoffed. "I want to see the darker side of Edwin Coldwell." Reaching in she pulled out two wicker baskets and a black yoga mat. "How are these sex toys?"

His eyes went wide as he remembered buying the baskets and their purpose, a twinge twisting his heartstrings. "I intended on using them as part of a ritual, but never got the chance."

She glanced up at him, one brow cocked. "A ritual? So, there's more than just hot, kinky sex in this for you?"

He gave her a soft smile. "The rituals can be a part of that hot, kinky sex," he told her as he draped the flogger over the box. "It's all a part of foreplay, really, setting the mood for whatever happens next and putting the submissive into the proper mindset."

She nodded, her lips pressed into a thin line as she studied the two baskets and the mat. "All right, I get that. So, tell me what this ritual was supposed to be." She then glanced up at him, her eyes a little wide as she obviously feared crossing a line. "If it's not too personal, that is."

He smiled at her as he moved over to sit on the arm of his couch, picking up his coffee cup as he did. "It's not. Hopefully, I get to use it one day. I still think it would be hot as hell." He pointed to the baskets. "Both baskets would be placed by the front door. One would be empty, but the other would hold whatever outfit I wanted my submissive in that day. When she walked through the door, she would strip, placing her clothes neatly in the empty basket and then get dressed in the clothes waiting for her in the other. Sometimes, I might not have any outfit in the other basket, preferring her to be naked around the apartment. She would then kneel on the mat until I came to give her permission to finish entering the house. I even had a pose for when she waited, kneeling. Her legs would be spread as she sat on her heels, hands resting palms up on her thighs, head bowed." He turned and stared at the doorway, a smile decorating his lips. "I think in that pose, the submissive would be gorgeous.

"Wow," Andrea said with a breathy whisper. He glanced over at her, worried she thought he was being silly. However, her expression showed she wasn't mocking him at all. "That sounds beautiful." She shook her head, glancing down at the baskets. "Brian never thought things out like this for us. Instead, he was all about sex and dirty pictures. I didn't realize there was anything else to it."

Edwin nodded as he lifted his cup to his lips. "So much more. For me, anyway." He took a sip of his coffee, licking his lips when he was finished. "For me, it's about structure and rituals, about what happens inside a submissive's mind before I even touch her body." He chuckled. "Now, don't get me wrong. I love the sex *and* dirty pictures, even videos, but there's so many different aspects of the BDSM lifestyle that those who never really dig into it miss out on. Those are the parts that truly grab my attention."

She nodded. "I like it," she said as she lifted the baskets in her hands, turning them over and examining them. "I love the idea." Her lips pressed into a thin line, she nodded again as if making a decision. Glancing up at him for a moment, she smiled and then walked over to his front door, carrying the baskets and mat. He watched as she placed each one against the wall, the mat rolled up in one of the baskets. Turning back to him, she shrugged. "You'll use them one day, I'm sure."

He smiled, nodding. "They look good there."

As she crossed back over to Edwin's toy box, she smiled as she pointed to the flogger. "A purple flogger? And is that, what, rabbit fur?" She cocked a brow at him. "You whip your submissive with rabbit fur?"

He shrugged. "It looked playful. I like playful, too. And it gives a different feeling than the leather ones. It's all about the sensations when using toys such as these, making the submissive feel different things to get her into subspace."

"Subspace?"

He nodded again. "That place, almost dreamlike, a submissive can be transported to if the scene goes well. It's almost euphoric at times. And can be dangerous if the dominant doesn't know his submissive well. She might not know when to use her safeword if she slips too far. It's then up to the dominant to know the signs of her body."

"Brian never gave me a safeword," she said, her brows pinched. "He said it wasn't important."

"Brian was a kid in a toy store, playing with things he didn't know much about, or rather just enough about to be dangerous. Sorry, but it's true."

"No need to be," she told him with a smile. "You're right, and we both know it. I guess I'm just glad it ended before I got hurt."

"So am I."

She grinned as she held up the flogger. "So, what does it feel like to be flogged with rabbit fur?"

~ ~ ~ ~ ~

His grin after she asked the question sent heat straight to her sex, soaking her panties. She couldn't believe she even asked it. *Oh, god, what was I thinking?*

"Do you really want to know?" he asked her, studying her with his head cocked.

She sucked in a breath, wondering if she did really want to know. But then again, wasn't this part of the lifestyle she wanted to explore? Brian never took it this far, his thrills being in other areas. So, what had she been missing?

With another deep breath, she nodded. "I do. Would you show me?"

He studied her a little longer, and at first, she thought he was going to refuse her, but then he set his cup on the end table as he walked over to her. "Are you sure about this? I don't mind doing it, but it's going to require you to take your top off to truly feel it. You can leave your bra on, but you won't have the whole effect through your T-shirt. And it's all right to say no. I can do it as you are, as I said. It just won't feel the same."

She shook her head. "No, I want it." She stood straighter, reaching for the hem of her shirt. She was about to pull it off when Edwin told her to stop. Dropping her arms to her sides, she stared at him, confused. Had he changed his mind? Maybe he still didn't trust her that this wasn't a setup of some kind.

Draping the flogger over his shoulder, he took her hand and led her to one of the walls without pictures or family photos yet. Setting the flogger on the wood floor, he looked at her and grinned. "I'm going to ask one more time. Are you sure about this?"

She nodded. "I am."

"All right. Your safeword is your first name, Andrea. If at any time you want to stop or things get to be too much or too intense, just say your name, and I promise to stop. Understood?"

His gaze was intense as he stared into her eyes, making sure she comprehended what he was saying. She did.

"Good. Now, not saying your safeword when you need to is just as bad as not having one in the first place. There's no shame in using one, and it's there to protect us both." He stepped closer to her, a mischievous grin on his face. "And I wanted to be the one to take your top off." He winked at her as he reached for the bottom of her shirt. Keeping his gaze locked onto hers, he slowly pulled her top up her torso, slow and deliberate, showing no signs of being in a hurry.

Andrea felt her arms being lifted as he raised the shirt, sliding it over her head, up her arms, and off.

He held it as he stared at her, her ample breasts in a black lacy bra. Grinning at her, he said, "Gorgeous."

She felt the blush warm her cheeks, as she sucked in a breath between her teeth. He had told her she could keep her bra on, but suddenly, she wanted Edwin to see all of her. At least the top part of her. Still keeping her gaze fixed on his, she reached behind her back and unhooked her bra, watching as his eyes widened with his excitement. She then slid the straps off her shoulders and down her arms, letting her bra fall to the floor at her feet. Standing straighter, she waited for his reaction, the cool air conditioning making her nipples hard buds of pleasure.

His grin grew as he raked her with his gaze. His tongue between his lips, he reached out and caressed her breasts, his callused fingers gliding over her sensitive pearls. She moaned as she pushed her breasts into his hand, begging for his touch. She wanted him, whatever he wanted. It didn't matter. She knew right then that she would give it to him.

"You are beautiful," he said, and she could hear the lust dripping in his voice.

She bit her lower lip, but said nothing as he massaged her tits, her eyes never leaving his.

With a grin, he asked, "Are you ready?"

"Yes, sir," she said, her body trembling slightly with the unknown.

"Remember, just say your name if things go too far, no matter what those things are," he said. "It doesn't have to be the flogging." He grinned at her. "It could be me tweaking your nipples or just you feeling uncomfortable."

As he said it, she felt him pinching her nipple harder, making her moan louder. She swallowed, nodding, still unable to speak.

Edwin turned her to face the wall, telling her to place her palms on the wall and hold herself up. He made her spread her legs, so she was braced and steady. Leaning forward, she felt his breath on her ear, which sent tremors of heat to pool between her legs. "This is not going to hurt so much as feel like a deep, heavy thud. Some of it will sting, especially as the tips strike your bare flesh." He rubbed her back with the flogger, allowing the rabbit fur to glide across her body. "I'll strike you five times, on your upper back and across your legs. Do not move until I say so. Understood?"

"Yes, sir," she said, closing her eyes as she realized it was the second time in such a short period that she had called him sir.

He stepped back, and Andrea felt her body tighten, braced for the first swing of the flogger. She didn't have to wait long before she felt the heavy thud just below her right shoulder, the pain slight except where the tips of the strands struck her, bringing a tight sting. Then she felt it on her other side, a gasp slipping out of her mouth as she lowered her head, forcing herself to breathe. A second later the tongues swiped across her upper left leg and then in the other direction across her right leg. Each stung, but the flogging also set her pussy on fire, a deep hunger to be stuffed with his cock filling her.

The final swing landed on her jean-covered ass, and she could tell he put a little more strength into it for her to feel it through her shorts. She moaned as she pushed her ass out toward him, her head dropped as her hair fell around her face. A second later, she felt his hand glide across her back and then down over her legs where he had flogged her.

"The red marks look gorgeous on your flesh," he said as he leaned in, his lips brushing against her ear once more.

She sucked in a breath as she felt the tremor of excitement ripple throughout her body. "Thank you. I'll have to peek in the mirror."

He slid a hand around her waist and up to her breasts again, kissing the side of her face softly. "Good girl for taking those so well on your first time. I'm proud of you."

And for some reason, the fact that he was turned her on even more.

"Here, let's stand you up away from the wall," he said, and she felt him lifting her into a standing position as opposed to where she had been leaning over.

When she turned around, she fell into him, her arms going around his neck as she kissed him hard, her tongue slipping between their lips to taste him. She felt his hands wrap around her waist, holding her tightly against him, her tits practically in his face, as he returned her kiss with just as much fire, his cock hardening and pressing against her.

Breaking the kiss, she grinned up at him. "So now, what about that riding crop and the restraints? How do they work?" She waggled her brows at him as she bit her lower lip.

Twenty-Two

Edwin finished swallowing his hamburger as he stared out at the creek. Once they finished sorting through all the boxes, Andrea slipping her bra and top back on, he had ordered some lunch from one of those places that delivered for other restaurants and cracked a couple of beers open. Andrea sat in the chair beside him, eating a chicken sandwich, and he wished she was still topless. It would have definitely been a sight he would have enjoyed while eating. He told her they would explore with the other toys later if she really wanted to, but most of it had been a dodge for the time being. He worried that in her heartbreak, she was jumping the gun on things she would have shied away from if she wasn't hurting. He wanted to give her that chance to think rationally before taking her to his bed and plunging his cock into her. He didn't want to risk their work relationship, or friendship, by rushing the part he wanted, her submission.

"How do people get into your type of relationship?" Andrea asked, holding a French fry in her hand. "When Brian and I started, it was with just some flirting and teasing. He made a crack about bossing me around and then he just did it. I obeyed because most of what he asked me to do turned me on. But, you're saying there's more to it than that."

He shrugged slightly. "Depends on the couple, really. Some leave it at that, and if it works for them, then more power to them. It's all about finding what you want. Some want it just in the bedroom and can even bounce between roles. I prefer the structure in everything, fulltime, and I always want to be the one in control." He glanced over at her and winked. "But you kind of figured that out already, I bet."

She giggled, nodding. "Yeah, you're pretty bossy. But still, I haven't seen you thump your chest and demand things your way or else. It's like you have a balance there."

"If you're going to be fair, you have to be balanced. Anything else to me is just being a bully. A dominant is not a bully, even though they may enjoy spanking their submissive's ass a bright red." He winked at her, smiling.

She giggled before biting into her sandwich.

"Submission is also offered, not taken," Edwin continued, not sure how much Andrea knew about the lifestyle. "The submissive offers her submission much the way a person proposes. That in itself can be done with a ritual or simply offered. Depends on what the couple prefers."

"I thought the dominant took the submissive?" She stared over at him, her brows pinched.

"Oh, there's plenty of taking to be had afterward, but that first step is the submissive offering herself to the dominant. Then, once he accepts, he takes her in oh so many ways." He chuckled again, just thinking about it. Shaking his head, he leaned back, picking up his beer as he thought about it all. "There's a lot of conversation in the beginning, learning what each other likes or doesn't like, what their limits are. How much control is to be given. I've seen people only submit in the bedroom, as I said earlier, as well as others who have turned their entire lives over to their dominant. I'm not much for micro-managing. I prefer to allow my submissive some leeway, but I do love structure and rules. It's all about exploration and setting the stage."

She turned her gaze back out to the creek. "I'm not sure I know what my limits are or even my likes or dislikes."

"That's what makes it so fun to explore. As you do, you discover things about yourself you never even knew." He grinned over at her, waggling his brows. "It's all about the experiences, and every scene is different, even if it's the same one you did last week. Your mood will be different, your frame of mind, the temperature, the pace, every little nuance that makes the scene complete. With the right person, the sex is mind blowing."

She giggled as she leaned back in her chair. "I bet it is. I don't even know some of the things that are out there. Before moving to Savannah, most of my fun with Brian was video chat, him telling me to do different things while he watched."

He glanced over at her, smiling, making sure he kept the shock that she was sharing something so personal with him off his face. He could only imagine the things Brian made her do while he sat back, more than likely jacking off while she performed for him. Of course, the more he thought about it, the more he truly wanted to know. He was kinky that way.

"Then when we both moved here, it was most of the same stuff because he was worried about someone catching us. We went out a few times, and I went to his place after dark. There was some light bondage while we had sex, making me kneel and such, dressing me up slutty and taking me out to show me off.

That sort of thing. We barely had time to explore anything because he decided to go to Florida suddenly."

"Are you wanting to explore more?" he asked, trying not to focus on the other parts of what she shared. She was still so new to everything that was out there. He would love to open her up to new experiences.

She sat there staring out at the water, a couple drifting by in a kayak.

Edwin just let her mull it over, not rushing her. She needed to make her own decisions, no matter how much he wanted her to decide she wanted it, that she wanted him.

"What you said earlier, about things still being raw after Brian and all, that's the truth," she finally said. "The hurt is still there, but to be honest, I, uh," she shifted in her seat a little, looking uncomfortable, "have been thinking more of you these days than Brian."

~ ~ ~ ~ ~

There, she said it. Whew. But now what would he do with it now that she had?

She glanced over at him when he didn't say anything, worried she may have said too much. Instead, however, he was looking at her, a smile decorating his face. "What?" she asked.

"I've been thinking of you, as well, to be honest," he told her, a sparkle in his eyes. "But as I said, I don't want you regretting anything once you're through being pissed at Brian." He shifted in his seat, turning more so he faced her. "I would love to share things with you, give you some of those experiences you never had." He grinned at her as he added, "Maybe even watch you repeat some of the things you've already done." He waggled his brows at her.

She felt her grin grow. "Is that so? You'd want a show like that?"

"Well, I can only guess at what 'like that' means, but," his grin grew, taking on more of a lascivious look, "I'm a full-blooded male with a kinky bent. I'd love to see whatever you want to show me."

She felt the blush warm her cheeks as she squirmed a little at his words. Grinning, she said, "I was told what to do. I'm not sure I could remember it all on my own like that."

He chuckled, shaking his head. "Sneaky little minx, aren't you? I can see someone's going to be a little brat at times."

"Is that when I get spanked? Or even flogged more?"

"Did you like that?"

"Yes," she admitted. "I was wet as hell afterward. You could have taken me right then, and I wouldn't have stopped you. Hell, I would have begged you."

His grin grew as he lifted his beer up to his lips. Before he took a swallow, he said, "I love to hear a submissive beg."

"I'll remember that," she said as she stood. She moved her chair so that the back faced the creek, causing her to face Edwin. She stood there, hands at her sides as she stared at him, her nerves wound tight. She wanted him to give her a command, wanted him to take that step. Needed it, actually.

He stared at her a moment, running his gaze over her body. "You know this doesn't mean you're my submissive, right? I still want you to take a few days and let your emotions settle down first."

She nodded. "Yes, sir. I understand."

"And you still want to do this?" he asked, his eyes narrowed as he studied her.

She glanced down, noticing the bulge in his pants even as he sat there. Nodding, she said, "Yes, sir. I want to do whatever you want me to right now."

He stared at her for a moment longer, waiting to see if she

would change her mind, she assumed. However, she wasn't going to back down. Her pussy burned with hunger for him. Finally, he nodded as he leaned back in his chair, scooting down in his seat a little, legs spread as he rested his hands on his thighs, staring over at her. "Do you remember your safeword?"

She nodded that she did. "Yes, sir."

"You're to use it if you start to feel uncomfortable and want to stop. Is that understood? There will be no repercussions and no shame." After she said it was, he grinned at her, giving an uplift of his chin. "Then take off your top."

She reached for the hem of her shirt, pulling it over her body and off, tossing it to the side as she stood there in her bra. She could feel her nerves causing her body to tremble slightly. Somehow, this seemed even more intimate than when he took her top off earlier to flog her.

He cocked an eyebrow at her. "Now your shorts."

She sucked in a breath, but she obeyed him, reaching for her buttons, and unfastening them. With another deep breath, she slid her shorts down her legs, kicking them off toward her shirt. Standing back up, she stood there in her bra and panties, her boss in front of her, admiring her body.

He nodded, smiling. "You are beautiful," he told her. "Simply beautiful."

She felt the blush warm her cheeks. "Thank you." Her voice trembled, and she bit down on her bottom lip to calm her nerves. She could feel her wetness soaking her panties.

"Now your bra." His eyes twinkled as he gave the order, grinning like the Cheshire Cat. God, his smile made her even wetter.

She reached behind her, unclasping her bra, and slipping it off her shoulders. She let it fall on top of her other clothes, the breeze caressing her nipples, adding to her excitement.

"Your panties." He cocked his brow, and she knew he expected her to use her safeword, backing out before she stripped completely.

She wasn't going to back out. Hooking her thumbs into the waistband of her panties, she slid them down her legs, kicking them off and to the side. She stood back up, her hands back at her sides as she stood in front of Edwin, completely naked, waiting for his next order.

"Now, sit down and show me what you did for Brian before you moved to Savannah," Edwin told her, and her pussy throbbed at what he wanted her to do.

"Yes, sir," she said as she sat her naked ass in the chair, spreading her legs in front of Edwin. She couldn't believe he actually wanted this, but that he did drove her wild with desire.

His brows arched as he saw her slick slit, his grin growing. "Beautiful. Absolutely beautiful."

~ ~ ~ ~ ~

He expected her to back out. But she didn't. He was surprised to be honest, but definitely pleased. And she was more than beautiful. She was absolutely gorgeous.

She kept her gaze fixed on his as she slid her hands up to her breasts, cupping them for him and holding them out for his viewing pleasure. He could tell she bit her lower lip and could only imagine how her nerves had to be twisting in her stomach right then as she exposed herself this way to him. She slid her fingers over her hardened nipples her areolas already shriveled into tight circles of pleasure around the sensitive buds. He watched as she pinched her nipples, twisting them as she pulled on them a little. A groan slid past her lips, making his cock throb in his pants. She slid her hand to the bottom of her left breast, holding it up to her mouth where she sucked on her nipple, her eyes never leaving his.

Edwin groaned, shifting more in his seat as he felt his eyes widen a little. Andrea was definitely giving it her all.

As she sucked on her nipple, she slid her other hand down her stomach toward her pussy. Grinning around her nipple, she slid a finger over her clit and down between her wet folds, toying with her entrance.

"Slide a finger inside," he told her.

Her brows arched slightly as she obeyed, dipping her finger down into her wetness. Lowering her breast from her mouth, she continued pulling at her nipple, pinching it as she fingered her pussy, the heel of her palm rubbing back and forth against her clit. Her moans filled his back porch, her chest rising and falling with her heavy breathing, her lips parted slightly. "Oh, god, Edwin," she moaned. "Do you like it? Do you? Am I pleasing you, sir?"

"Oh, you're pleasing me," he assured her. "Add another finger. Fuck that pussy of yours. I want to see you come."

"Yes, please, yes," she groaned as she opened her legs wider, dipping two fingers into her pussy. "I want to come for you. I want to so badly. I need it. God, do I need it."

His grin grew, remembering something she said just a little while ago. "Do you? Do you want to come?"

"Yes," she said, her voice a husky breath of air. "I need it. Please."

"That's it," he told her. "Beg for it. Show me how much you want it. Beg, my little minx."

She shoved her fingers into her pussy harder, faster, her other hand still manipulating her nipple. Closing her eyes, she surrendered to the sensations rippling through her body right then, and he loved watching her.

He could see the lust on her face, the desire, the passion. He watched as her hips started to rise to meet her hand, the sound of her juices reaching his ears as she fingered herself. His cock throbbed in his pants as he watched her, wanting to see her go over that cliff of her orgasm, the first of many he wanted her to have with him.

Her eyes popped open as her back arched, shoving her pussy up to meet her pounding hand. "I'm going to…" Her mouth fell open, her eyes going wide. "Oh, god, sir! Sir! May I… God," she cried out, her body twisting slightly in the chair as she continued to rub at her clit and finger her pussy. "Please!"

He grinned, his breath heavy in his chest. She was intoxicating. He thought about torturing her and making her wait but didn't want her to feel like she failed if he made her wait too long. "Come." One word. A simple word. And Andrea rocked, her body one tight knot of sexual release as she grunted, long and loud, her hand releasing her breast and gripping the arm of her chair.

He stared as her orgasm broke over her, his cock aching to take her and fuck her right then and there. Her mouth opened as she groaned, her body shuddering until her climax finished, her body slumping back down in the chair once she was finished. Her breasts rose and fell with her heavy breathing as she glanced over at him, her body still slid down in the chair, her ass dangling off the edge. He had yet to see that bare ass of hers, but god, he wanted to so badly.

With a deep breath, she slid back up into her chair, clutching the arms. "Well?" she asked. "Did, uh, I mean, was that what you wanted to see?"

He grinned at her. "Oh, yes. Definitely. You were amazing. I could watch you do that for hours."

She glanced down at the bulge in his pants. "And you don't need release of your own?"

"It's not always about my release. Oh, I'll get it eventually," he assured her. "But when I take your body, I want you to be mine. I can wait until then."

She blushed, and he loved the color on her cheeks.

"For now, though, you can stay naked." He grinned over at her, making her blush deepen.

"Yes, sir," she said, his cock throbbing at her words.

Twenty-Three

Edwin stared down at another contract, this one for a daycare center west of Savannah. The owner, a charismatic woman in her twenties, had already signed the contract and issued them a check. All he needed to do was put his signature on it and pass it off to Andrea to get the surveys and permits started. Luckily, they didn't hire the man Andrea wanted for the bullpen. She finally admitted to only picking him because she was pissed at Edwin at the time and wanted to make some random point that now didn't even make sense. Instead, they sat down and went over the other applicants, picking a lady named Beth Crowley who would be interviewed tomorrow. Hopefully, she would be the one handling permits and contracts soon, which would free Andrea up for the things she was best at, helping to run the office and the teams out in the field.

A knock came at his door, jarring him out of his concentration. Glancing up, he saw Andrea standing there, and immediately, a smile creased his face. "What's up?"

She leaned on the doorframe, her arms under her breasts, holding them up for his pleasure, he knew. After she had masturbated for him on his back porch Saturday, they spent more time talking about the lifestyle, and to his delight, she did remain naked while she sat out there. After a while, she got dressed, and then they went out for dinner, the topics of conversation switching to more mundane things other than sex and rituals. Sunday, he stayed home, putting his house back in order after all the boxes had been sorted through, and she had done her dreaded laundry. Of course, they did spend the day, as well as the couple of days after that, texting back and forth, and Edwin even called her each evening to say goodnight. There had still been no word from Brian, which Edwin took as a sign the man had given up. Five days was plenty of time for Brian to send an email, call her at work, or make some other lame excuse to show up on her doorstep. He was ether licking his wounds or relieved that he had made it out with his balls still attached.

"Ryan's in the warehouse helping Ethan organize it the way he wants," Andrea said. "They seem to be getting along all right, which is good for everyone around. I haven't seen Ryan and Sammy making goo-goo eyes at each other, so for now they're keeping it professional." She shrugged. "The closer they get to each other, the harder it will become, I'm sure."

He nodded, wondering if she was thinking about the two of them in the same situation. He hadn't pushed her on submitting to him since their talk Saturday. He had meant it when he said the decision would be hers if she decided to travel that route with him. Oh, he gave her small orders Sunday and that morning before she arrived to work, but nothing too serious and nothing she couldn't refuse. Not surprisingly, she had obeyed every one of his commands, saying, "Yes, sir," behind each instruction. She had flirted and teased him, asked more questions as they discussed things that intrigued both of them, but had not come out and offered her submission yet. That was all right with Edwin, though. He was a patient man, and Andrea was worth waiting for; of that, he had no doubt.

"We'll just keep an eye on them," he told her. "They're grown adults, so they can make their own decisions as long as it doesn't interfere with the workings of this office."

She nodded as she pushed herself off the doorframe, entering further into his office until she stood in front of his desk. "May I ask a question, please?"

"Always." He leaned forward in his chair, hands clasped together and resting on the top of his desk.

"When you were controlling Faith, how did that work in the office? Did she answer to you there, as well? I know you said something about playing around at work, but how did the other aspects play into it all?"

"Well, I was actually her boss, so it was a natural outflow of that," he told her, his head cocked to the side as he smiled over at her. "However, with you being my second here, if this is where you're going with this conversation, there would have to be some rules on boundaries." He glanced around Andrea to where the others sat at their desk, making sure no one was there to overhear them. Glancing back at Andrea, he continued. "I would never use my role as your dominant to force you to go against what you think is best for this company. I want your honest opinion about everything we do here, just as you've been doing, even if they go against mine. I want your ideas and thoughts. There would be a line that would separate us in that way and for which you couldn't be punished." He saw her eyes widen at the word "punished".

"That's good to know," she said, nodding. "Thanks."

"My pleasure," he said. "Anything else?"

She shook her head. "Nope, just trying to think it all through."

"Smart on your part," he told her. "Now's the time to ask all the questions you want if you're considering what we discussed this weekend."

She nodded again, her lips pressed into a thin line before turning and walking back out of his office.

He stared at her ass, cupped firmly in her jeans as she walked away. The fact that she was still asking questions about how everything would work inferred she was considering submitting to him, and that made his cock twitch. He wanted her as his, but he needed her to surrender to him. That first step of surrendering her control to him was the sweetest part.

With a sigh, he picked up the contract again, adding his signature at the bottom.

~ ~ ~ ~ ~

For the past few days, Andrea had found it hard to focus on work. She couldn't stop thinking about everything she shared with Edwin: the flogging, her masturbating for him on his back porch, and all the conversations of the BDSM lifestyle. Everything he described just intrigued her more. It was sex, but it was also so much more than that. It was a way of life, just like a married couple, only with more structure and a lot more kink. She had to admit, both of those had her attention. She had remained constantly wet since he flogged her and had even masturbated nightly thinking of Edwin's hands on her body again. What would it feel like to have his cock pounding into her?

Sighing, she forced herself out of her chair to check on the new guys, just so she would have something to do. However, her mind was still locked onto Edwin Coldwell. What would it be like to submit to him, surrender control over to his desires, and allowing him to have his way with her? In everything she had seen so far, Edwin was a gentle, patient man. There had been plenty of times he could have just fired her for how she treated him when he first arrived, but he never even threatened it. Instead, he went out of his way to make her like and accept him. He had been firm when he needed to be, no doubt, but he had also always been fair, giving her a chance to voice her opinions whether or not he agreed with them. She couldn't see him behaving in any other way in his personal relationships. After all, he was the one to protect her, to tell her how risky it was that Wednesday night when Brian sent her out to flirt and tease strangers. Edwin would be that way in everything, she just knew it.

Jana was in the warehouse when Andrea arrived, taking notes and making lists as the others moved things about, sorting and organizing. They all seemed to get along, and whereas she expected to find Jana territorial over the equipment, not wanting anyone to touch what she had already done, the woman was more giving in allowing Ethan to set up the warehouse the way he wanted it. It confused Andrea a little bit, and she had no problem admitting it.

With her arms over her chest, she walked up to the woman as Jana scribbled more notes down on paper. "You seem to be handling this all right."

Jana finished what she was writing and then looked up at Andrea, her lips twisted in a lopsided grin. "It's his baby," she said. "With him here, I'll hardly have to come out here other than to pass off requisitions or do some inspections. I'm more than happy to hand this area over to him." She shrugged. "Besides, everyone needs their little area that's theirs, something they have control over."

Andrea nodded but said nothing. If she surrendered to Edwin the way he wanted, would she have any area left that was just hers? If she gave him everything, what then was left to her? He had told her Saturday that people explored at different levels, but he had also told her he would not be satisfied in the shallow end of the BDSM pool. He wanted to be fully immersed in it. The man even had rituals for when his submissive arrived at his house! She sighed, shaking her head. Every time she thought she had all the answers she needed to make her decision, there appeared to be even more questions.

She left the others to finish what they were doing as she turned back toward the main office. Edwin stood just outside the back door, a cigarette dangling from his fingers as he watched her cross the parking lot, a playful grin toying at his lips. She smiled as she felt the blush warm her cheeks. There was just something about him that caused her panties to be constantly soaked.

"How's it going out there?" he asked as she drew nearer.

"Better than I thought to be honest. I assumed Jana would throw a fit with the changes he's making, but she seems to be handling everything all right."

He nodded as he flicked his ash to the side. "Good. We need all of this to go smoothly."

"Have you thought about what Neal will do if he finds out about us?" she asked, needing answers to the myriad of questions that kept popping up in her mind.

Edwin shrugged. "I'll just tell him. Neal's not opposed to couples being together. He's opposed to chaos disrupting his workplace. Neither one of us are married, we're not sneaking around, and we're both adults, allowed to fall for whoever we want."

Fall for? She tilted her head. Was Edwin falling for her? "If I go this deep the way you want, will I lose myself?"

He stared at her, his eyes soft, his expression tender. Finally, he shook his head. "No. Actually, I think we'll both find ourselves."

She nodded, slipping her hands into her pockets. "And if I decide I can't do it?"

"Then we regroup, talk it out, and decide what's best for both of us." He grinned at her. "I promise never to do anything to you that you don't want done. I also promise, I'm not wanting to change you. Just explore with you." He shrugged. "Of course, there will be some change in both of us. That's just natural. But I honestly think it'll be a change for the better. I won't bully you. I'll protect you, treasure you, and cherish you." He leaned forward, a conspiratorial grin spreading his face. "And if you want to know the truth about it all, the dominant winds up serving the submissive as much as she serves him, just in different ways." He straightened back up. "I think you'll be surprised at how much you come to thrive in this lifestyle. I can promise you'll definitely be turned on by what we do."

She felt the blush on her cheeks again. She didn't doubt what he told her. Everything about the man in front of her kept her excited.

He studied her, his eyes narrowed and his head tilted to the side slightly. "You also always have your safeword, which you can use for anything, not just physical scenes. No matter what we're doing or where we're at, if you use your safeword, I'll stop whatever is going on and see to your well-being. You have my word on that."

She smiled over at him. "I don't doubt that."

"And are there other things you doubt?" he asked, still studying her. "We can go at your pace if you want to explore this. If you don't, then we just keep being great friends and coworkers. No harm, no foul."

"I'm not sure what I'm feeling," she admitted. She ducked her gaze to her feet, toying with a pebble on the ground with the toe of her shoe. "I guess I'm just worried about disappointing you."

She looked back up into his eyes. "I never want to do that."

"I really don't think you could, minx." He winked at her as he lifted his cigarette to his lips and took another puff.

She felt her chest swell with his confidence as she blushed again. God, how many times would he cause her to do that? "I hope not." She smiled at him, adding, "Sir," to the end of her sentence.

He grinned at her as he tossed the rest of his cigarette into the ashtray by the back door. "I love that word coming from your lips."

"So do I."

And she did. The question was, however, could she give her all to this man who had so captured her heart and world? She honestly didn't know, but she knew she desperately wanted to try.

Twenty-Four

Edwin opened his front door, allowing Andrea inside his apartment. The week was over, and he was looking forward to the weekend and spending time alone with the blond minx. She had continued to ask her questions over the past couple of days, but they had turned into asking about more of the things that he enjoyed during sex, like flogging or the restraints she had discovered last weekend, rather than the formalities and logistics of things. They had tried to keep everything under the radar at work, but it was more than obvious that they were spending quite a bit of time together. They had even gone out to lunch together today, which didn't seem to surprise anyone. Sammy had just winked at him as he ushered Andrea out of the office.

"I'm returning the bottle of Glenfiddich I gave you and then drank last week," Andrea said as she entered the house, slipping out of her sandals as she did. Turning, she shrugged. "Again, I'm sorry about that."

He took the bottle from her, chuckling. "No problem. Promise. However, no drinking right now."

"Oh?" She cocked an eyebrow at him. "And why is that? I thought we were going to enjoy a night on the back porch."

"We will but later. You have asked what all turns me on, so I thought if you were willing I would give you a little sample. I don't want alcohol to impair either of us. What do you think?"

"I think I'm curious," she said.

He grinned as he reached out and took her hand, leading her down the hallway to his bedroom. When they entered, he heard her gasp at the way he had it set up. Candles burned all around the room, and soft jazz played subtly in the background. He kept his eyes on her as she glanced around, noticing the toys on his dresser, the riding crop, restraints, and even a feather.

"Wow," she said as she scanned the rest of the room. "Is this another ritual?"

He shook his head as he guided her over to the bed. "No. This is part of that kinky sex I was telling you about. You remember your safeword, correct?"

"My first name," she told him.

He nodded once. "Use it if anything starts to feel uncomfortable, even if it's just your emotions or mind. Understood?"

He watched as she took a deep breath. "Understood, sir."

"Good. Now, let's strip you." He reached for her shirt, pulling it up and over her head. Folding it, he laid it gently on his dresser next to the toys. She reached for her bra, but he stopped her. "I didn't give you permission to move," he told her, grinning. "That'll be two swats with the crop."

She visibly gulped, nodding. "Yes, sir. Sorry, sir."

"Just stand there while I strip you."

He then walked behind her and unhooked her bra, sliding his hands up her back and under the straps. Slowly, he glided his hands over her shoulders and down her arms, taking the bra with him. Moving over to his dresser, he folded the bra in half and laid it on top of her shirt. He then moved back to stand in front of her. Staring into her eyes, he unbuttoned her shorts. Hooking his thumbs into the waistband of both her shorts and her panties, he slid them down her legs, lowering himself to his knees as he did. When he was eye-level with her slit, he leaned in and kissed the top of her mound, gliding his tongue over her flesh.

Andrea moaned but didn't move.

Glancing up at her, he grinned as he indicated for her to step out of her shorts. Once they were off, he folded them and added them to the pile of clothes.

Turning back around, he walked over to her, took her hand, and led her to the bed. "Lie down," he ordered.

She obeyed, moving her naked body on the bed until she centered herself, and then stretched out for him as he asked. Her gaze went straight back to his, and he could see her chest rising with her steady breathing, nervousness but expectation masking her face.

He took her arms and lifted them above her head, putting her wrists beside each other. Then he retrieved the restraints from the dresser and bound her arms, hooking the restraints into a notch on the headboard. Grinning at her, he slid a finger over her breasts, down her stomach, and dipped it between her folds. "God, you're already so fucking wet. I love it."

Reaching under a pillow, he pulled out a dark burgundy scarf. "I am going to blindfold you by simply draping this across your eyes. If it's too much, just tell me."

She nodded. "Yes, sir."

Edwin laid the scarf over the upper portion of her face, leaving her mouth and nose uncovered. "I am not going to tell you what I plan on doing to you, but you will feel the crop and other things, different sensations each. I will use them on your entire body wherever I see fit."

Moving over to the dresser, Edwin gathered the riding crop, the feather, and one of the candles. When he turned around, he stopped for a moment and just soaked her in, her body gorgeous as it stretched across his bed, bound at the wrists just waiting for whatever he wanted to do to her. God, she was perfect.

Setting the candle on his nightstand, he put the other implements on the bed, keeping the riding crop in his hand. He took the tip and glided it across her hardened nipples, flicking them every once in a while as he moved from one to the other. Her body tightened under his machinations, a moan slipping past her lips. He then pulled the crop up and smacked her tit with it, making her flesh jiggle slightly as she yelped. Still, she laid there, waiting, her mouth slightly ajar, her breathing growing heavier. He then slid the crop down her stomach to her pussy, slapping at her thighs until she parted her legs. He rubbed the tip of the crop up and down her folds, focusing on her clit. Her body remained braced, her legs slightly parted as she waited for him to smack her there, but he just kept rubbing her.

With his other hand, he picked up the feather, gliding it over her sensitive nipples while he toyed with her wetness. She wiggled slightly, pushing her hips upward to try and apply more pressure on her clit. He grinned at her attempts but said nothing. Instead, he brought the crop up quickly and smacked her pussy with it, another cry bursting from her lips.

Laying the crop across her stomach, he slid a finger down between her folds, dipping it inside her wetness, making her gasp. She was soaked, as he knew she would be. He fingered her for a while as he used the feather and toyed with her nipples, brushing it back and forth, barely caressing her skin with it, just enough to make her tremble with the sensation. Her body squirmed as he played with her, drawing as many reactions out of her as he could. When she felt as if she was on the brink of an orgasm, he stopped, sliding his finger out of her passion. Picking up the crop, he brought it down on each breast, one at a time, and then placed it to the side.

"How do you feel?" he asked, reaching out and pinching her hard nipple.

"Like my body is on fire," she answered. "Everything felt so intense. I'm soaked and would really love your fingers again. Please."

"Not yet, my sweet minx. I have one more thing I want to do to you first, and then I'll see about some release for both of us."

She groaned. "Yes, sir."

Reaching over to the candle on his nightstand, he said, "With what I'm about to do to you next, you'll feel a little burn, but I promise, it's not doing anything to your skin but giving you the feeling of heat. Your flesh will be red afterward, and sensitive, but there will be no lasting marks. It'll be hot, but it'll feel good all at the same time."

She nodded, and he watched as she took a deep breath, her breasts rising slightly in the air.

Holding the candle about two feet over her left breast, he tilted the votive cup until a couple of drops of wax rolled over the edge to fall onto her skin.

Andrea arched her back, shrinking away from the burn as she cried out.

He moved over to the other breast and repeated the action, causing her to suck in a breath through clenched teeth. The wax hardened on her flesh, having cooled almost before it hit her skin thanks to the distance between where he held the candle and her body. Reaching out, he glided his fingers over her nipple, making her jump slightly at the change of sensation. "See?" he said. "It burns, but then again, it doesn't. The sting fades almost as quickly as the wax hits your body."

He then tipped the candle over her cleavage, pouring the wax out in a straight line down her stomach to her sex, allowing a drop to hit her clit and then her folds.

Andrea sucked in another breath, her body twisting slightly as if trying to get away from the wax. "Oh, god," she groaned, her arms pulling at her restraints. "Sir, I need you. Please. God, I'm so wet. Please finger me. Fuck me. Something. Please!"

He picked up the riding crop and smacked her breast with it, two quick, hard swats. "I'm the dominant here," he reminded her. "You'll get something in that hungry pussy of yours when I'm ready."

"Yes, sir," she said, practically moaning.

He slid his finger down her stomach to where the wax hardened around her belly button, toying with it as he raked her flesh with his fingernails. It was then that he realized he wouldn't be able to wait until she surrendered to him formally. He wanted her now. Right then.

Stepping away from the bed, he quickly stripped, his clothes clumped on the floor unlike how he had carefully folded hers. "Do you want to taste my cock?" he asked her as he climbed back onto the bed, slipping the scarf from her face and letting it fall to the pillow.

She glanced up at him with hunger in her eyes. "Oh, please, sir," she begged. "I want it. God, do I want it."

He knelt beside her head, slipping his hand into her hair and turning her so that her mouth faced his cock. With his other hand, he glided the head of his shaft back and forth over her lips, and to his surprise, she didn't open her mouth, waiting for him to tell her what to do. She was definitely a good girl. He smiled down at her as he commanded, "Open."

Andrea opened her luscious lips, her tongue gliding over the tip of his cock as he slid his manhood into her mouth. "That's a good girl," he told her, still gripping her head as he guided her mouth back and forth on his cock. He could feel her tongue twirling around his hardness, lapping over every vein and ridge, circling the head as he slid it back to the edge of her mouth. Her slurping noises mixed with her moans as he started to thrust into her mouth, pounding her face, his balls slapping her chin and cheek. As he held her head, he slid his other hand down to her chest, pinching and tweaking her nipple, making her whimper around his cock.

"God, your mouth feels so fucking good," he told her. "I will make sure to use you a lot."

He could tell he was close to coming in her mouth, but that's not where he wanted to put his load. Instead, he slid his cock from between her lips and then helped her roll over onto her stomach, unhooking her arms from where he had them restrained, and then hooking them back in place so she would remain bound while he took her. He pushed her legs together as he straddled her, his cock aimed at her entrance as he studied her round ass. "Do you want it?" he asked her.

"God, yes!" she cried out, pushing her ass back toward him. "Please."

He swatted her rump hard. "I said I will give it to you when I'm ready," he told her. "Lie still until I do."

"But I want it, Edw...sir. I need it. God, I've never needed to be fucked so badly in my life."

He could still feel her squirming underneath him, her body almost out of control. He aimed his cock at her pussy's entrance as he straddled her legs, teasing her. "Are you sure you want it?

I'm going to fuck you until I come in that tight little pussy of yours. Are you sure you're ready for it, my hot little minx?"

"Please," she groaned. "God, sir, I'm going crazy with need. Please fuck me. Use me. I want it. I want you."

Edwin gripped her hips as he thrust deep inside of her wetness, Andrea crying out, her fingers spreading wide with nothing to clamp down onto. She couldn't move as he held her tight, pounding her from behind as she stretched out prone underneath him. He knew the bedspread would be rubbing at her clit as well as her nipples, driving her just as crazy as his cock was. She kept begging for more, crying out for him to fuck her harder, faster, telling him how much she needed his cock, wanted to serve his cock, serve him. He focused on the side of her face as she turned her head toward his dressed, her mouth open as she made soft, sweet mewling noises while he fucked her, her wetness sounding loud mixed with her cries. She felt so fucking good in his hands, around his cock.

Then she cried out just before he felt her body tighten underneath him. "Oh, god, sir! Sir! I'm going to... God, can I.. Please!"

"Do it," he growled as he shoved his cock back and forth into her honey. "Come for me, minx. I want to feel you come on my cock."

Her body trembled in his grasp as she tried to stretch, her cries bouncing off the walls as her orgasm exploded through her. He drove into her over and over, his fingers digging into her flesh as he fucked her. He could feel her inner walls milking his cock, feel her juices coating them both as he slammed into her. And then he felt his cock twitch and throb just before his own orgasm ripped from his shaft. He shoved himself down into her, thrusting deep, and stayed there while he emptied his load into her, his mouth open as he grunted over her.

When it was over he almost felt like collapsing on top of her, his breathing heavy in his own ears. He leaned over, sliding a hand up her back and into her hair as he kissed the side of her face. "Now, that was amazing," he said, pulling the scarf further away from her face from where it sat clumped on the pillow and tossing it onto the floor.

She smiled over at him as he slid his cock from her drenched pussy and laid down beside her. "Um, yeah, that's one word for it. God, you felt so good."

Pulling the hair out of her eyes, he kissed her nose before reaching up and unhooking the restraints around her wrist, massaging each arm where the restraints had held her, slight marks in her flesh from where she struggled a little. He rolled her over so that she faced him, laughing slightly as he noticed the flakes of wax falling off her body and onto his bed. "We're going to have a slight mess to clean up."

She glanced down at the bedspread, grinning. "Oops. Well, it was your idea." She winked at him as she slid an arm around his neck, pulling him closer for another kiss, her lips soft and warm against his. Breaking away from him, she gazed up into his eyes. "Can we clean it up in a bit, though. I really just want to hold you."

Edwin nodded as he caressed her shoulder. He stood up real quick, pulling the bedspread down and helping Andrea slide underneath it. Then he slid in beside her, wrapping her in his arms as he pulled the covers up to her shoulders, tucking her in tight against his side. "Aftercare is just as erotic to me as the scene itself," he told her.

She had already laid her head on his shoulder, but she nodded as she mumbled, "You'll have to tell me what aftercare means later." And then her breathing grew steadier as he felt the weight of her head resting fully on his chest.

He turned slightly, kissing her head. "You got it, minx."

Twenty-Five

When Edwin woke up the next morning, the bed was empty except for little flakes of wax stuck everywhere. He shook his head as he brushed as much as he could off the bed and himself and then searched the room for Andrea. She was nowhere in sight, however, not even in the master bathroom. Glancing at his dresser, he noticed her stack of clothes was also missing. Surely, she wouldn't have just got up and left without telling him.

He jerked the covers off and reached for his robe, concern creasing his brow. The entire house was quiet, the sun barely creeping through the curtains as he walked down the hallway, passing the other rooms. She wasn't in any of those, either. Where the hell did she go?

As he stepped out of the hallway, he glanced toward the kitchen but heard nothing, no glasses clinking or coffee cups, no water running, nothing. The house was dead quiet.

He turned toward the front door to see if her sandals were there at least and froze, a lump filling his throat as he stared at Andrea kneeling on the black mat, her clothes in one of the wicker baskets. She knelt there in the exact position he had described to her last Saturday, her legs spread, palms face up and resting on her thighs, head bowed. He could see her shoulders rising with her deep breaths, and he had to wonder how long she had been kneeling that way.

"Andrea," he said as he stepped closer to her. "Are you okay?" He felt a heaviness in his heart as he stared at her, knowing the special gift she was giving him.

"I've only been up for a little while, sir," she told him, her head still bowed. "I tried to sleep, but my mind would just not stop going. I replayed everything you said over the last couple of weeks, and I know what I'm surrendering myself to. I've loved the things we've done, and I want to do even more with you. I will obey you and make you proud." She glanced up into his eyes, and he felt his chest constrict with emotion as he saw the twinkle there as she gazed up at him, the intensity and depth. "I will be your perfect little minx if you'll take me as yours. I want to be your submissive, and you to be my master." Then her expression changed to one of worry. "This is the way you said it was supposed to be done, right? I had to offer you my submission?" She nodded once. "Then I offer it. I want to be yours. Will you accept me as your submissive?"

He couldn't stop the grin that creased his face or the joy that beat in his chest, threatening to undo him. Walking over to her, he stretched out his hand, waiting for her to take it. Once she was on her feet, he pulled her tightly against him, his finger under her chin keeping her focused on his eyes. "I eagerly accept it, love, and I am eager to show you what a true dominant can do and the fun we can have. I promise to protect you, guide you, and give you all of me in every way you need. I will always listen, never judge, and always help you grow. I accept your submission and vow to be the best master for you that I can be. You are mine. I am yours. We belong to each other."

She bit her lower lip as she stared up at him, and he slid his hand down to cup her ass, squeezing her tighter against him. "Yes, sir," she whispered. "We belong to each other."

He grinned at her, digging his fingers into her ass. "Mine," he said. "Your body. I will use it as I see fit to give each of us experiences that will drive us crazy while keeping us safe and healthy, as well."

He heard her suck in a breath as she nodded.

He slid a finger up to her head, touching her forehead gently. "Mine," he repeated. "Your mind. I will help you grow and guide you in the ways to serve and be the best person you can be."

Her smile grew.

He slid his finger from her forehead to her chest, flattening his hand over her heart. "Mine," he repeated one more time. "Your heart. I will not share it, and I promise to protect it with everything I have in me. This is the promise I make to you."

Still biting her lower lip, she nodded. "I'll hold you to that promise."

"Good," he said, slipping his arms around her waist again. "And since that basket was empty, I guess you're going to be naked all day." He winked at her, chuckling.

Andrea giggled. "Yes, sir. Your wish is my command."

He smiled down at her. She was his to command, to protect, and to love. He would make sure he honored each of those promises and more.

"Now what?" she asked, still holding onto him.

"Well, I suppose we could get some coffee going," he said, his eyes narrowed as he thought out their next steps. "And then I think I should probably call Neal and give him a heads up about us. Assure him I won't make you walk around the office naked."

"At least when the others are there, right?" she said, leaning back and studying him with confusion. "I mean, I gave you one of my past experiences. I definitely want some of yours." She shrugged. "It's only fair."

He laughed, turning her toward the kitchen as he dropped his arms from her waist, and smacked her ass, making her yelp. "It is only fair, minx. God, this is going to be so much fun. Now, let's get things started with coffee."

"As you wish, sir," she said, giggling.

He watched her ass as she sashayed across the floor and into the kitchen. The view in Savannah just got a whole lot better.

About the Author

Basking along the beaches of Central Florida, R. C. Wynne is a romantic at heart. R.C. loves writing heart-throbbing stories with strong, but sassy heroines, hunky heroes who love their women to have an inner fire, plenty of sexy times to melt your panties and keep your heart racing, romantic happily-ever-afters, and an abundance of emotions to keep you laughing, crying, and even sometimes screaming.

When not writing, R.C. is often found on his back porch enjoying a cigar, a scotch, and some Dean Martin tunes. He derives pleasure from his large family and his crazy group of friends who provide the inspiration for his blog, *The Mess that Is Me*.

His series include, *The Rutherford Series*, *Fangirls*, *The Best of Both Worlds*, and the popular *The Harper Twins*. For more information about his new releases, upcoming events, and sneak peeks into his crazy world, visit R.C. at rcwynnebooks.com.

Connect with R.C. Wynne online:

Website ~ www.rcwynnebooks.com
Facebook ~ https://www.facebook.com/R.C.WynneAuthor
Twitter ~ https://twitter.com/RCWynne2
Pinterest ~ https://www.pinterest.com/robbie9652/
Goodreads ~ https://www.goodreads.com/user/show/128870802-r-c-wynne
Instagram ~ https://www.instagram.com/r.c.wynneauthor/

Bookbub ~ https://www.bookbub.com/profile/1566963280
MeWe ~ https://mewe.com/i/rcwynne

For up-to-date news on R.C. Wynne's latest releases, book signing events in your area, and giveaways, follow his newsletter - https://landing.mailerlite.com/webforms/landing/l7q0q7

You can also join R.C. Wynne's reading group, Wynne's Romance Hideaway, for more updates, extra giveaways, and even more fan involvement - https://www.facebook.com/groups/wynnesromancehideway

Other Books by R.C. Wynne

The Rutherford Series
Losing Faith
Roll the Dice
To Be Cherished
His to Command
Sharing Hearts

Fangirls
Nikki
Lily
Cassie
Olivia
Willow
The Collection

The Harper Twins
Sibling Rivalry
Taming Karla
Always Aimee
The Harper Twins Box Set

Best of Both Worlds
Ribbons & Bows
Under the Wrapping
The Best of Both Worlds

Visit www.rcwynnebooks.com to find out more about these great books by R.C. Wynne!

Writing as Robbie Cox

Warrior of the Way
Reaping the Harvest
Lore Master
The Warrior's Blade
Summerlands

The Cauldron Coven
Death's Shroud
Daughters of Darkness
Chaos Magicians

Halloween Seduction
Come Halloween
Behind the Mask

Life's Moments
Green is the Grass
Waiting Room
Second Light
Saturday at the Inlet
Life's Moments

The Witches of Savannah
Enter the Witch

Short Stories
Circle of Justice

<u>Bull Creek Chronicles</u>
Alpha Rising
Panther Hunted
Bear Necessities

<u>Destined Mates</u>
Magic's Mate
Mate's Appeal
Mate's Touch
My Lover's Mate
My Mate's Wife

Visit www.robbiecox.com to find out more about these great books by Robbie Cox!

THE MESS-Y STORE
Robbie Cox's Books & Merchandise
CELEBRATE YOUR LOVE OF READING ROBBIE'S STORIES

Books. Shirts. Totes. Socks. Mugs. And More.

SHOP NOW TO FIND YOUR FAVORITES!

www.robbiecox.net/merch

Get all your great merchandise at The Mess-y Store, from coffee mugs to T-shirts to laptop sleeves! Visit www.robbiecox.net/merch to order your fun swag today!

Milton Keynes UK
Ingram Content Group UK Ltd.
UKHW030143180324
439604UK00005B/685